Winter
of Secrets

To
Rina
Happy ~~~~~

Winter
of Secrets

Vicki Delany

Poisoned Pen Press

Poisoned Pen Press
6962 E. First Ave., Ste. 103
Scottsdale, AZ 85251
www.poisonedpenpress.com
info@poisonedpenpress.com

Printed in the United States of America

*For all the people in Nelson, too numerous to mention,
who make me feel so welcome. You know who you are.*

Acknowledgments

As always I'd like to thank the officers of the Nelson City Police and the Nelson RCMP detachment for their help and advice, particularly Brita Wood, Constable Janet Scott-Pryke, Corporal Al Grant, and Detective Paul Burkart. Any errors in police procedure are either for the sake of the story or because I forgot to ask. Thanks also to Staff Sergeant Kris Patterson and Constable Laura Portt of the Belleville Police Service. Help with swift water rescue procedures was provided by Al Craft, Fred Doefler, and Chris Armstrong of Beasley Fire and Rescue. To Ken Campbell who kindly took time to talk to me about his many years working with police dogs, Shenzi says "woof". Skiing tips were provided by Maureen Jansma, Jennifer Muller, Ken Semon, and Deborah Turrell Atkinson. Madeleine Harris-Callway and Verna Relkoff helped fine-tune the drafts.

Chapter One

They don't often get big snow storms in the Kootenay area of British Columbia. Lots of snow, that's a given; sometimes the air is so full of snow that the daytime is as white as the night is black. But there isn't much wind in these mountains, and the snow falls thick and fast and straight down, where it lies deep on the ground. The word "whiteout", meaning when high winds whip falling snow around, reducing visibility to nothing, isn't often heard in Trafalgar.

Tonight it would be.

It was Christmas Eve, and as Constable Molly Smith began a twelve hour shift the storm of the decade was settling in over Trafalgar. She'd scarcely had time to say hi to the earlier shift, the lucky ones who got to enjoy the evening with their families, before the first 911 call came in. The first, of what would be many.

Pedestrian struck by a car on Front Street. Appear to be injuries.

Smith reached for the keys to the truck, but she wasn't fast enough. "I'll drive," Constable Dave Evans said, tossing the keys in his hand and heading toward the back door and the parked vehicles.

"You'll be with Evans tonight," Sergeant Caldwell, the shift supervisor, shouted after her. "It's going to be rough in this. And it's supposed to get worse."

Grumbling under her breath, Smith climbed into the passenger seat. Evans flicked on the wipers to get rid of the snow that accumulated since the vehicle had been parked. Which hadn't been long: the truck had turned in as she'd walked up the steps to the station.

Caldwell's prediction came all too true, and Smith and Evans spent their Christmas Eve running from one call to another.

Cars in the ditch. Cars spinning out of control in the middle of the highway. Pedestrians slipping and sliding all over the place. Holiday revelers who'd started into the Christmas cheer a bit too early, and too heavily, but thought they could still drive.

In late December, in a town surrounded by mountains, it was dark before four-thirty. The night was a strange shade of shifting white as the lights of cars and homes and streetlamps reflected off snow cutting through the black sky in near-horizontal slashes. The snow was blinding; there were times when Smith could barely see the front of the truck as they drove.

The radio crackled with activity, everyone was out, and even Caldwell had grabbed a car and was answering calls.

A few minutes before midnight they were called to an accident on Cottonwood Street.

Smith and Evans arrived to find a fender bender. Two vehicles, a top of the line, fully-loaded SUV, and a rusty old van, had met in the middle of the road. Not hard to do, as drifts of snow had reduced the road, one of the steepest in a town built on the side of a mountain, to a one-lane track.

When the police arrived, blue and red lights reflecting off falling snow like manic Christmas decorations, the drivers were standing in the road, inches apart, screaming in each other's faces. Additional yelling came from the ditch and Smith could see two women on the far side of the cars, waving arms. Wide-eyed children peered through icy windows of the SUV. Cars began lining up in both directions, horns honking as drivers leaned out of windows.

Evans glanced at the clock on the dashboard. "Merry Christmas, Molly," he said. It was one minute past midnight.

"Let's go spread some seasonal cheer," she replied.

It was a battle just to get the truck door open, but she proved to be stronger than the storm. Snow and wind hit her full in the face. If it were possible, the power of the blizzard seemed to be increasing.

Without discussion, Evans approached the arguing men and Smith walked around the cars. The two women stopped fighting at the sight of the police officer, trying to keep her footing in the calf-high drifts lining the road.

"What's going on here?"

Whereupon the women resumed screaming, at each other and at Smith.

She wanted to ask them what had happened to their Christmas spirit. Instead she flashed a light into the back of the SUV. Two small, round white faces looked back at her.

"Why don't you get into the car, Ma'am. Your children seem distressed."

"They're fine," the woman snapped. She wore a beige fur coat, either real or a good fake, and leather gloves. Knee-high boots were planted firmly in the snow. Her chin-length blond hair was a wet mess and thick lines of black mascara ran down her face. "That fool came out of nowhere, and…"

"Don't you call my Ed a fool. If your goddamned husband had been watching where he was going he wouldn't have…"

"Wait in the car, please," Smith interrupted. "My partner's taking the details of the accident. Your children are bound to be upset and in need of some care."

The woman had the grace to look embarrassed. Her shoulders lost their fighting stance, and she put her hand on the SUV door.

"You tell her, Molly," the other woman said.

That was not helpful.

The fur-clad woman swung around. "What the hell's this? You're going to pin this on Roger because they're locals, is that it?"

"I'm not going to pin anything on anyone. You can look after your children or I'll radio for someone from social services to come and do it for you."

"You can't…"

"And as for you, Mrs. Morrison," Smith said, "if you don't get back into your vehicle, right now, and sit and wait quietly while Constable Evans talks to Mr. Morrison, I'll arrest you for interference. Decide ladies, but do it fast."

A tree groaned and let loose its full weight of heavy snow. A substantial portion of which found its way down the back of Smith's neck. Involuntarily, she yelped.

United in their anger at the female police officer, satisfied at her small bit of humiliation, the two women returned to their vehicles. Both doors slammed hard.

The radio at Smith's shoulder crackled. Two people were waving liquor bottles and screaming at each other outside the variety store on Aspen Street. The caller reported that she knew them: the LeBlancs. Smith groaned under her breath. Them again. She'd been called to their house in the summer. Husband and wife each as drunk as the other, both of them off to spend a night in the cells. Police had been at that address at least once since. Tonight, Dawn Solway responded and said she'd take it.

Evans put his notebook into his coat pocket and told the men to move their cars. People trying to get past were getting restless, and a few figures stepped out of the swirling snow to see what was going on. There didn't seem to be enough damage to either car to prevent them from moving.

Grumbling, and with shouts of 'see you in court' and 'I'll sue you for everything you've got,' the men joined their families.

"Five-one?"

Smith answered the call. "Five-one here."

"Car off the road at the bottom of Elm Street."

"We're almost clear."

"The car has gone into the river."

"On our way. Move it, Dave, we gotta go. This could be a big one." She jumped into the truck, heart pumping. Evans climbed behind the wheel. "What we got?"

"Car in the river."

"Jesus." He started the engine, while Smith punched lights and sirens on.

Chapter Two

Elm Street was decorated like a Christmas fairyland. It was a pleasant street of small shops, coffee bars, casual restaurants. Tonight, everything was closed, but windows shone with muted lighting illustrating holiday displays. Tiny white lights glittered from lamp posts, illuminating eddies of snow swirling like the skirts of ballerinas. The snow was falling so heavily that all traces of afternoon foot traffic had been eliminated, leaving the sidewalks white and pristine.

Visibility was poor, and the truck's windshield wipers weren't doing much more than stirring the white stuff around. Smith wanted to tell Evans to slow down or they'd end up in a fender bender of their own. She bit her tongue instead.

Elm Street descended from the upper town in a long straight line before taking a sharp turn at the river, where it carried on to the east. It used to be a street of industrial docks and warehouses; modern, expensive homes now lined the river. To the west lay the beach, Riverside Park, and city hall.

At the bottom of the hill a car was sprawled across the street, front end buried in a snow drift, rear end blocking the road.

Evans slammed on the brakes, and the front of the truck stopped within inches of striking the car broadside. "Close one," he said, trying to sound casual.

Smith stifled a grin, and jumped out of the truck. Either the wind had died, or they were facing in a different direction, but she had no trouble getting the door open.

"Oh, God, Officer. He was there. He was just there. I tried to get out of the way, and then he was gone. Oh, God."

The man was young, wiry, long-haired, and long-bearded. His brown eyes showed too much white, like a horse smelling fire, and his gloved hands flapped in the air. A purple toque, with a cheerful pink ball at the crown, sat on his head, and a black scarf had come unwrapped from around his neck. The long tasseled ends dragged in the snow.

"Who was there? Where? Dispatch said someone in the river?"

The man turned and pointed. "He went in, Officer. He went in."

Smith and Evans ran. The river was black and moving fast. Snow flew in their faces, sharp as the needles of fir trees. Cold wind sought gaps in necks and cuffs.

"I can't see a damned thing," Evans shouted.

"There." Smith grabbed his arm. "Look there."

About twenty-five feet from shore the undercarriage and wheels of a vehicle were pointing up. Some of the rear was visible, bright yellow, otherwise she might never have seen it.

Smith turned to the man with the long scarf, who'd followed them. "Did you see anyone? Did anyone get out?"

He shook his head. Ice was gathering on his beard. "Don't think so. I sat in my car for a few seconds, trying to get my head back. When I got out, he was in the river, going down. I didn't see anyone."

"Five-one to dispatch. We need Fire, now. Swift water rescue team."

"On their way."

A siren screamed down the hill.

"See anyone?" she asked Evans, who was passing the beam of his flashlight across the water.

"No." The wind whipped the normally placid Upper Kootenay River into tall peaks. Waves crashed against the sides of the car and washed over the exposed undercarriage.

Black water and white snowflakes covered the tops of the rocks lining the riverbank. The snow at the side of the road was piled as high as her waist. Smith climbed onto the snow bank. The snow was hard, packed by the plow. She'd swum in this river many times, and knew it was shallow for a long way out; the roof of the car must be resting on the bottom. People were trapped in there. How long had it been since it went in? Ten minutes at least. Time for the long-scarfed guy to get out of his car, run to the water's edge, pull out his cell, call 911. And then for Smith and Evans to arrive. More than time enough to drown.

People had survived for longer in a trapped car, if they had an air pocket. She moved to undo her gun belt.

Her boot slipped on a rime of ice, and she would have fallen into the water but for the hand on her arm. "You can't do it, Molly." Dave Evans was strong enough to almost lift her off her feet with one hand. "That water's freezing. You'll be incapacitated in under two minutes, and the rescue guys'll have to waste their time trying to find you."

He was right, much as she hated to admit it. She followed Dave Evans' hand back to solid ground. "We can't stand here and do nothing."

Another siren—the fire truck this time.

"Get that car out of the way," Evans said to the fellow with the long scarf. "There's going to be a lot of traffic coming this way and you're blocking the road."

"I'll try, but I'm pretty much stuck."

"Constable Smith'll give you a hand. Get that car moved. If not, the fire guys'll hit it so hard we'll be looking for pieces into next year."

They ran uphill to the car buried head first in the snow bank.

People were beginning to gather at the edges of the street-lights, ghostly shapes, faint outlines in a swirling white world. The curious, drawn by blue and red lights, the sense of urgency, the promise of excitement.

"You there," Smith called to a man in a good overcoat and black scarf. "I'm Constable Smith, Trafalgar City Police. Can you get your neighbors together and help this gentleman get his car out of the road. We need it cleared."

An ambulance made its way down the hill. It edged carefully around the stuck car, as if illustrating Smith's point.

"Glad to help," the man turned and with a single step he disappeared.

Fire truck. Top of the hill. Moving fast. Smith yelled into her radio to tell them to slow the hell down, a vehicle was in the way.

Whether her request got through or not, she didn't know. But the fire truck climbed the sidewalk to miss the obstruction and pulled parallel to the river. The occupants jumped out. Two were already dressed in yellow and black dry-suits. They fastened helmets as they ran. Another firefighter followed, carrying bundles of rope.

A group of locals, some in their Christmas Eve best, some in overcoats thrown over pajamas, came running, carrying shovels of various sizes. Snow flew everywhere as they began to dig. Smith tried to direct them, but she was ignored. The man with the long scarf jumped behind the wheel.

"Okay," a woman yelled, Santa Claus-patterned pajama bottoms sticking out from beneath her jacket. "Stand back everyone. I think we're free. Give it a go."

The car roared to life, and with a great burst of black exhaust, accompanied by applause from the snow shovel heroes, it backed into the road. The driver stuck his hand out of the window and gave everyone a wave. He pulled into a driveway, switched off the engine and joined them on the sidewalk.

The crowd moved toward the river's edge. Their euphoria at getting the car out of the way didn't last long as word spread that someone was in the river.

Feeling perfectly useless, Molly Smith watched the two firefighters moving in the black river. They'd made it to the vehicle. The shorter one ducked under the water, checking for signs of life.

The emergency tow truck was next down the hill. It turned into a driveway, and reversed to come in rear first. Smith and Evans guided onlookers out of the way.

Police radios sounded and dispatch said the RCMP were sending someone to keep the road closed.

They gathered at the water's edge. Police officers, EMT, fire-fighters, citizens, and neighbors. A man prayed softly. The tow truck moved as close as it could to the edge of the river.

On her radio, Smith heard Solway report that Mr. and Mrs. LeBlanc were being escorted to the station. *Nice Christmas for their daughter, Lorraine,* she thought.

Sergeant Caldwell reported from the scene of a three-car pile-up just outside of town. He needed an ambulance, but they said they had every vehicle out and would get to him when they could.

An aerial fire truck arrived. The ladder was raised and used to bathe the scene in strong white light. The tow truck driver got ready to fasten to the car. The people in the water, tethered by lines to their truck, moved with care, and signaled to each other with hand gestures. One came back, walking slowly in the heavy dry-suit. Chunks of ice drifted around her legs. Her face was dark and grim beneath the clear visor of the helmet. Firefighters clambered down the riverbank, dragging the end of the cable attached to the tow truck. The woman in the water grabbed it. Washed in the powerful lights of the ladder truck, snowflakes falling around her, up to her knees in black water, reflective stripes on her suit glowing, she looked like an alien, heading back to the mother ship after taking samples of Earth life forms.

Something soft, gentle and cold landed on Molly Smith's cheek. She looked up. Snowflakes drifted down from the heavens. She put her hand to her head. She'd lost her hat long ago, tossed into the back of the truck, hopefully, although she didn't remember. Her hair was soaking wet from snow melting against her scalp. Her boots were good, but even so her feet were getting cold. She wiggled her fingers inside her gloves.

But all this, she knew, was nothing compared to what the people trapped in that car must be feeling.

If they were feeling anything at all.

◇◇◇

Eliza Winters snuggled up against her husband. It was Christmas Eve, Christmas morning now, and she was delightfully warm and content. He was on vacation, and, wonder of wonders, still on vacation. No one had called, sending him back to work, tossing apologies over his shoulder. Nothing urgent, nothing only he could handle.

In the early days of her marriage, she'd seriously considered unplugging the phone and hiding it behind the sofa, before leading her husband into bed with languid glances.

But, she'd realized, that would work exactly once.

And so she'd decided simply to accept the role of the wife of a street cop, a detective, and then, the most unpredictable of all, a homicide detective.

And thus the last twenty-five years had generally passed quite well indeed.

"I think we need another log."

"I think I need another log," she said with a giggle.

"Eliza, you're drunk."

She lifted her crystal flute. "I am not. But I am out of Champagne."

He reached over and took the bottle out of the silver cooler. Ice, melting and soft, clinked. He filled her glass. Let her drink as much as she liked; she rarely did, and she wasn't driving anywhere tonight.

She'd regret it in the morning, though.

The seven-foot Douglas fir sparked with miniature white lights and colorful decorations, and the scent of the freshly cut tree filled the house. Eliza had arranged groupings of white candles on the coffee and side tables. The smaller ones had gone out, and the larger ones were flickering. The lamps had been turned off, and the only other light came from the wood-burning fireplace. The Ely Cathedral Choir sang carols in the background.

Their home was out of town, high in the mountains, on five remote acres. When John Winters had gone to the kitchen to fetch another bottle of champagne, he'd looked outside. Nothing but night and wind and snow.

He checked his watch. "It's past midnight. Merry Christmas, Eliza."

She smiled up at him. Her eyes were losing some focus around the edges. "Does that mean I can have my prezzie now?"

He hit his forehead in mock horror. "I knew I forgot something."

"I didn't, so you can open yours."

A handful of brightly wrapped presents sat under the tree. From their families and Eliza's friends in Vancouver. A single simple gift to each other, as was their custom.

He selected two boxes. Her gift to him was wrapped in heavy silver paper tied with a shimmering blue ribbon twisted into curls and spirals. His to her was stuffed into a gift bag with a candy cane pattern and fastened with enough Scotch tape to keep Fort Knox secure. He had, as always, forgotten about wrapping it and ran to the dollar store moments before closing to be faced with nothing but leftovers.

By common agreement, they didn't spend much money on gifts. Eliza was a reasonably wealthy woman. She'd been a top-ranked model in her youth and had invested most of her earnings. She now worked as and when it suited her. He was a Sergeant in a small town police department, and had never been anything other than a cop. She could afford to buy herself anything she wanted, but seldom did, and he was notoriously bad at handling money.

"You go first," he said, smiling down at her.

"Nice bag."

"Sarcasm does not become you."

The bag was very light, probably a gift certificate. She pulled at the tape. "I need a knife."

He handed her one from the cheese plate on the side table, and she sliced through the wrappings. An envelope, as she'd suspected. She opened it and laughed out loud. "Oh, John, I do love you. Now open yours."

His fingers picked at the ribbon. Still laughing, she handed him the knife. "Just cut it."

He opened the box. A book had been placed inside to provide a disguising weight. An envelope lay on top. He ripped it open. "It's true," he said, "great minds do think alike."

They had given each other gift certificates to the Greenfields Spa. Hers was for the 'Deluxe Spa Escape', his for the 'Men's Experience.'

He grinned, and she felt her heart turn over. After twenty-five years of marriage she still loved him so much.

A log on the fire fell over, spitting sparks. The last of the candles went out, and flames danced on the high ceiling. The CD player clicked off.

"I'm ready for bed," he said.

Eliza had been worried all evening that someone in Trafalgar would get himself murdered and John would be called out.

Apparently not tonight.

She hiccupped.

◇◇◇

The crowd continued to grow as people stood around, bundled up in winter wear, silently watching. Smith kept her eyes on them, but no one seemed inclined to think they could do a better job than the rescue team.

"Take this, Constable." A pair of purple wool mittens handed Smith a mug. Steam rose from the top and the cup was hot in her gloved hands. The smell of chocolate rose in the snowy air. She muttered her thanks. Evans stood beside her, sipping from his own mug.

Dave Evans didn't like her much. Which was fine with her, as she didn't like him either. But for some reason she felt she'd been stuck in the role of representing all female police officers whereas the fact that Evans was an arrogant, swaggering jerk reflected only upon himself.

She stopped worrying about Dave Evans and looked across the faces of the watchers. In the middle of the crowd, she saw someone she wouldn't have expected to see out on Christmas Eve. Meredith Morgenstern: ace reporter of the *Trafalgar Daily Gazette*. Meredith was pretty much *persona non grata* with the City Police these days. Over the summer she'd interfered in an investigation with potentially disastrous consequences. Rumor ran wild that she was going to be fired because of it, but somehow she hung onto her job.

Meredith was dressed as if she'd left a party, which she might well have done if she'd gotten a call from a *Gazette* staffer bored enough to spend his holiday evening listening in on the police radio. Sparkling in black fur and diamonds, she might have arrived in the back seat of a Russian troika pulled by matching stallions. Fake fur and fake diamonds, doubtless, but they looked good against her white skin, thick black hair, and large dark eyes.

Catching Smith watching her, Meredith turned away. There would be no exchange of seasonal greetings here.

While Evans impressed the young women in the crowd earlier by directing Fire to the scene (or pretending to direct—they needed no help), Smith had taken the report of the driver of the other vehicle.

Now that his car was safely off the road, and someone had tossed a warm blanket around his shoulders, he'd recovered his wits and could talk about what had happened. He was heading west, he told her, going home after the holiday dinner at his parents' house, took the big bend in the road and was turning north up Elm, driving carefully because the visibility was, in his words, like sticking your head into a snow bank and opening your eyes, when a yellow SUV came down the hill. Moving fast, really fast. Probably too fast even for normal conditions.

Snowplows had been out all night, but they couldn't keep up with the fall and the roads were thick with drifting snow. There wasn't enough room for two cars to pass comfortably. He wrenched his wheel in an attempt to get out of the way of the approaching car, skidded on a patch of ice or packed snow, and headed straight off the road where he, luckily, made a soft landing into a snow bank. It was likely that the yellow car had also swerved, trying to miss him, and, losing control on the slick road, failed to make the turn. It had been moving so fast it sailed over the bank only to come to a halt when it met rocks and ice and water.

"Hey, Molly, Merry Christmas." The deep voice pulled her out of her thoughts. Constable Adam Tocek, RCMP, stood in front of them, smiling.

"Merry Christmas," she said, suddenly feeling warm. "But not, I'm afraid, for them." She nodded toward the river, where the firefighters had attached the cable to the yellow SUV. It was slowly, very slowly, being dragged toward shore. Two people in dry suits walked beside it. "Yellow submarine. Hey, forget I said that. It was callous."

"No problem. Dave, how's things?"

"Okay," Evans said. "What brings you out?"

"Norman's in the truck," the Mountie said, "in case he's needed." Tocek was the RCMP dog handler for the district. Norman, he of the unlikely dog name, was Tocek's bushy-tailed partner. "When they reported that no one had been seen to get out of the vehicle, I got a call. People are washed away sometimes. Alive or dead. Seat belts undone, car window smashed. Washed down river to end up stuck in the branch of a tree."

"And a dog can find them?" Evans asked.

"It's happened."

"Would you like some hot chocolate?" Smith nodded to her cup. "They gave me this, but I don't want it."

"Sure. Thanks." He took the drink with another smile.

"Better check what's happening," Evans said, heading for the fire truck.

"You do that," Smith said to the retreating back. "Oops, sorry. Something else I shouldn't have said."

"Not a problem. We've all had partners we didn't care for. Why I like working with dogs—never met a dog I didn't like."

He was good looking, Constable Adam Tocek. He loomed over the five-foot-eight Smith, and his uniform shirt probably came in size XXXL, just to fit across the chest and around the upper arms. His hair was dark, and cut very short. All of which would have made her dismiss him as a professional tough-guy, were it not for the warmth in his brown eyes that reminded her of Sylvester, her mother's dog, and the soft smile that he seemed to have whenever he was talking to her.

"I hear," he said, "congratulations are in order."

Her face burned, even as snow fell against it. "Thanks." She'd passed. There'd been times over the last year when she'd been so sure she couldn't cut it she'd found herself surprised to realize she made it out of her probationary period. She was now a Constable Third Class with the Trafalgar City Police. Chief Constable Paul Keller had called her into his office, shook her by the hand, and told her he'd notified payroll to move her up a grade.

Bands had not played. Fireworks had not gone off. A giant banner had not been strung across Front Street announcing the good news. Barb Kowalski, the Chief's admin assistant, congratulated her, but no one else said a word.

She hadn't told her parents or her best friend, Christa.

She was now a "real" police officer.

"After that business in the summer, at the resort," Tocek began, staring at his feet and making patterns in the snow with the toe of his boot, "I didn't get a chance to say…"

"Coroner," Smith said, nodding toward a tall man who'd stepped into the light. "You think they found anyone?" She dropped her voice. "Alive I mean?"

"No."

"I'd better start trying to move people away. They'll be bringing the vehicle out, and if the coroner's here…well, we know what he's here for. It's tough, seeing dead people brought up, when you've been hoping for a miracle. Particularly on Christmas morning. See you, Adam. Give Norman a scratch for me."

"Sure, Molly. I'll do that."

Constable Smith waded into the crowd. She felt Adam Tocek's brown eyes on her back.

She didn't turn around.

◇◇◇

After the car in the river, things began to slow down. The bars were all closed, so there was nothing to do on that front. The storm continued, unabated, but by one o'clock most everyone was off the roads, helped by the early closing of the bars, and there were no more vehicular incidents.

"I think the convenience store on Aspen is still open," Evans said, as they were heading back to the office. "I feel like a chocolate bar. Want one?"

All she wanted was a bathroom.

"No, thanks."

A figure passed by the truck, as indistinct in the swirling snow and black night as a cloaked Sherlock Holmes moving under fog and gaslight. But Smith recognized the walk, which leaned slightly to the left. The result of a childhood injury, apparently an accident, but the parents had been too drunk to take the girl to the hospital until several days had passed.

Smith hopped out of the truck. "Hey, Lorraine, wait up a sec."

The girl turned. A sneer settled over her face when she saw who was calling, but she waited for Smith to catch up.

"What are you doing out?" Foolish question. Lorraine LeBlanc, sixteen years old, daughter of the town's number one drunks, went where she wanted, when she wanted. It wasn't as if anyone cared.

"Fuck off, will ya," was the girl's customary greeting.

"It's sure cold," Smith said. "I don't think I've ever seen the wind blow like this. Have you?"

Lorraine shrugged. She let down her guard, just a fraction. "It's pretty bad. They say someone went into the river. And didn't come out."

Even on Christmas morning the town grapevine was working.

No one had come out. If by that one meant no one alive, Lorraine was right. The car had been hauled out of the frozen river. Smith had cleared the onlookers while Evans held up a blanket to shield the coroner from public view. The coroner had leaned into the car, done what he had to do, and pronounced them dead. Two young males, looking to be in their early or mid twenties, faces as white as the falling snow, lips blue. They were both clean shaven, with short hair. Smith and Evans had looked at the cold faces and discreetly shaken their heads at each other. No one either of them recognized. The men had been removed from the vehicle and zipped into body bags on waiting stretchers. The ambulance headed up the hill, toward the hospital, not bothering to switch on the siren. The remnants of the crowd watched in respectful silence.

"What are you doing here, Lorraine?" Smith waved her arms in the air. "The town's shut down. Everyone's gone home. The bars and restaurants are all closed. Even the dealers have left."

"I'm not looking for a dealer, Molly."

"I didn't mean you were. I just meant there's nothing happening here. It's Christmas morning. Hey, I've an idea." She spoke before she thought. "I'm off shift soon, heading home. Why don't you come with me? I mean it's just me, my place, but warm and quiet. I'll pull out the couch to make up a bed."

Lorraine's upper lip twisted. "As if," she said, "I'd go anywhere with a dyke cop. I value my reputation, you know."

"It's not like that." And it wasn't. Molly Smith had a BA in Social Work from the University of Victoria. She'd been about to get her MSW when she'd dropped out and, after a year of aimless wandering, applied to the Trafalgar City Police.

Police and social workers sometimes stood on opposite sides of the fence. And, as if she didn't have enough problems, Molly Smith occasionally found herself straddling said fence.

"I have a boyfriend, Molly. A nice guy, okay? I'm going to his place now." Lorraine's make-up was thickly applied, dripping in the snow melting off her hair. She wore a proper winter coat, although one elbow and a seam in the right shoulder were patched with duct tape. Her boots were good, but they looked too big for the girl's small feet. Probably from the Salvation Army. Her scarf was full of holes, but at least it protected her neck.

"We're gonna have a real Christmas," she said. "With presents and a tree and everything."

"That sounds good." And it did. Too bad the boyfriend couldn't, or wouldn't, pick Lorraine up and escort her to this Christmas wonderland. Although, Smith had to admit, Lorraine LeBlanc had good reasons to keep a prospective beau well away from her family.

Particularly as Mom and Dad were spending the night in the drunk tank.

"The sidewalks are icy, Lorraine. Watch your footing."

"I've been out after dark before."

"Night, Lorraine."

"Hey, Molly."

"Yeah?"

"Merry Christmas, eh?"

"Same to you, Lorraine. Same to you."

Evans came out of the shop, ripping the packaging off an Oh Henry. He stood beside Smith, watching Lorraine slipping on the icy streets. "What'd that slut want?"

"Come on, Dave, give the kid a break. You know what her life's like. Dawn hauled Mom and Dad off to the cells tonight. Nice family Christmas."

"Tough. But she's still a cheap slut."

Chapter Three

"He's not here, and I don't know where he is. There's nothing unusual in that. He likes to play at keeping people waiting for him." Wendy Wyatt-Yarmouth looked the girl standing in the doorway up and down, not trying particularly hard to hide a sneer. No matter: the stupid girl didn't seem to know an insult when one scored a direct hit on her butt.

The girl's lanky hair and the shoulders of her second-hand coat were covered in snow. She was making a puddle on the mat at the front door.

"You might as well go home," Wendy said. "If, and I mean if, he comes in, I'll tell him to call you."

"But…I don't…I mean, he promised. He said he'd call before he came to pick me up. He didn't, so I came over anyway. I figured his cell phone ran out of juice." Her voice trailed off.

"My brother promises a lot of things. To a lot of people. Sorry to disappoint you, kid, but he doesn't believe promises are worth fuck all." What she said was true, and Wendy wasn't too bothered by the tears that welled up in the girl's eyes, or the way her chin quivered.

"Nonsense." Mrs. Carmine helped the visitor divest herself of her coat. "I'm sure the young men will be back soon. In the meantime, I've prepared a lovely meal. You're welcome to join us, dear."

Whatever. Wendy went back to the common room. Where, she had to admit, *lovely* was the appropriate word. A fire roared in the fireplace, spreading warmth and light. It was only gas, but was a good imitation of a real wood fire. The Balsam Fir in the corner was green and tall and fat, brimming with delicate ornaments and colored lights. The side tables held wooden decorations, small and lovingly carved, of a manger scene, an Alpine village in winter, and Santa's workshop. Nine big red stockings, names painted on them in bright glitter, crowded the mantle above the fireplace.

The interloper gasped at the sight. She stepped toward the mantle and reached out her hand, stopping just short of touching the stocking with her name. "It's beautiful." Her voice cracked.

Wendy rolled her eyes.

"I made one for you, Lorraine," Mrs. Carmine said with a big smile. She was short and fat, her hair gray and badly cut, her eyes small and dark like a rat's. She wore a red velour tracksuit covered with a white apron decorated with gingerbread people. Except for the eyes, she looked exactly as one might imagine Mrs. Claus.

Mrs. C, as she insisted her guests call her, had gone all out to create the perfect Christmas setting.

It would be hard not to enjoy it.

Wendy was not enjoying it. They'd accepted Mrs. C's suggestion—okay, her quiet bullying—to have a traditional Christmas Eve in the common room. But Jason had left hours ago, and hadn't come back, and no one had seen Ewan since yesterday.

"We're going to get old waiting for them," Sophie said. "It's long after midnight. Hi, Laurie."

"Lorraine."

They'd flown in from Ontario and Quebec. A group of friends getting together for a ski vacation in British Columbia. A cozy B&B in Trafalgar. Days on the slopes, nights in the bars. Christmas cheer and New Year's revelry.

It had all gone wrong, almost immediately. *Although that shouldn't have been any sort of a surprise*, Wendy thought. She shouldn't have come. These were her brother Jason's friends, and she didn't like any of them. Now Jason had taken off, leaving her to celebrate Christmas with his university buddies. And the awkward local girl he'd collected like a dog collects fleas—a wide-eyed child who was anything but innocent.

God fucking bless us, every one.

Wendy threw herself onto the couch. "Jason'll be here soon. I don't want to open our presents without him. It was his idea to have our party tonight, so we could hit the slopes first thing tomorrow."

"Get real, Wendy," Jeremy said. "Jason found something more interesting than us, and he's snuggled up in someone's bed getting his private Christmas present."

"He wouldn't," Lorraine said. Light from the fire reflected off her washed-out blue eyes. "He invited me to come. For his away-from-family-Christmas, he said. He wouldn't forget that."

Wendy pulled out her phone, one more time, and dialed Jason's cell. Again, it went to voice mail. Maybe he had run out of juice, like Lorraine said. But that didn't explain why he wasn't here. He had to know she was waiting for him.

"You can sulk all you want." Alan said. He switched his smile to "on" like the actor he was and turned it full force onto Mrs. C. "I'm in the mood for Christmas. And speaking of something better, I'll bet there's something here for me."

The landlady laughed. "You have to wait, just one minute. Kathy, help me in the kitchen. You stay right there, Sophie," she said to the girl who'd only leaned over to nuzzle the back of Alan's neck. "I don't need any help."

Mrs. Carmine and Kathy, her daughter, returned moments later, carrying trays precariously balanced with glasses of pale yellow eggnog, platters of sliced shortbread, mince tarts, cheese and crackers.

"I have something to add to that." Alan ran up the stairs and was back a moment later, clutching a bottle of Champagne. Being Alan it was the real stuff—*Moët et Chandon.*

"Nice," Jeremy took the bottle from him. Sophie, Alan's girlfriend, ran toward the tree. "You have to open mine first. You must."

Alan swept Sophie up as she passed. "Let me get you some Champagne first."

Everyone jumped as the cork popped out of the bottle. With a big grin, Jeremy held it high. Wendy was still looking at Alan and she saw the cloud flash across his handsome face. He'd wanted to do the ceremonial opening, to continue being the center of attention, but Jeremy had upstaged him. Alan never liked to be upstaged.

Rob and Kathy held the glasses while Jeremy poured the drinks into an assortment of champagne flutes, beer mugs, and wine glasses. Kathy beamed at Rob who seemed impervious to her charms, modest as they might be. Alan threw himself into an armchair, smile fixed in place. Lorraine accepted her drink with wide eyes and brought the glass slowly to her lips.

Pearls before swine.

When everyone was served, Mrs. C clapped her hands in delight. "Presents, presents. We must have presents."

Alan opened his gift from Sophie. Good, reliable ski gloves, just shy of being top notch.

Like Sophie herself, solid, respectable, but most definitely not the best.

Wendy sipped at her champagne and watched the rest of them opening their gifts, enjoying the refreshments, laughing and flirting.

Lorraine sat alone on the edge of the sofa, clinging to her glass. If she were a nice person, Wendy would feel sorry for the girl. Thinking she was in love with a good looking guy from a good family and a great university with a highly-promising future, who'd do nothing but screw her and wave bye-bye out the car window as he left town.

But she wasn't a nice person, and so Wendy didn't bother herself to care about pathetic little Lorraine.

"There must be a present for our Lorraine," Mrs. C said, having trouble getting her lips around the words. Wendy suspected she'd been into the Champagne already. Alan had a secret store in his room, and he always knew how to butter up the hired help.

"I'll have my Christmas at home in the morning," Lorraine said, "with Mom and Dad, of course. There'll be plenty of presents." Her eyes slid to one side, and Wendy knew she was lying.

"Nevertheless there must be something for you under our tree."

Kathy, Mrs. C's daughter, another precocious teenager you might as well crush under your shoe as you would a cockroach, rolled her eyes. "As if," she muttered.

Jeremy laughed.

"Keep digging, Kathy," Mrs. C said. No sugar was left in her voice.

And sure enough Kathy came up with a small box. She handed it to Lorraine.

The girl hesitated before taking it, looking as if she'd bolt. Then she accepted the box and rubbed her fingers, nails bitten to the quick, across it. "It's so beautiful." She pulled at the ribbon, all the colors of the rainbow, and then at the paper.

"Who's it from?" Sophie asked.

"Jason, of course." Lorraine's eyes shone. "See, it says right here on the label. To Lorraine, Merry Christmas, from Jason."

"What's in it?" Sophie again, sounding as if she were actually excited.

Lorraine opened the blue box. She gasped, and they all, Wendy included, leaned forward.

Gold earrings. Small, perfectly round hoops.

"How lovely." Wendy reached out her hand. Lorraine hesitated, but Wendy kept her hand in place, and Lorraine reluctantly put the box into it.

Gold. Pure gold.

The hour hand of the clock in the lunch room approached three.

Evans leaned back in his chair and stretched. Like Smith, he'd taken off his coat and Kevlar vest. "I'm going to Emily's soon as I'm off. She made something she calls a late supper and told me she's looking forward to celebrating our first Christmas together."

How nice of you to let me know you have food and sex in your immediate future.

Smith herself would stagger home and go to bed where she'd eventually wake to welcome Christmas day alone. All alone. As every Christmas since…

Enough. Adam Tocek had asked her on a hiking date in the summer, and she'd made a feeble excuse not to go. Undeterred, he was still sending her loud and clear signals. She'd chosen to ignore them, and that was her choice.

It was still too soon.

The hands of the clock touched three. Evans grabbed his coat.

"Say Merry Christmas to Emily for me." Smith got to her feet.

He was in such a rush to get out the door and off to his girlfriend's place he didn't hear her.

"Have a nice screw," Smith muttered.

"What's that, Molly?" Ingrid, the night dispatcher, asked.

"I was wishing Constable Evans the complements of the season."

"My aunt Fanny."

"Night, Ingrid."

"Night, Molly."

"See you tomorrow."

"As there is no lottery draw on Christmas Day, that will probably be the case."

The radio spat to life. Smith listened as Ingrid answered. 911. House fire. Christmas tree in flames.

"Forty-two, forty-two," Ingrid said. Solway answered and Ingrid gave her the details.

"This has been one miserable Christmas Eve," Smith said. "But at least it's over."

"Maybe not."

"Hold on, I'm going home."

"Halton called back." The dead men in the car pulled out of the river were both carrying wallets containing Ontario licenses. The driver, Jason Wyatt-Yarmouth, was from Oakville, and Ingrid had called the regional police to request they contact the address on his license. The yellow SUV had been a local rental.

"They went to Wyatt-Yarmouth's address," Ingrid said. "Merry Christmas. Your brother/son/husband/father/friend/ life-long enemy's bought the farm. Don't let us spoil your turkey dinner. Night. Couldn't possibly be our Jason, the parents said, as he's in Trafalgar, B.C., skiing. He's staying at the Glacier Chalet B&B with his sister and a group of friends."

"Tough."

"You got that right, Molly. Tough enough for the sister to hear the news straight off. Not to sit up all Christmas Eve wondering where her brother is."

"Come on, Ingrid. Tough stuff happens all the time. Why are you laying this on me?"

The dispatcher pulled a tissue out of the box beside the screen monitoring the cells. Tonight's only guests of the city were Jake and Felicia LeBlanc. The town drunks. They'd been at a party and had gotten into a screaming and hitting match on their way home. In a breach of seasonal spirit they were not sharing a family cell.

Ingrid wiped at her eyes. "I hate Christmas, okay. My sister, my big sister who I adored, died on Christmas day. Cancer. I was twelve and she was sixteen. My parents wouldn't take me to the hospital to see her one last time. Didn't want to spoil my Christmas."

"Gee, Ingrid. I'm sorry."

"You tell anyone that, Smith, and you'll be answering every domestic we get for the next year." Ingrid blew her nose. She was in her late fifties, with short hair the color of a rusty battleship, and hard eyes. Smith didn't know anything about Ingrid's background. Other than over the radio, they'd never exchanged more than five words at a time.

"Why don't the parents phone the sister? This isn't news that should come from a stranger."

Ingrid threw up her hands. "I don't know. They asked us to send someone around to inform the group in person."

"Ingrid…"

"Dawn's gone to the fire. Might be there a long time if they have trouble controlling it. Caldwell's at an OD. Found a nice package of white power while he was there."

"Send the Mounties."

"Molly."

"Okay, okay. I'll pop round. Not as if I have anything to do Christmas morning anyway."

◇◇◇

Try as she might to remain aloof, Wendy found herself forgetting her troubles and falling into the spirit of things. Presents were opened, snacks eaten, champagne drunk, more champagne drunk. The presents the friends gave each other were frivolous stuff: chocolates, bath salts, silly puzzles, costume jewelry.

Alan gave Sophie a barely-there peach nightgown. Sophie turned red and covered her face with the thin fabric while Mrs. Carmine broke into giggles. Their landlady had definitely had too much Champagne.

Mrs. C's gift to Kathy was a set of flannel pajamas, and Kathy gave her mother an electric kettle.

Lorraine clutched the tiny blue box that was her present and watched the festivities with a gentle smile on her face.

Wendy refused to open her gift from Jason without him present.

As they hadn't seen Ewan since yesterday, and everyone assumed he'd found more hospitable accommodations, they opened the gifts from him.

Finally there were only a handful of wrapped presents under the tree. Gifts to Jason and Ewan, and Wendy's from her brother.

"Something must be wrong," Lorraine said, staring at the small pile of gifts. "Why isn't he here?"

"Because he doesn't wanna be," Wendy said. She took the last piece of shortbread. Homemade, packed with so much butter it melted in her mouth.

"Per'aps 'e and Ewan caught up," Sophie said in her strong Quebec accent, rubbing her fingers through the fabric of her gift as if she were already imagining the feel of it against her body. And the feel of it being taken off. "And 'e 'ad to go wherever Evan's been."

"I'm sure you're right, Sophie," Mrs. C said. "That's a perfectly sensible explanation. Good heavens look at the time. Kathy, help me do up the dishes. What time would you like breakfast in the morning?"

"Breakfast," Rob shouted, throwing up his arms in mock surrender. "Perish the thought. I can't think of breakfast."

"Well you have to if we're going to be on the slopes early," Alan said.

The seven of them—Jason, his sister, and five of his friends—had come to B.C. for two weeks' skiing. They were all university students. Jason, Ewan, and Alan had grown up together in Oakville, allowing, sometimes, Wendy, the kid sister, to tag along. Alan had gone to McGill, the University in Montreal, where he'd met Sophie, the *Québécois*.

Rob had been Jason's roommate first year and they'd stayed friends. Wendy didn't quite know where Jeremy fit in.

For as long as Wendy could remember Jason and Ewan had been best friends. Ewan-Jason, Jason-Ewan. So close they might as well have hyphenated their names. She'd grown up tagging along after Jason and his friends, and she'd always had a bit of a crush on Ewan. Who never paid the slightest bit of attention to her. He'd disappeared only a few days into their two-week vacation, but no one even considered worrying about him. *Typical Ewan*, they all thought. As he'd been temporarily between girlfriends, he'd started looking for something to lay before they'd even gotten off the plane at tiny Castlegar airport.

This vacation was Jason's idea, formulated after last year's incredibly dull New Years Eve at a house party. He'd found the

B&B on the Internet and had been early enough to book the entire place. The group had gathered at Toronto airport. Flown to Calgary and then to Castlegar. Jason had arranged the rental of a seven-seater SUV with a ski compartment on the roof. Bags, friends, skis, presents were loaded aboard, and they'd headed for Trafalgar and their Christmas vacation.

They were gathering their gifts, leaving the cleaning up and dishes to Mrs. C. and Kathy—they were paying guests, after all, no matter how homey Mrs. C. made the place—when the doorbell rang.

Lorraine ran to the door like a greyhound out of the starting gate. Wendy followed, prepared to give her brother a piece of her mind. She'd only come on this stupid trip because he'd asked her. She had plenty of other things she could have done with her vacation.

"*Alain*," Sophie said, "I am going to *bed*. You can come with me or stay to 'ave a drink with your *ami*, Jason. Not both."

Alan's feet hit the stairs, hard.

"As for me," Jeremy said, "I'll have another drink. Tell Jas and Ewan to get in here. I hope to hell they brought more booze."

Lorraine threw open the door. Wendy and Mrs. C. crowded behind.

It wasn't Jason.

The woman was young, probably not much older than Wendy herself. Very pretty with an oval face, sharp, high cheekbones, pert nose, and large blue eyes. Cheeks and plump lips were reddened with cold. She was tall and, much as one could tell with the way she was bundled up, in good shape. Snowflakes fell on the shoulders of her blue coat and blue-trimmed hat.

For a brief moment Wendy dared hope this was a strip-o-gram, bringing a raunchy holiday greeting from friends back in Ontario. But the police uniform was too perfect. And the woman was not smiling.

The cop shifted her feet and took off her hat, revealing short hair the color of ripening corn.

"Lorraine?" she said, blinking in surprise. Behind her, reflected in the street lights, snow fell steadily.

"Are you following me, Molly? You can't come in here. I know my rights. I haven't done anything. Mrs. Carmine." Lorraine darted to safety behind the landlady's chubby form. "Tell her to go away. Tell her to stop bothering me."

"I'm sorry," the officer said. "Lorraine, I didn't know you were here. Honest." She sounded hesitant, unsure of herself. It was none of Wendy's business, but she never minded seeing pretty young women slapped into place. Interesting, that this representative of the law and Jason's holiday amusement were on a first name basis.

"You didn't?" Lorraine squeaked.

"No, I didn't. Sorry if I frightened you, Lorraine. I'm looking for Ms. Wendy Wyatt-Yarmouth and I've been told she's staying here."

Wendy looked around in confusion. Attracted by the voices, Kathy had stuck her head out of the kitchen, and Jeremy and Rob were in the doorway to the common room.

"You'd better come in, Moonlight," Mrs. Carmine said. *What the hell did the light of the moon have to do with any of this?* Wendy thought. "Or you'll catch your death. Dreadful night, isn't it? We're cleaning up. Such a lovely party we had. I'll make up a plate for you. Kathy, put the kettle back on and lay out the remainder of the shortbread. See if there's enough cheese left. How dreadful you have to work tonight, dear. Lucky can't be at all happy about that, now can she. Come in, please."

"Thank you, Mrs. Carmine. But I need to speak to Ms. Wyatt-Yarmouth. Is she here?" The woman's voice was recovering some of its confidence.

Wendy stepped backward. Pushing Jeremy and Rob aside, into the common room, where the tree was almost devoid of presents. Someone had switched the lights off on the side tables and the beautiful Christmas scenes had gone dark. Only the fireplace still cast a soft yellow glow. The room looked like the set of a play, coming to the end. Wendy's heart was in her stomach and, for some strange reason, she was aware of a vein throbbing in her neck. She considered making a run for it, but she didn't know where the back door was.

The police officer walked into the room. She hadn't bothered to remove her boots and coat, as any well mannered visitor would do.

"You must be Ms. Wyatt-Yarmouth. I'm Constable Smith, Trafalgar City Police. I'd like a few minutes of your time, please." Her big black boots spread sand and snowmelt across the floor.

Wendy looked around. Jeremy was holding his beer bottle behind his back, and staring at the place where the woman's jacket was pulled up, revealing the black gun at her hip. Mrs. Carmine was ringing her hands, finally understanding that this was not a social call of the sort that necessitated tea and short-bread. Kathy and the boys just stared. Lorraine had disappeared. Upstairs, in Alan and Sophie's room, a floorboard creaked and a toilet flushed.

The heat of the gas fireplace was hot against the back of Wendy's legs. "It wasn't my fault. Go away."

"I'd appreciate it if you and your guests could give us some privacy, Mrs. Carmine," the cop said.

Mrs. C waved her hands as if she were gathering chickens into the hen house. "I'm sure it's nothing to worry about. Let's go into the kitchen, shall we. My late husband was rather fond of his Cognac, nothing but the best would do, and there's something in the back of the cupboard. Why don't I fetch you one, Wendy. I'm sure Moonlight would enjoy a sip as well. Kathy," Mrs. C snapped. "I said, come into the kitchen."

They fled. Leaving Wendy alone with Barbie-plays-cop.

"I'm very sorry, Ms. Wyatt-Yarmouth, but I have to inform you that…"

Chapter Four

Smith stepped into the night. Snow was still falling and the wind was still blowing. The street was deserted, everyone at home with their loved ones.

She pulled her collar up around her neck and dug in her pockets looking for her gloves. Light from the streetlamps was dim in the falling snow. It was only two blocks to her apartment, and she walked through deserted streets, enjoying the sound of snow crunching under her feet.

The wind was a problem, but all this snow promised great skiing. She had to work tomorrow, Christmas day, much to her mother's dismay, then she had four whole days off. The hills would be packed with tourists, but it would still be quite wonderful. Even at the height of the tourist rush, there wasn't too much of a crowd at the double black diamonds, where Molly Smith went to ski.

What a miserable business that had been. Many officers said that informing people of the death of a loved one was the worst part of the job. Tonight had been Smith's first time. Evans was senior to her, he should have done it. Sergeant Caldwell should have done it.

Anyone but her.

As she tried, gently as possible, to inform Wendy Wyatt-Yarmouth of the death of her brother and his friend, she couldn't help but be aware of the piles of cast-off gift wrap littering the floor, the glasses stained with reside of eggnog and wine, half-eaten cookies and crackers and smears of cheese and pâté on paper plates decorated with a cheerful assortment of holiday motifs.

And, under the huge, perfectly shaped and decorated Christmas tree, one heartbreakingly small pile of gifts, waiting to be opened.

Wendy Wyatt-Yarmouth had crumpled to the floor like a rag doll left out in the spring rains, while Smith shifted her feet and stuffed her hands into her pockets. Obviously Mrs. Carmine and the whole crew had been listening at the door; they'd come running into the sitting room at Wendy's moan.

Assured that Wendy would be taken good care of, Smith left. Feeling like absolute crap.

Mrs. Carmine walked Smith to the door. She looked like Mrs. Santa Claus, all steel grey hair and red clothes and white apron. "They forget, these young ones, so proud of themselves, so sure of their invulnerability, protected by money and arrogance, they forget what weather can do."

She touched Smith's arm. "Say Merry Christmas to your parents, will you? Tell Lucky she left her plate here after our pot luck the other night."

"Sure, Mrs. Carmine. Sure." Smith had stuffed her hat onto her head, faced the wind and headed back to the patrol car.

It might be time to start looking for a job in a big city, Vancouver, say, or Calgary. Even Toronto. Toronto was advertising for experienced police officers, but Smith was, she admitted to herself, afraid to venture too far away. She'd never been further east than Calgary; Ontario was as foreign and exotic as the Orient. Although the advantage of Toronto was that she could be pretty much guaranteed that the citizenry would not tell her to say hi to her parents or know that her given name was Moonlight. Moonlight Legolas Smith. Legolas being a character in *The Lord of the Rings*, of which her parents, hippies, draft-dodgers, idealists, had been exceptionally fond. *What a name for a cop.*

Smith's mother, Lucy, whom everyone called Lucky, was no less idealistic now than she'd been back in the day. Which also didn't make it easy to be an Officer of the Law in this opinionated, left-leaning, artistic, independently-inclined town nestled in the mountains and forests deep inside British Columbia.

That it was also beautiful, creative, invigorating, and a place of independent minds, was, well, something she'd rather not think about as she pondered whether she'd have to move to the big city. If she wanted her career to go anywhere, she probably did. Trafalgar was generally a peaceful town. No gun battles in the streets, no gangs, no organized crime or street prostitution. Not much in the way of hard drugs, although there were almost as many grow-ops as citizens, and marijuana was, despite being illegal, the area's most famous, and most profitable, crop. Murder was rare, and when it did happen, was usually solved quickly.

Trafalgar wasn't a place to get good policing experience.

But it was her home. And she didn't want to imagine living anyplace else.

She made her way up the back stairs to her apartment. She particularly enjoyed her new place when she got off duty at six a.m. to be welcomed by the scent of fresh bread and croissants, straight out of the ovens of the bakery below, wafting up the stairs. Tonight, a brown bag full of left-over baking sat on the landing in front of her door. She scooped it up, peeked at the contents, and let herself in.

She'd moved out of her parents' house in the fall, realizing that it was time to become a real adult. She'd never lived alone before, and was afraid she wouldn't like it. She'd moved out of the parental home into res at university—all giggling girls, parties, booze and drugs, and serious study—then an apartment with Graham, her fiancé. When Graham was knifed and left to die beside a garbage container in Vancouver she returned to her parents' house by the river.

She loved living on her own. She could play her choice of music, watch what she wanted on TV, cook what she wanted to eat, leave the bed unmade for days, and the dishes unwashed, and the floor unswept, if she felt like it.

She'd been lucky to get this place. She'd seen the apartment in the summer when they investigated a murder in the alley behind, and had loved it even while poking around looking for evidence. But the time hadn't been right for her to move, and when she did inquire, someone else had taken it.

That someone else only stayed for a month and when he left, Alphonse, the landlord, called to ask if she still wanted it. The apartment was on the second floor of an old building on Front Street, Trafalgar's main thoroughfare. Alphonse's traditional French bakery took up the ground floor, filling her dreams—and the clothes hanging in her closet—with wonderful smells. She thought she'd miss the dark nights and clear skies and quiet of her family home, but found that she liked living in town. Still, the first thing she'd done was to hang a couple of big heavy blankets over the thin blinds at the bedroom window directly across from a street lamp.

She'd placed a small chair at the door, so she could sit down and take off her boots the minute she stepped inside. She walked into the bedroom, took off her belt and locked her gun in the safe. Back to the kitchen for a closer inspection of the contents of Alphonse's brown paper bag. A slice of apple tart and a half-sized whole wheat baguette. Did they make whole wheat baguettes in France?—maybe not, but despite advertising his bakery as traditional, if Alphonse wanted to survive in Trafalgar, British Columbia, he had to make what the customers wanted.

And people in Trafalgar wanted organic, natural, local, and healthy.

She tore the loaf into hunks, spread butter on the exposed ends, and took a bite.

She should go to bed, but she was still wound up from the shift. Imagine going off the road and into the river. Imagine sitting there, in your car, and not being able to get the door or windows open. Sitting there while the car filled with water and the air ran out.

Better not go there. Second rule of the job—don't take it home.

She filled the kettle and poured hot chocolate powder into a mug. When the drink was ready, she carried it and her food into the living room. She was expected to be at her parents' house first thing in the morning for presents and spend the day with them, suitably cheerful and brimming with holiday spirit. She'd help her mom in the kitchen, go for a walk with her dad and the dog, eat an enormous turkey dinner, and then head home to change and be at work by three. She wouldn't even be able to have a glass of wine with the meal.

She switched on the TV and DVD player and settled down to watch the end of the boring movie she'd rented yesterday. She should have known better than to choose a film the guys in the lunch room were talking about. She finished her baguette, sipped hot chocolate, and started in on the apple tart. Even better than her mother made. There would be apple pie for dinner tomorrow—later today, that was—and banana cream, her dad's favorite. Smith liked banana cream pie just fine, but some years ago her mother had gotten it into her head that her daughter's favorite was apple. And so there was always an apple pie.

She'd rather sleep for eight hours and pop over to the house for a quick exchange of presents and brunch. But, particularly as her brother Sam and his family were not coming this year, her mom was determined to fit the whole Christmas experience into the few hours Molly had off work.

By the time the final credits of the movie ran, she was asleep on the couch.

Dead. Jason was dead.

Wendy lay in bed, her eyes wide open. A street lamp burned outside her window, throwing yellow light through the thin curtains.

Mrs. Carmine had been all brisk efficiency. Showing the cop to the door, shooing the onlookers away, telling Rob to use her car to take the sobbing Lorraine home, taking charge of Wendy, who'd been reduced to having as much muscle control as a rag doll. Mrs. C had ordered Jeremy to take Wendy upstairs to her room, which he'd done in sort of a half-carry. Mrs. C followed, ordered Jeremy out, flicked through the wardrobe and found pajamas and a warm blue robe. She unbound Wendy's hair and stripped her down to bra and panties. Pulling and stuffing, pajamas had gone on. She placed the robe at the end of the bed, in case it was needed in the night, pulled the homemade quilt up to Wendy's chin, switched off the light, and whispered goodnight.

Jason was dead, and Ewan along with him. Fitting somehow, that they went off the road together.

Or so the cop had said, but the police weren't perfect. They got things wrong all the time, didn't they? That officer, the woman, she was young, obviously inexperienced. Embarrassed and awkward, in her big boots, dripping hat, and ill-fitting gun belt. Who knew what mistakes she might make.

Yup, that was it. The cops had, typically, made a mistake. Jason would be here in the morning, shouting for coffee and breakfast, apologizing for keeping everyone waiting. Charming Mrs. Carmine and yelling that they were going to the hill and he'd leave anyone behind who wasn't ready in five minutes.

And Ewan?

No one would care what happened to Ewan.

As long as Jason was all right.

Wendy closed her eyes. Something hit the wall. She rolled over, gathering the blankets around her chin. All would be revealed tomorrow. Mom and Dad would be having quite the fit tonight. She almost chuckled at the thought. Why, they'd be so upset at the (incorrectly reported) death of the precious son and heir they might spare a thought for their daughter and give her a call.

But she wouldn't wait up for that.

The walls in this place might as well have been made of rice paper. Her room was next to Alan and Sophie's. Their headboard hit the wall—again. And again. A steady rhythm started up.

Wendy studied the ceiling. There was a crack in the right corner.

Everything would be settled tomorrow. She might lay a complaint against Constable Smith for causing her undue worry and stress.

Just for something fun to do in this bumpkin town.

<><><>

John Winters walked into his office as the phone began to ring. It had been one of the best vacations in a long time. He and Eliza had gone nowhere, done nothing. Just relaxed at home, enjoyed long walks in the winter woods, dined out twice, went to a surprisingly pleasant cocktail party at the Chief Constable's house. He'd even shoveled the driveway a couple of times without waiting for the snowplow service to come and do it. It was their first Christmas in their home in the Kootenays, and they'd wanted simply to enjoy it. And they had.

Winters had taken two weeks off leading up to and over Christmas, and his partner, Detective Ray Lopez, got the days on either side of New Year's off. A yellow post-it note was stuck to Winters' monitor. "Do NOT, repeat NOT, attempt to care for my plants. P.S. Happy New Year."

The office housed GIS—the General Investigative Section— the detectives for the Trafalgar City Police. All two of them. Lopez, by virtue of being here longer, had the desk by the window. Where he carefully and lovingly cultivated a row of small pots of African violets. The first time he went on leave, he'd asked Winters to care for the plants. They'd almost died from neglect and Lopez was now afraid Winters would over-compensate.

No need to worry about that.

Between Christmas and New Years not much was likely to happen. He planned to fill his days reading two weeks' worth of accumulated e-mail and finishing up overdue paperwork.

He answered the phone. "Sergeant Winters."

"Merry Christmas, John. Or is it too late to wish one Merry Christmas?"

"Happy New Year is the accepted greeting for now until…I don't actually know when you stop saying Happy New Year. Sometime in February, I think. Perhaps by Groundhog Day."

"I probably don't want to know what Groundhog Day is. But I feel compelled to ask. Do you go shooting these groundhogs and cook them up in some sort of native ritual?"

"Doc, you wouldn't believe it if I told you. But I will anyway. We stand around a groundhog's hole and watch it pop its head up to see if it sees its shadow."

"I shudder to think."

"It's more common in the east than out here. What's up, Doc?"

Childishly he always loved to say that to Doctor Shirley Lee, the pathologist. She never got the joke. Doctor Lee had lived in Canada since she was eight years old but, so sheltered had she been by a rich, insular family, there were plenty of cultural reference she didn't get. She didn't even know about Groundhog Day.

She said, "I've stopped the autopsy on Mr. Williams."

Winters sat up. Ewan Williams had gone into the Upper Kootenay River on the early hours of Christmas morning. In the company of Jason Wyatt-Yarmouth and a yellow SUV. Both men had been trapped in their vehicle, in the ice-coated river, for more than thirty minutes before being pulled out. Cause of death should have been easy to determine: drowning and hypothermia. Which was why there'd been no big rush for the autopsy over the holidays.

For Lee to stop an autopsy meant she'd found something significant.

"Why?" he asked.

"I did Mr. Wyatt-Yarmouth first. I found what I expected to find. Healthy, well-fed male in his early twenties in excellent physical condition. Judging by the muscles of his arms and legs, he was a keen athlete. Death by drowning, no doubt about it. Massive trauma to the hands and forearms as he attempted to bash and claw his way out of the vehicle. I recommended that the body be released to the family. I've withdrawn that recommendation."

"Why'd you do that? Because of Williams, I'd guess. What's funny about Williams?"

"Ewan Williams had been dead for twenty-four hours, at a minimum, before he went into the water."

Chapter Five

Molly Smith floated into work on a cloud of champagne powder. Although not literally; the big storm had ended by mid-morning on Christmas Day, and nothing but a dusting of snow had fallen in the valley since. She'd come back to work early, having agreed to take someone else's shift, but she'd spent two great days on the ski hills. Doing run after run; double black diamond after double black diamond. The snow was so dry and light they called it champagne powder. She'd been at the resort when the day began, leaving the slopes when the unlit hills closed down at four o'clock. Holiday time, and the parking lot of Big Sky resort had been full to overflowing, the lines for the lifts long. But the weather was good, the sun bright in a blue sky, and the powder deep and fresh on the hills.

Graham had been the ultimate outdoor adventurer. With one exception. He consistently refused to go skiing with her. She'd tried to talk him into it, assuring him that she wouldn't laugh, she'd show him the ropes—in school she'd been a skiing instructor and worked ski patrol. He refused to even try it, and one wet winter's evening in their apartment in Victoria, the night before she was to go up-Island to the slopes of Mount Washington with friends, he'd finally confessed he was afraid. He'd skied as a child, taken a bad fall on a grade four trip, and dislocated his shoulder. Rather than letting him get right back onto the proverbial horse, his skittish mother had gone on and on about what a dangerous sport skiing was, and she'd refused to sign his permission slip for the next trip, when the shoulder was back in place. Her fear had made him fearful.

He'd never been on skis again, and he wouldn't try even for Molly.

Other than her work, skiing was the one thing that took Molly Smith away from the ghost of Graham Buckingham.

"Anything happening?" she asked Jim Denton, the day dispatch officer.

"Quiet as a mouse. One guy in cells. Picked up last night for drunk and disorderly. Tisk, tisk. We should start getting busy tonight as folks practice for a big New Year's blow out. You can be glad you're on days, Molly. It should be a nice, Q, shift."

As superstitious as actors who never mentioned the name of the Scottish Play or wished each other luck, break a leg being the accepted alternative, police never said the Q word, afraid it would bring on the opposite and the shift would be anything but quiet.

"But not too calm." John Winters appeared out of nowhere, and both Smith and Denton jumped. The Sergeant could walk on cat's feet sometimes. "I've been reading the report of an accident that happened on Monday. Car went into the river. Two males who didn't survive. You were at the scene, Molly?"

"Yes. Hell of a shift. We answered more traffic calls in that night than we usually have in a month. The big storm. My dad said nothing's been seen like it in the Kootenays for decades. Why?"

"What with the holiday season, and vacations, and the flu outbreak at the Seniors' Residence, and the apparently obvious cause of death resulting from the car in the river, the autopsy wasn't done until today."

"So they've been busy and understaffed at the morgue. Nothing new about that," Denton said.

"Apparently?" Smith said.

Winters hid signs of approval. Molly had zeroed in on the right word. She had a long way to go, a very long way, but she just might make detective some day.

"Appearances are sometimes deceiving. You're with me, Molly. Who's the shift sergeant?" he asked Denton.

"Peterson."

Peterson. Who never left an 'i' undotted or a 't' uncrossed and would never let a new constable off the beat without an argument.

"I'll call Al from the car. Let's go."

"Where?" she said.

"Trail. The hospital. Doctor Lee's stopped the autopsy pending my arrival. As you were there, at the scene, I thought you'd want to be involved."

"Gee, thanks, I'd like that. But, well, why'd she stop the autopsy?"

"An autopsy's performed in any unexpected death, you know that. Ninety-nine times out of a hundred, it's none of our business. But this time, Shirley stopped in the middle of it. Left the cadaver sliced open on the table. She backed away and told her assistant to pack him up as is. Why would she do that?"

"She found something that made her think it's our business?"

"Yup. Jim, find out where they took the wreck of that car. I want it confined until we can look into it."

They took the unmarked van, heading for the hospital in Trail, about an hour from Trafalgar. Most of the trip passed in silence.

Smith wasn't going to break the quiet by saying anything. She'd learned that Sergeant Winters didn't care for idle chatter or useless speculation.

It hadn't snowed in town for a few days, but the trees lining the mountain road were heavy with fresh powder. Easy to see why evergreen trees were conical: their branches drooped under the piles of snow dragging them down. Every once in a while something, a puff of light wind, a passing animal, a settling bird, shook a branch, and the snow drifted down in a white cloud all of its own.

The road, slick with patches of ice or hard-packed snow, twisted and turned through the mountain passes. The sky was heavily overcast, and as they drove past the airport at Castlegar, she couldn't see the mountains. No planes were likely to be getting in or out today.

"Do you know what they call Castlegar, John?" she dared to ask.

"No."

"Cancel-gar." Long pause. "'Cause of the number of flights that are cancelled 'cause of the weather."

"Thank you, Molly, I understood the reference."

She concentrated on the road. The last thing she'd want would be to put the Sergeant in a ditch, and have to wait for a tow while he called the RCMP to come and get him.

She hadn't liked John Winters much the first time she'd worked with him. In fact she hadn't liked him at all. But he was kinda growing on her, and she thought they were getting on okay. As long as she didn't screw up. She was more afraid of John Winters' displeasure than that of the Chief Constable or Staff Sergeant Peterson.

"Uh, John?"

"What is it now?"

"I don't think you called Peterson."

"Why would I do that?"

"About taking me off the road?"

"Right." He pulled out his cell phone. Nearing Castlegar, he had a signal.

She could tell by the one side of the conversation she was party to that Peterson was arguing. But as long as he wasn't arguing with her, it was all okay.

Wendy Wyatt-Yarmouth leaned on her poles and looked down the hill they called Blonde Ambition. Then she took a deep breath and pushed off, swallowing her fear. She'd constantly avoided taking this midlevel, or blue, run despite Jason and Ewan's nagging, but today she decided to ski it. Some sort of tribute, perhaps. Or maybe just to prove to Jason, for the last time, that she could accomplish something.

When Jason had suggested spending their Christmas break skiing in the Kootenays—for the powder, he'd said—she'd agreed, thinking that Blue Sky would be like Whistler. Her parents gave her a holiday in Whistler as a high school graduation present, and she'd loved every minute of it. Whistler was full of the sort of restaurants that were featured in *Gourmet* magazine, designer shops, luxury hotels. And, incidentally, good skiing.

Blue Sky was full of good skiing. Period. The so-called lodge was nothing other than one long, low, two-story building with a cafeteria, a twenty-seat bar, and plenty of room for people to sit on wooden benches to enjoy lunches carted in in paper bags, backpacks, or family-sized coolers.

Despite the death of their friends, the group had decided to continue their ski vacation. They had to do something, or they'd go nuts just hanging around waiting until it was time to go home.

And Wendy did not want to spend any more time with her parents than she had to.

They'd left home the day after Christmas, as soon as they could get a plane heading west. They'd flown to Calgary, where they sat, fuming, for a day because Castlegar was socked in. They could have taken the Greyhound bus, but Doctor (PhD) and Doctor (MD) Wyatt-Yarmouth did not travel on buses. And now they sat in town, at a third-rate hotel because it was the only place with a vacancy, both of them fuming some more, and her father complaining to everyone who'd listen, and many who didn't particularly want to, about the incompetence of small town policing.

They tried demanding that Jason's body be released for them to take home, but the police were still waiting for the result of the autopsy.

Didn't they know that Doctor Wyatt-Yarmouth Number One was on the board of the Halton Regional Police Service?

The Trafalgar City Police, apparently, didn't give a flying fuck.

Soft white snow flew into Wendy's face, and she almost smiled. Her smile died when she remembered why her parents were here. To take Jason, and her, home. Yes, she wanted to go home. Get through the ordeal of loading Jason's coffin onto the plane, making the arrangements, the visitation, the funeral.

Mr. and Mrs. Williams, Ewan's parents, were spending the holidays sailing in the Caribbean. No one had been able to contact them. Jeremy and Rob decided to stay in Trafalgar until things were settled. Alan didn't seem so sure. At first he'd said he was leaving, but then he changed his mind. Which might have had something to do with the fact that Sophie, who hadn't met Jason until this trip, most definitely wanted to finish her vacation.

Wendy reached the bottom of the hill, and pulled off her goggles and helmet. Alan and Rob had headed immediately for the Black Diamond runs. She'd gone up the hill with Jeremy, who was the same level of skier as she, but she'd lost him soon after stepping off the lift. Sophie, lucky Sophie, was spending the day at the spa. Wendy would have liked to join her but she was afraid of running into Doctor Wyatt-Yarmouth Number Two (aka Mom) who'd announced a similar intention. Also, as Wendy didn't care to admit, even to herself, she couldn't afford a spa day. If Jason hadn't bribed her into coming by paying for a good chunk of her expenses, including room at the B&B and a two-week ski pass, she couldn't afford to be skiing either. She had barely enough room left on her credit card to go shopping in Toronto for ski clothes. The ones she'd worn to Whistler three years ago were so out of date.

She joined the cafeteria line, picked up a tray, and ordered a chicken Caesar salad. She'd waited until close to two o'clock before coming inside for lunch in order to snag one of the wooden benches that served as seating.

She handed her money to a strikingly beautiful woman with a trace of Asian features and grabbed a place by the window. The air was heavy with the scent of soggy clothes, damp woolen hats, exposed socks, fragrant food. She munched on her salad and watched people enjoying the day's skiing.

A woman threw her tray onto the table next to her. Wendy looked up, mildly annoyed. There was plenty of room, why couldn't the woman sit somewhere else?

"Mind if I join you?" The interloper sat down without waiting for a response. She wore a knee-length purple sweater over a black T-shirt that emphasized her most valuable assets and snugly fitting blue jeans. Every piece, Wendy couldn't help but notice, looked pretty high-end.

Although nothing at all like one would wear for a day on the slopes.

Wendy speared a slice of chicken and turned her head to the window.

"Good skiing?"

"It's okay. I was expecting a better quality of resort."

The woman laughed. Her teeth were straight and unnaturally white. Her long black hair was gathered into a wild bunch at the back of her head. "You're not here for just the powder then?"

Wendy's head turned. Something was not quite right about this woman's appearance or her demeanor. She was not here to ski, nor did she appear to be all that interested in the beef stew on her tray.

"I'm afraid I have the advantage of you, as they say in the classic English novels. You're Wendy Wyatt-Yarmouth."

"For my sins, as they say in the more contemporary English TV shows. Who the hell are you and what do you want?"

The woman smiled. She held out her hand. "Meredith Morgenstern. *Trafalgar Daily Gazette*, for my own sins. My condolences on your loss."

"Thank you."

Wendy hadn't accepted the handshake. The woman didn't seem put out and picked up a whole wheat roll. "If you don't mind, I'd like to ask you about the death of your brother and his friend."

Wendy looked down her nose and snorted. "I don't think so. Take your tray and find another table, before I call security."

"Please, Wendy, hear me out." Meredith thrust her fork into the bowl of stew on the table in front of her. Brown liquid bubbled up. "The police will not be releasing your brother's body any time soon, nor that of his friend. Never mind that your distinguished parents are cooling their heels in town. Recipient of the Order of Canada, eh? Impressive. That makes your family newsworthy. I'm interested in finding out why the police have suddenly started paying attention to the accident, and when I saw you sitting here, by yourself, I thought you also might want to know what's going on."

Wendy looked at the black-haired woman on the far side of the large, battered wooden table. Stew had splattered across what were probably surgically-enhanced boobs.

She hadn't happened upon Wendy having lunch. She'd probably gone looking for her at the B&B, and Mrs. C or Kathy had told her the group was skiing. Wendy'd have a thing or two to say about that. She had a right to her privacy, and the reporter should have been sent packing.

How good could she possibly be anyway, working for the *Trafalgar Daily Gazette*? Rather than sticking her nose into the Wyatt-Yarmouth family business, she should be reporting on the results of the Ladies Bridge Finals or the Men's Curling Quarterly.

Wendy pressed the paper napkin she'd picked up at the checkout to her eyes. "My brother," she said, "was the most important person in my life. Not only did I love him, but I respected him as well. Jason...well, Jason believed in the dignity of every human being. It was his dream to become a doctor and go to Africa and help the suffering humanity. As for my parents," Wendy lifted her eyes to check that what-ever-her-name-was was paying attention, "they are quite naturally inconsolable with grief, and I request that you respect that."

What a perfect lot of rubbish. Wendy adored her brother, that was true, but she had no illusions about him. Jason Wyatt-Yarmouth was no more interested in the suffering people of Africa than she was.

Meredith gave her a smile full of sympathy. "I can tell you loved him very much. May I quote you?"

"If you must."

"Thank you."

"But you're full of garbage. My parents were told this morning we can take Jason home."

"The situation's changed."

"You're lying."

"Seriously, Wendy, I am not. I have contacts, well placed contacts. A good reporter needs contacts. How close were you to Ewan Williams?"

"If I thought this was any of your business, I'd tell you he was my brother's friend, nothing more to me than that."

"Then I don't mind telling you that the pathologist found... complications...with Ewan's death."

Wendy picked up the almost full plate of Caesar salad and threw it across the table.

Chapter Six

John Winters wasn't going to speculate about Doctor Lee's startling discovery to Smith. He wasn't even going to speculate to himself. The only thing he needed to know, right now, was that Ewan Williams had died before the car accident. That meant one of three things: Williams died naturally, in the car prior to the accident, and no one noticed; Wyatt-Yarmouth had killed him and was taking the body to dispose of it; Wyatt-Yarmouth had not killed him and was taking the dead body who knows where or why. The direction they'd been going in took them away from the police station and the hospital. Which might not be relevant: it was possible that, being an outsider, Wyatt-Yarmouth didn't know where the hospital was.

Did Wyatt-Yarmouth know Williams was dead? Winters would have to check with Lee about the condition of the body at the time of the accident.

All this was speculation. Jason Wyatt-Yarmouth would not be sitting up to answer John Winters' questions.

But Ewan Williams might have something to tell Doctor Shirley Lee.

Winters looked out the window, not that there was much to see. Gray clouds, fat with unshed snow, hung so low they covered the mountains. Puffs of mist rose up from the river, black and cold, to his left.

"Have a nice Christmas?" he said to Smith about half an hour outside of Trafalgar.

"Very nice," she said, automatically. The rote answer to a standard question.

"I mean, well," she added, "it was okay, I guess. Mom wasn't at all pleased when she found out how much I'd be working. Dad wasn't pleased either, but he doesn't say so. And when my brother, Sam, told them he and his family were going to Hawaii for the holidays, after spending last year at his in-laws, poor mom." John Winters knew Molly's mother well, so he wasn't surprised that she'd chatter about her family. Lucky, as everyone called Mrs. Smith, was *known*, as the phrase went, to the police. Not that she'd ever been a criminal but if there was a controversy in the town of Trafalgar, British Columbia, you could be sure Lucky Smith was on one side or the other. And probably the leader of her side at that.

"Christmas was okay, but my days off were great. The conditions at Blue Sky can't be beat. Do you get up there much?"

"I don't ski."

"Brought up in B.C. and you don't ski! You should give it a go. It's the best thing on earth. You know we get free skiing if we carry a radio and help out if they need it? It's a great deal. I've never been called, although some of the guys've had to break up fights or look into someone's pack being snatched."

"Can't teach an old dog new tricks, Molly."

The period at the end of that sentence was so strong, even Smith, young and chatty, knew to drop the subject.

They arrived at the Kootenay-Boundary Regional Hospital in silence.

Before he got out of the car, Winters pulled a tube of Vaseline out of his pocket and dipped his finger in. He handed it to Smith and she also applied a touch of the gel to the inside of each nostril. Otherwise the smell of death would stay with them for days.

"Okay, Doc," Winters said, at the first sight of Doctor Lee standing inside the swinging doors leading to the morgue. "You've got my attention. You know Constable Smith."

Lee nodded. She wore a regulation white lab coat over a cream blouse and blue skirt cut perfectly to the middle of her knees.

Her stockings were sheer and her shoes leather. Her heels were so high that the doctor, who probably had to stretch to reach five feet in her bare feet, didn't appear to be all that much shorter than Constable Smith. Her black hair was tied into a stiff knot at the back of her neck.

"I have no doubt about it," Lee said, turning and heading down the hall, her heels sounding as out of place as a marching band on the industrial-white floor. "Mr. Williams was dead at least twenty-four hours, perhaps more, before his body was retrieved from the water."

"Why do you think that?"

She launched into a description of the degrees of rigor mortise and the stages of decomposition of various body parts.

"You didn't notice right away?" Smith said. "Wouldn't that have been kinda obvious?"

The doctor stopped walking. She turned. Her perfectly made-up black eyes threw chips of ice at the young Constable.

"I mean," Smith said, digging herself further into a hole of her own making, "Bodies start decaying right away, right?"

"When I need to be interrupted in my observations, I will call on you, Constable," Lee said. "Provided you're still in the room and paying attention."

That was a dig. The first time Smith had been present at one of Lee's autopsies she'd run from the room before the business even began. The second time she lasted it out, only by looking at everything but the table, and thinking, for all Winters knew, of England.

Lee might be catty, but she was a non-sexist cat. She'd dripped scorn all over Ray Lopez, when, for all the detective's years of experience, he'd vomited when Lee ripped the toupee off a heart-attack victim they initially suspected might have been done in by the ex-wife. Lopez had thought Lee'd scalped the man.

"Condition of the body would indicate," Lee continued walking down the hall, heels tapping, a chastised Smith tiptoe-ing after her, "that it was kept in a cold setting post-mortem. Of course any place outdoors in the last week would provide cold conditions. Locating that place, is, fortunately for me, not my concern, now is it, Sergeant Winters?"

"I'll take it from there, Doc."

"One other thing that might be of interest," she said. "He was fully dressed, in outdoor clothing, but his gloves were in his pocket. His fly was unzipped and his penis was partially out."

She threw the double doors open, and the group walked into the autopsy room. Lee's assistant, Russ, was waiting.

A man lay on the table, on his back, naked, lit up as if for his Broadway debut. He was white, about five foot eight, slender and lean. Fingernails trimmed, clean. Brown hair, well cut, with an artificially streaked blond bit falling over the forehead.

Face as pale as, well, as death.

It was not hard to notice that, shriveled in cold and death though the man might be, Ewan William's penis was enormous.

"You do something to that?" Winters asked, pointing.

Behind him, he heard Smith suck in air.

"Is that some sort of joke, John? If so, it is not in good taste. I do not *do* anything." Unlike other pathologists he'd met, Doctor Lee did not indulge in black humor. Nor did she allow her staff to do so. Which meant that they indulged out of her hearing.

"At first, I assumed the trauma to the back of the head had occurred during the accident. A foolish presumption on my part." She paused to allow him to agree.

He did so.

"As soon as we removed his clothing we could see that Mr. Williams' blood had settled along his side. It had achieved complete lividity. When the heart stops pumping, blood stops circulating and begins to settle. In the same way that if you pour colored liquid into a glass of water and stir, it will move through the water. Once the stirring ceases, the colored liquid will settle on the bottom of the glass."

"I'm aware of that, doc."

She ignored him. "Mr. Williams was placed on his back while awaiting the autopsy. The admission report also indicated that there had been a minor degree of rigor mortise when he was brought in. Rigor begins to settle in about three hours after death, and achieves maximum at around twelve hours. That is assuming ideal conditions. Regardless of the conditions, Mr. Williams should not have been in any stage of rigor less than an hour after his death, nor should his blood have settled along his right side. I can only assume such sloppy observation on the part of the night clerk was due to the pressures of the holiday season."

Meaning, Winters interpreted, that someone's head was going to roll down the morgue corridor.

"Once I realized that the time of death pre-dated the accident, I stopped work and phoned you."

"So you did."

"I've been thinking about it since, of course."

"Of course."

Doctor Lee was an exceptionally competent pathologist. But, like many highly intelligent people, she got more than a mite prickly at times. Winters considered it one of the qualifications of his job to be able to massage her gently to get her to spit out the damned point.

"I believe he was kept outside after death. The temperature over the twenty-four to forty-eight hours prior to the vehicle going into the river did move a few degrees on either side of the freezing point. Further investigation will no doubt reveal more." Lee pulled on her latex gloves, and reached overhead to switch on the microphone and recorder. Russ handed her a hacksaw.

Smith swallowed, audibly.

Chapter Seven

They arrived back in Trafalgar shortly after noon. Cause of death determined by Doctor Lee: hypothermia aggravated by a single blow to the head. She found minute traces of wood and charcoal in the wound, and some ash. She might have been reciting her shopping list, but it was enough to get Winters' heart pumping.

What contained wood, charcoal, and ash, but the instruments used by a common household fireplace?

He said nothing until they'd thanked Doctor Lee. She promised to have her report ready in a day or two, and told them she'd go over Wyatt-Yarmouth one more time, to make sure she hadn't missed anything the first time. "As unlikely," she'd sniffed, "as that might be."

Smith hadn't thrown up, run from the room, or broken into hysterical laughter. She'd stood somberly out of the way, pressed up against the wall, but when on the one or two occasions Winters glanced up, his attention drawn by something Russ was doing, Smith had been watching the procedure.

"Getting easier, Molly?" he asked, as she turned the key in the van's ignition.

"Can I throw up now?"

He laughed and grabbed the radio. "Jim, remind me of where Williams and Wyatt-Yarmouth were staying."

"Glacier Chalet. It's a B&B at 1894 Victoria Street."

"Who's the officer who informed the sister and friends of the deaths?"

"Give me a sec," Denton said.

"Me," said a small voice from his left.

"What?"

"Me. I was the one who told Wyatt-Yarmouth's sister."

"Never mind, Jim. I'll get back to you." He put the radio down. "You informed the family?"

"Yes."

"At the Glacier Chalet B&B?"

"Yes."

"Did you go inside?"

"Yes."

"Right inside the house I mean, not just stand in the doorway?"

"Yes," she said, daring a sideways glance away from the icy, steeply sloped, curving road. "Wyatt-Yarmouth's sister, Wendy, guessed why I was there and pretty much ran until her back was up against the wall. I followed her in. I don't think Ellie Carmine liked my boots tromping on her clean floors. Why?"

"Did you see a fireplace?"

"Let me think. Yeah, I'm sure of it. We went into the living room, nice Christmas tree and party stuff, and I remember thinking that it had been so cold outside and now I was too hot standing by the fire."

Winters picked up the radio again. "Jim, contact Ray Gavin, tell him I want a full forensic team at the Glacier Chalet B&B ASAP. Call me back with their ETA. I also need a patrol car and two," he glanced at Smith, "make that one, uniform to be on site when I get there. Which will be in about forty-five minutes."

"Got it," Denton said.

"The Glacier Chalet B&B, Molly."

Due to the road conditions, Smith was driving a touch under the speed limit. She pressed her foot to the gas.

"You know the saying 'better ten minutes late than forty years early'?"

"No."

"It means don't speed. Did you hear what Doctor Lee found in the wound in Williams' skull?"

He waited to hear her answer. She'd been chastised before for pretending to have heard something she hadn't.

She hesitated before speaking. "Damage?"

"Damage indeed. Caused by being struck by the proverbial blunt instrument. She also found a few visible wood fragments, perhaps singed, and a fine gray powder that might have been ash. She'll examine the particles under a microscope to be sure, but Shirley never guesses unless she's practically positive. Can't imagine what it would be like playing poker with her. All of which suggests he was hit by a fireplace poker, and fell into either the fireplace itself, a pile of wood, or perhaps even tipped over the ash bucket. What makes it more interesting is that he lived long enough to go outside and let the cold get him. Or to be taken outside."

Smith turned and gave him a bright smile. "So he was attacked in the B&B?"

"Plenty of fires in town, Molly, and outside of it." Many of the houses dotting the hillsides and bottoms of mountains in the Kootenays were heated by wood stoves, and many that weren't, such as his own home, used fireplaces for atmosphere. He remembered Christmas Eve. Eliza, arranging candles, nibbling on canapés with her small white teeth, opening their presents, the light from the fire turning her green eyes the color of dragon fire. Sipping *Veuve Cliquot*. Later, around the time Santa could be expected to be tossing his big bag down the chimney, rubbing her back as she vomited into the toilet.

"However, as I can't drag Ray and his truck around to every fireplace in the valley, we'll concentrate on one. So, yes, I need to find out if the Glacier Chalet B&B is missing a fireplace poker, check it out if it's not, and see what we can find by sifting through the ashes. Most people keep a bucket for cold ashes and only throw it out when it's full. More time has passed since Williams' death than I'd like, but I'm sometimes astounded at what Ray can pull out of what looks like a pile of nothing." The Trafalgar City Police was small, boasting twenty sworn officers. When needed, they called on the closest RCMP detachment to do the forensics. He swung the car's computer around and began typing.

"Don't we need a warrant?" Smith asked. "It is a private home."

"I'm starting the ITO"—information to obtain a warrant—"now. It won't come though in time, but if I have to I can claim exigent circumstances. We have to get into that fireplace before evidence can be destroyed, even accidentally." He'd ask the B&B owner if he could have a look at her fireplace. He and about ten of his best friends. And that would get him started. According to Smith, the fireplace was in the common room. A semi-public place in which no one should have any expectation of privacy. If he needed to look further, particularly into Williams' room, he'd need that warrant.

A police car was sitting outside the Glacier Chalet B&B when they arrived. Dawn Solway got out. Winters and Smith joined her. From the homes surrounding, he could see faces pressed up against windows. He glanced at the house. A sign, topped with a foot of snow, hung out front with all the stamps and official notices indicating that this was a top of the line establishment. It was a big Victorian, as proud and stately as the old Queen herself, in a street of recent tear-downs and glass and steel and concrete gentrifications. The house was painted cream with dove gray veranda pillars, window and door frames, and gingerbread trimmings. The front yard was large; several feet of snow covered a carefully tended lawn trimmed with perennial beds, sleeping until the first kiss of spring. A porch, clear of snow, outfitted with a black iron table and chairs, filled the front of the house and ran around each side.

"Molly," he said, looking at the imposing front of the magnificent old house, "you're with me. Dawn, keep busybodies away, and that includes anyone we flush out of the house."

As they'd passed into the Trafalgar town limits, Denton called to say that Ray Gavin and his scene-of-the-crime van would be on site in ten minutes. Winters and Gavin went back a long way. He'd known he could count on the Mountie. In the absence of a warrant, the home owner could turn him away on the spot, but he hoped that the proprietor of a Bed and Breakfast, of all respectable places, would allow the police access to the public rooms.

Winters walked up to the front door. The path was neatly shoveled, lined with walls of snow level to his knees. The door opened before he reached the first step. A woman in her late fifties, stout and gray haired, peered out. She spoke before he had a chance to open his mouth.

"I can't imagine what you lot think you're doing parked outside my door as if you're raiding a house of ill repute."

He blinked. He wasn't about to accuse her of operating a cathouse.

"Sorry," the woman said, "Didn't see you there, Moonlight. Are you looking for your mom? We're having tea. Come on in." She held the door open. Winters hadn't even had to produce any I.D., much less a search warrant. They stepped into the B&B.

The entrance hall was small, but keeping with the Victorian theme, decorated in heavy wallpaper, wooden wainscoting, and a period painting of a brooding old man, military uniform, whiskers, and attitude. The scent of household cleaning products, overlaid by something warm and fresh and touched with cinnamon filled the air.

"Moonlight?" A gray head, shot through with threads of fiery red, topping a short, solid, plump frame came out of the kitchen. "Thought I heard your name. Hello, dear. John, how nice. Did you have a pleasant Christmas?"

"I did, Lucky. Nothing special. Just a quiet time at home with Eliza, my wife." Winters' back was to his constable. Her sigh could have stirred snow on the mountaintops.

Chapter Eight

Try as she might to be accepting of her child's life choices, and all that garbage, Lucy (Lucky) Casey Smith hated to see her beautiful daughter wearing that hideous uniform, all bulk and intimidation. When Moonlight joined the police, everything changed, even her beautiful name. No longer Moonlight Legloas Smith, a name as soft as butter melting on the tongue, but Constable Molly Smith. Authority and aggression.

John Winters accompanied Moonlight. Lucky and Sergeant Winters had sparred like medieval swordfighters, but for some strange reason she'd become rather fond of him. She lifted a hand and checked that her hair was tucked into place.

"Mrs. Eleanor Carmine?" Winters said, the statement sounding like a question.

"That's me." Ellie's voice quavered.

"You don't have to answer their questions," Lucky said, forgetting about trying to look nice for John Winters and worrying about Moonlight. "Not without legal advice."

"What? I don't need a lawyer. I don't know what any of this is about." Ellie's voice shook. Understandable, Lucky thought. anyone would be frightened when faced with the full force of the law. Particularly after two of her guests had been killed in a tragic car accident.

"If you wish to consult counsel that is, of course, your right, Mrs. Carmine," Winters said, in a voice as deep and smooth as blackstrap molasses. "But if you have no reason to do so…"

Lucky tried to catch Moonlight's eye, but the girl was looking at everything but her mother.

"Is there anyone else in the house?" Winters asked.

Eleanor Carmine glanced toward Lucky Smith.

"No," Lucky said.

"No," Mrs. Carmine repeated. "My guests have gone out."

"Before we continue with this conversation," Lucky said, "I must insist, Sergeant, you tell me what's going on here."

Moonlight coughed. "I'm sorry, Mrs. Smith, but as far as I can see you have no right to insist upon anything. If you're acting as counsel for Mrs. Carmine, please identify yourself. Otherwise." Moonlight coughed again. "This is none of your business, and...well...please be quiet, Mom."

Lucky stared. John Winters was regarding Moonlight with an expression like someone gazing upon a garter snake that had turned into a python. Ellie Carmine rubbed her hands together.

They all turned at the arrival of Ron Gavin and his forensic bag, clomping up the sidewalk. He'd parked his van half into the road, not able to pull to the side because of the snow drifts as high as a man's chest. An RCMP patrol car joined Solway's vehicle in washing the street in red and blue lights.

Curtains moved and doors opened in the neighboring houses. More than a few people came out to their front steps or wandered down to the sidewalk to see what was going on. Solway told them to keep back.

"What on earth is going on here? You need a warrant to bring those people and their equipment in here, Mr. Winters. Do you have one?"

"Mrs. Carmine," Winters said, ignoring Lucky. "I'd like your permission to search the fireplace in your common room. Due to the highly volatile nature of the search area, I don't have time to get a warrant. I promise you I'm only interested in the fireplace and its immediate surroundings. I won't examine anything outside that area at this time. You are entitled to refuse us entry. I'll then have to wait for the warrant to arrive, in which time vital evidence might be destroyed. Your decision."

Ellie looked at Lucky again.

What a ridiculous situation. Lucky was here to have tea with a friend and listen while her friend talked out her troubles. She had not planned to engage in a debate over the finer points of the law with the police. Who were, on this occasion, represented by her own daughter.

Moonlight stood slightly behind and to one side of John Winters. She shifted her big black boots, looking at everything but her mother.

"The fireplace is in a common area, open to all your guests, is that correct?" Winters said.

"Yes."

"May we have a look at your fireplace, Mrs. Carmine?"

"I have nothing to hide," she said. "Come on in. You too, Moonlight. And I guess all those other folks behind you."

"Whether or not you have anything to hide," Lucky said, "is completely beside the point. It's a matter of the right to…"

"If you'd please step outside, Mrs. Smith," Winters said. "Mrs. Carmine will ensure we don't exceed our legal bounds."

"Ellie," Lucky said. "I'd suggest…"

"Mom," Moonlight said keeping her voice down. "Will you get out of here. Sergeant Winters knows the law as well as you do."

Lucky blinked. "I need my coat."

"Get it then," Constable Smith said.

Lucky scurried into the kitchen. She came back, moments later, fastening buttons, pulling on gloves, knotting a blue scarf around her neck. She should stand her ground, convince Ellie Carmine, insist that John Winters produce a warrant before searching…the fireplace? What the heck would be the point? Let them have at it.

Besides, it wouldn't look good to be seen having a public confrontation with her daughter. Moonlight's face was set in dark, serious lines. The house was over-warm, and snow melted off Moonlight's hat and dripped down her collar. She didn't move. Just alternately glared at her mother, and stared off into space as if wishing she were somewhere else.

It wasn't easy, Lucky knew, for Moonlight. "I'll be outside if you need me, Ellie," she said.

Winters and the RCMP man passed her, and went into the common room.

"Oh, for God's sake," Winters shouted.

Moonlight ran. Lucky followed her.

John Winters was standing in the middle of the living room, staring at the fireplace on the far wall. The room was beautifully decorated for Christmas with a mixture of old ornaments lovingly preserved and glistening new ones. A miniature Santa's village ran across the top of the mantle over the fire, which was now dark and cold. Lucky couldn't see anything wrong.

Winters turned around. His color was high and his arms stiff at his sides.

"Constable Smith," he said, his voice very low. "Is this the fireplace you told me you saw when you were here last?"

"Yes." Moonlight's voice broke. Lucky knew her daughter tried to deepen the pitch of her voice, to make herself sound more authoritative, more serious. But it did have a tendency to squeak under stress.

"Outside, now," Winters said, molasses replaced by pure iron. "Ron, sorry to have dragged you away from home. Mrs. Carmine, Mrs. Smith, I apologize for disturbing you. A misunderstanding. We'll get out of your hair."

All the blood had drained from Moonlight's face, making the girl almost as pale as the moon on the snowy night she'd been named for. She almost ran out of the room. The policemen followed: the Mountie trying to hide a grin, John Winters looking about to bust a gut with suppressed rage.

"That was odd," Ellie said.

"You can say that again," Lucky said, wondering why they'd make such a fuss over a gas fireplace.

Chapter Nine

She chose deep red polish. In summer she preferred something much lighter, pink and flirty. Winter was for fire and passion. The esthetician put the bottle of polish on her tray and ordered Eliza Winters to lift her feet out of the warm water. Taking one soft naked foot in hand, the woman began to apply fragrant lotion. Eliza settled back to enjoy the sensations coming from her feet. Her day at the spa had been as delightful as advertised. She would have liked to have come with John, but she suspected she'd wasted her money on his Christmas gift. When they vacationed far from home, he made use of a spa, and always enjoyed it very much. But it was likely that in the close-knit, gossipy town of Trafalgar, he'd be afraid of running into one of the two policewomen he worked with, or, even worse, the wife of one of his colleagues, while dressed in a fluffy white robe and floppy sandals heading for his facial.

Men.

A low moan came from the chair beside her. Eliza opened her eyes. The woman seated there lifted her hand and wiped at her face. Her eyes were red, the delicate skin underneath puffy and dark. Otherwise her skin tone was almost perfect, although she must be well into her forties, perhaps even her fifties. The woman saw Eliza looking her way. "Pardon me," she said, forcing out a smile as frozen as the patch of ice Eliza had skidded on while parking the car.

Eliza came to the spa to relax and be fussed over. She did not come to engage in mindless conversation with complete strangers. But she felt she had to say something. "Are you all right? If the pedicure's bothering you, you can tell her to stop."

From her short stool at the woman's feet, the second esthetician looked up, alarmed.

"Continue, please. Not the pedicure, no. It's quite lovely. Do you come here often?"

"Not as often as I'd like. Yourself?"

"My first time. I'm only visiting."

"Here for the skiing?"

"Skiing? No, I won't be skiing."

Eliza settled back into her chair. The dead skin was being scraped off her heels. White flakes flew into the air and coated the girl's black smock. Quite disgusting. The woman beside her wiped at her cheek and closed her eyes. Conversation over. Thank heavens.

The pedicure was the end of the spa day. Eliza floated on a soft cloud of contentment to the changing rooms. She entered a tiny cubicle and dressed before standing in front of the mirror trying to arrange her hair. It was thick with lotion applied during the neck and forehead massage, and the best she could do was force it into some sort of reasonable shape to see her to her car and home.

The woman she'd spoken to in the pedicure room emerged from a cubicle. Eliza's expert eye took in the quality of her cream wool slacks, navy blue cashmere sweater over a tailored white T-shirt. And were those ox-blood leather ankle boots Jimmy Choo's? They might well be.

The woman smiled at Eliza and lifted a hand to her own hair. Her nails were perfectly groomed, cut short, the polish clear. Her eyes were red, redder than they'd been in the pedicure room. Eliza turned to her. "I don't mean to pry, but something seems to be wrong. If this were summer, I'd suspect you have allergies, and leave you alone. If I can help, please let me."

This small town friendliness seemed to be contagious. Eliza did not normally care to hear anyone else's problems.

The woman's smile was tinged with sadness. "I'm parched after all that. And hungry. I didn't manage to eat much of the lunch they provided. Is there a coffee shop nearby where I could get a drink and perhaps a muffin?"

"Big Eddie's Coffee Emporium is just around the corner. Rather an extravagant name for what's essentially a corner coffee shop."

"Sounds perfect. Will you join me? My treat, but I'm afraid I'm not very good company today."

The woman held out her hand. "I'm Patricia Wyatt-Yarmouth."

Quit. She should quit right now. Go back to university and finish her MSW. Or find a job at a ski resort. Perhaps she could work at Mid-Kootenay Adventure Vacations, her parents' store. No, that would be just too humiliating.

She'd driven Sergeant Winters back to the station in silence. Wishing he'd yell and scream and call down plagues and locusts upon her head. Instead his silent anger spread through the car like the monster in a cheap science fiction movie. He'd said nothing more since they'd walked down the neatly shoveled path outside the Glacier Chalet B&B and he'd said, very quietly, "A gas fireplace does not require stoking, Constable Smith. No use for a poker, no logs. No ashes to be discarded. I would have thought that, as a mountain woman, you'd know such things."

Smith got into the driver's seat while Winters told Solway and the Mountie to leave. Ron Gavin had followed them out of the house, lugging his bag of equipment, trying not to laugh.

At least someone was amused.

She concentrated on her driving. A SUV had skidded off the road at the corner of Front and Monroe Streets and was blocking the intersection. She could see the police station ahead, up the hill where Monroe met George Street, but was trapped in the snarl of traffic. Heat radiated off her face. She wanted to take her gloves off but was afraid of making a move.

Winters activated the computer. He'd sent the ITO moments before they pulled up in front of the B&B. Now he'd have to withdraw it.

Why the hell hadn't she noticed that the fireplace in the common room of the Glacier Chalet B&B was gas? Because no one had told her there would be a test later. She'd been there to tell a young woman her brother was dead. Not to examine the scene as if she were Sherlock Holmes crawling across the floor, peering into his magnifying glass.

No excuse. It was her job to see, to observe, and she hadn't.

A tow truck arrived, a man climbed out and he and the SUV driver stood back to examine the scene. "Looks like you might be here a while," Winters said. "I'll walk the rest of the way."

"Okay."

He put his hand on the door handle. "I need to go back to the B&B and ask very politely if I can check Williams' room. That will now be somewhat awkward. Ron Gavin came out on his day off because he's a good officer. Also because he owes me one. We'll both consider that debt to have been paid. The Horseman who followed Ray will no doubt make sure everyone back at the station gets a good laugh hearing about how I screwed up." Horseman, Smith knew, meant a Mountie. Winters opened the car door. Unfortunately he wasn't finished. "And this will be my screw up, Constable Smith. Eventually to become a story spread far and wide for the amusement of police officers everywhere. I'll wear it, because I will not embarrass myself, or the Trafalgar City Police, by trying to set the story straight." She ground her teeth and fought back tears. *Shut the fuckin' door. Just shut up and shut the door.*

"I will, however, be required to give a full, and honest, report to the Chief Constable."

The door slammed shut.

She gripped the steering wheel. Slightly ahead and to her right a bright red Toyota Echo, dotted with magnetic black circles that made the car look like a giant ladybug, backed out of a parking space. The ladybug hit a patch of ice and slid downhill, very slowly, coming to rest against the bumper of the police car.

A tall, slim middle-aged woman climbed out, spiked purple hair, red coat, blue scarf, yellow mittens, and clanging jewelry. She waved her mittens in the air, and mouthed apologies.

Smith could see Sergeant Winters climbing the hill. His head was down and his back bent as his boots stomped through packed snow.

Molly had two choices: she could tell the ladybug woman to leave her the hell alone and go home to bury her head in her duvet, or get out of the patrol car and direct traffic.

She took a deep breath, and got out of the car.

Wendy plunked herself down on a bench by the door. She was sick and tired of skiing. She didn't like it much anyway, but all the fashionable people skied, so she made the attempt. After tossing her salad at the odious reporter, who'd read her intentions in time to duck and avoid most of the barrage, Wendy wanted to head back to town. She'd arranged to meet the others when the lift closed at four. Jeremy had the keys to the SUV. They'd had to rent another car, seeing as to how Jason had driven the first one into the river.

Jason. Wendy's chest closed. Jason. She'd resented him for almost all their childhood. *Jason the Perfect*, she called him. Their parents' favorite. At the same time she'd loved him. He was the older brother, the one who looked after her, worried about her, protected her. He couldn't be gone. He'd be at the B&B when they got back. Laughing his over-the-top laugh at how he'd made fools of them all.

And Ewan. What had the reporter said about Ewan? That there was something suspicious about his death? What the hell did that mean? She chewed at a fingernail.

A young woman fell onto the bench beside Wendy, dropping helmet and goggles into her lap. "It hurts, okay. Get it? Hurt. Pain. Agony."

A man knelt in front of her. His long hair was black with yellow streaks. Real yellow, not blond. Yellow like out of a child's box of crayons. "Let me see," he said, reaching out. Like the woman he was dressed in mis-matching ski jacket and pants.

"Don't touch," she shouted.

"Let's take your boot off, at least."

"Don't touch me. It hurts. I want to go home."

"It might not be so bad. Maybe your boot isn't fitting right."

"I know when my boot fits and when it doesn't. I want to go back to town. Now. If you won't take me, I'll call for an ambulance. And you can be sure I'll remember you left me here, all alone."

"Okay, okay. I'll get the car. Can you at least hobble down the steps and meet me out front?"

"Absolutely not," she said, "it hurts too much. You'll have to carry me."

"For god's sake, Jackie."

"Why don't I help?"

Jackie, clearly enjoying her pain and suffering, gave Wendy a look that would curdle milk.

Wendy didn't care. "I'll help you down the steps while your friend goes for the car." She smiled at the black and yellow haired boy. "If you don't mind, that is?"

He jumped to his feet, throwing her a smile full of gratitude. "That would be so great. Thanks. It'll take about ten minutes for me to get to the car and bring it around front."

"We'll be waiting," Wendy said.

"I don't want to take you away from your skiing," the injured girl said. Her lower lip stuck out. Most unattractive.

"Don't worry about me. Hey, here's an idea. I've just about had enough today anyway. I'll come back to town with you, in case you need more help."

"Great." The boy ran for the door.

"Nice guy," Wendy said.

"Keep your paws off, hear me."

"I've problems enough of my own, thanks. But here's a tip for nothing: bad, bad idea to do the Prima Donna thing. Men tire of it so easily. Lean on my arm if you must and I'll deposit you at the bottom of the steps. I have to get my skis."

⟨⟩⟨⟩⟨⟩

John Winters stormed into the police station. He didn't say a word to Jim Denton at the front desk, or to the legal clerk who had to jump out of the way to avoid being knocked over. He marched into Barb's office. She was opening a package of cookies. A cup of herbal tea, smelling like someone's wet socks left to dry on a fireplace fender, emitted steam from beside her elbow. "Paul free?" he snapped.

Wisely, Barb refrained from making a crack about his mood. She glanced at the phone on her desk. A red button was shining. "Still talking to the mayor. If it's important, he'll be glad of the interruption."

Young, fresh, keen, rash. Sometimes so goddamned stupid. All words that would have fit John Winters when he was a shiny new recruit.

"Not important enough to drag him away from the mayor. I'll be in my office for a while. He'll want an update on the bodies pulled from the river. And it's a doozy."

"I'll tell him." Barb gave him a sideways glance as she returned to her cookies.

Winters went to the GIS office. He should have spent some time talking to Ellie Carmine about her guests, and he needed to have a look at Williams' room, to see if anything was out of order, but he was so frigging angry at dragging everyone and their dog around to the B&B for an urgent search—of a *gas* fireplace—that he knew he had to get out of there before he exploded.

He called the Glacier Chalet B&B. The guests, according to Mrs. Carmine, had all gone out first thing and weren't usually back until four-thirty or five, after the ski hill closed. He confirmed that they'd arrived under one booking, and wrote down their full names as Mrs. Carmine recited them.

The phone rang as soon as he put it back into the cradle.

"Chief's free," Barb said.

Back down the corridor he went. The legal clerk clutched a ream of papers to her chest as she saw him coming. He gave her what he hoped was a reassuring smile.

Paul Keller leaned back in his chair as his lead detective came in. Even from the other side of the room, Winters could smell the cigarette smoke that surrounded the man like an aura. The Chief Constable popped the top on a can of Coke. "Want one?"

"No thanks. You know I hate the stuff."

"Your loss." Keller took a long drink. "What's up?"

"Wyatt-Yarmouth and Williams. Car went into the river Christmas morning. All attempts at resuscitation failed."

"Oh, yes, I'm familiar with the situation. In fact, Doctor Wyatt-Yarmouth has been on to me, demanding that I accelerate the process of releasing his son's body. *Doctors* Wyatt-Yarmouth, I should say. The wife is, as her husband was quick to inform me, a member of the Order of Canada for her contributions to…" Keller waved his can of pop in the air…"the discovery of some thing that didn't make a word of sense to me."

"Just what we need. Someone who thinks they have political clout."

"Someone who might indeed have political clout, John. Is there a problem?"

"A big one." As Winters explained Shirley Lee's findings Keller's face grew more serious by degrees. "That," he said when Winters had finished, "is not good."

"Agreed, but is it a murder case? I can't say, yet. It's entirely possible Williams fell and hit his head and lay in the snow for almost a day before his friend found him and tried to rush him to the hospital. In my experience a 24-hour corpse looks nothing like a living person, but Wyatt-Yarmouth might have thought he was getting help for his friend. I checked the weather, and it was minus 5 degrees that night, so the body would have been cold even if he were still alive. Shirley has lots of tests to make still. Right now she's leaning toward a blow to the back of his head, hard enough to render him unconscious long enough for the cold and the concussion to kill him." A blow that was *definitely* not caused by the contents of a *gas* fireplace.

Keller drank more Coke. The staff joked, well out of the Chief Constable's hearing, that the copious cans of pop he drank were his security blanket now that he couldn't smoke in the building. To his credit, Keller restricted himself to two smoke breaks a day—ten a.m. and three p.m. Although every time he had to leave for a meeting, he could be seen sucking as much nicotine as possible into his lungs before getting into a vehicle.

"What about his friends? Didn't they notice him missing?"

"I haven't spoken to them yet."

"I'll take a wild guess and say they assumed he was snuggled up with some dolly bird, all warm and comfortable."

Dolly Bird? Keller sometimes tried to remind everyone, himself most of all, that he too had been hip once upon a time. Although his hipness pretty much remained locked in a time warp from the mid '70s when he'd been lucky enough to snag a couple of months in England on a course on counter-terrorism. Fortunately the CC's time warp was restricted to his speech patterns, and not to his understanding of fighting terrorism.

They made fun of the CC quick enough—his incredible tobacco addiction, the ten or more cans of coke he guzzled every work day, his unfashionable phrases, but they all knew he was a good cop and a fair boss. As far as Winters knew he was the only one who suspected the CC's big secret: the man was in love, had been for many years, with Lucky Smith, Constable Smith's mother.

"What hotel are they staying at?" Keller asked.

Winters hesitated. He could mention the Keystone Kops invasion of the B&B. He could mention what had prompted it. But he decided to keep quiet. Word might never cross the CC's desk, and if it did, Winters would admit he'd made a mistake.

He could withstand a mistake easier than Constable Third Class Molly Smith.

"Glacier Chalet B&B."

"Ellie Carmine's place. My wife adores that house. She told me once she'd dreamt that we bought it. I can't imagine a deeper level of hell than owning a B&B. I live in fear that's what Karen has in mind for when we retire. Until you have reason to believe otherwise, this is a highly suspicious death, John."

"Agreed."

"So young Mr. Wyatt-Yarmouth—I hate those double-barreled names—and Mr. Williams will remain in the tender care of Doctor Lee until she's learned all she can from them. Are you going to inform the Doctors Wyatt-Yarmouth, or shall I?"

Winters got to his feet. "I need to speak to them anyway. Find out what they know about their son and his friend." He had plenty of people to talk to. He needed Lopez. But his partner was on the coast, on vacation. In the past he'd taken Molly along, if he thought she'd be a helpful listener. Today he was in no mood to make her think she was anywhere near his good books.

He'd manage for now.

◇◇◇

Wendy Wyatt-Yarmouth tried to come in the front door as quietly as possible. She'd sat in the front seat of the rusty old Toyota Tercel while the girl with the sore foot smoldered away in the back, where, under Wendy's careful direction, she'd been placed in order to keep her leg straight and her foot up. Wendy gave directions to the Glacier Chalet. When they arrived, the boy leapt out to help Wendy unload her skis, thanking her profusely for her help. The girl glared out the back window with pure white rage.

Wendy wiggled her fingers in farewell as the Tercel slipped and sided up the hill. The boy had wanted to get her number so, he explained loud enough for the girl in the back to hear, they could buy her a drink to thank her for her help. Wendy considered it briefly—not that she wanted to see either of these people again, but just giving the guy her number would probably send the girl into a fit. She wasn't in the mood for that sort of fun, so Wendy said no, and didn't bother to make an excuse.

She tried to nip into the B&B without being noticed, but Mrs. Carmine, who probably heard every mouse in the place scratch its little mouse ass, stuck her head out of the kitchen. She wiped floury hands onto an apron featuring pictures of Mrs. Claus doing her Christmas baking.

Shoot me now.

"You're back early, dear."

Feeling that she had to say something, Wendy said, "I'm not in the mood for skiing, Mrs. Carmine. To be honest, Jason was the one keen on skiing." She swallowed, determined not to break down in front of this well-meaning, but nosy, stranger. "I left early. The others'll be back at the regular time. I'm going to have a nap."

"I'm sorry, dear, but that'll have to wait," Mrs. Carmine pulled a cell phone, a trendy little purple and silver piece, out of her apron pocket. She punched it only once, meaning a stored number. She turned and muttered something Wendy couldn't catch.

Snapping the phone shut, Mrs. Carmine turned with a smile. "They'd like you to remain here, dear."

"I told you, I need a nap. If I cared, I'd ask who would like what, but I don't." She headed toward the stairs.

"The police, dear, will be here shortly. They have questions about Jason and Ewan. Sad, so sad."

"Speaking of questions, you shouldn't have sent that woman from the newspaper after me. I'd call that an invasion of my privacy."

Mrs. C braced her shoulders. "I didn't…That might have been Kathy. I'll have a word with her. You can wait for the police in the common room, unless you want them in your bedroom. I'll put the kettle on. Would you like coffee or tea? It's afternoon, but police officers seem to like their coffee. You go ahead and get settled. Shall I send them up to your bedroom?"

"I'll be downstairs," Wendy said.

Which was where she was when the doorbell rang. After brief greetings, Mrs. Carmine led a man into the common room.

He was an older guy, about her dad's age, but a lot, definitely a lot, better looking. Most of his salt and pepper hair was cut short, not grown into hideously long strands to try, and fail, to cover a bald patch. He had a mustache, black streaked with gray, which suited him as it did few men these days. He was tall and lean, with nothing but a hint of middle-aged belly.

Sergeant John Winters, he introduced himself. He expressed his sympathy at her loss and launched into the questions.

Wendy answered them, as best she was prepared to. Here for two weeks of skiing, they'd arrived in Trafalgar on December 18th. They were friends, but they didn't spend all their time together. She pulled at a tissue in her pocket.

"Tell me about Ewan Williams," he asked. "When did you see him last?"

She could blow the cop off. Burst into tears and run upstairs to her room. But he'd be back. Guaranteed. She wondered whether to let him know that the reporter had told her there was something suspicious about Ewan's death. She decided not to.

"Sunday. The day before Christmas Eve. We went skiing and came back to town together when the hill closed. Then," she dug for that tissue, and began shredding it in her fingers, "we went to our own rooms."

"Mr. Williams as well?"

"Cookies?" Mrs. Carmine came into the common room, all smiles. She carried a tray, groaning under the weight of coffee carafe, cups, cream pitcher, sugar bowl, plate piled high with Christmas baking.

The cop's face tightened at the interruption, but Wendy was glad of it. "You are such a dear, Mrs. Carmine. Isn't she wonderful, Sergeant...uh...whatever? I'll have to spend the next month in the gym, non stop, to get over all these treats."

Mrs. Carmine made to settle into a comfortable arm chair. Sergeant Winters wasn't shy about telling her, politely, that she wasn't wanted.

She left in a barely concealed huff.

"You were telling me about the last time you saw Mr. Williams. Sunday evening, after skiing?"

"Right."

"What time was that?"

"Five, at a guess."

"You didn't have dinner together?"

"I told you no. We didn't necessarily all eat together every night."

"Who did you have dinner with?"

"Why are you bothering me with useless questions? My brother is dead. It was a car accident, plain and simple! Can't you just leave me the hell alone?"

"For what it's worth, I am sorry for your loss. But I have my reasons, and my questions are not useless. Dinner, Sunday night?"

"I went with Jason and Alan and his girlfriend Sophie."

"What did the others do, Jeremy, Rob, and Ewan?"

She took a deep breath and studied the wooden Santa Claus on the table. Jolly old Saint Nick. Fuck him too. "I don't know. They went their way, we went ours."

"What did you do after dinner?"

"Came back here. Alan and Sophie like to go to bed early. They're tired after a day's skiing."

"Did Jason go out again?"

She knew exactly what Jason had done and Ewan as well, but she wasn't going to tell the cops. She tried to look as if she were struggling to remember. "Sorry, Mr. Winters," she said at last, "but I can't say for sure. I didn't see him leave, but he might have." He had, in fact, phoned Lorraine, his bootie call, from the sidewalk outside the restaurant. He drove the group back to the B&B, went to his room for a few minutes, and then left, without telling anyone where he was going. Jason and Ewan were a couple of tom cats, always on the make. And that was none of this damned cop's business. She looked at the tissue in her hands—it was shredded to ribbons. She wiped at her nose with the back of her sleeve. Winters got a box of tissues from the table and handed it to her. She pulled one out, and blew her nose, resisting the urge to be polite and say thank you.

He walked to the window and looked out on the snow-covered garden, allowing Wendy a few moments of privacy to wipe her face and compose herself.

Sunday night she'd been lying in bed, not able to sleep, when she heard footsteps in the hall and Jason's voice. A female said something in return. Jason had been alone at breakfast the next morning.

Sergeant Winters turned from the window. "You didn't see Ewan Williams again, after approximately five o'clock on Sunday evening?"

She wiped her eyes. "No."

"I'll need to speak with the rest of your group, Ms. Wyatt-Yarmouth." He handed her his card. She took it. "I'd appreciate it if you'd ask them to give me a call the minute they get in."

Nice words: *Appreciate it.* As if he wouldn't hesitate to clap them in irons if they didn't call.

He hadn't touched his coffee or the homemade cookies. Mrs. Carmine would be disappointed. Wendy could imagine the old bat leaning up against the kitchen door, ears flapping.

"We want to help," she said, getting to her feet to show him out.

Mrs. Carmine came out of the kitchen wiping her hands on her apron.

"I'd like to have a look at Ewan's room, if I may," he asked her. "Have you cleaned the room since they died?"

"Of course I have. And I removed their things. Wendy wasn't up to it, so Sophie helped Kathy pack their suitcases."

"I'd still like to have a look."

Mrs. Carmine led him back through the common room and up the stairs. Wendy threw herself into a chair. She heard Sergeant Winters ask Mrs. C if she had noticed anything out of order. She answered in the negative.

It wasn't long before they came back down. Wendy was still sitting in the common room, a pile of soggy tissues on her lap.

This was all such a nightmare. Her parents wanted her to wait in Trafalgar and go home together. She wanted to leave but the effort of organizing a flight home seemed beyond her.

It was just so unfair.

Mrs. C gave her what she probably thought was a sympathetic smile. Wendy got to her feet and followed them to the hall, wanting to see for herself that the cop got through the door and wasn't about to jump out and say "One more question."

"Isn't he just the cutest thing," Mrs. Carmine said, as the two women watched John Winters walk to his van. "His wife is a famous supermodel."

Yeah, right. Kate Moss secretly living here in back of nowhere British Columbia.

"Enjoy your nap, dear." Mrs. Carmine returned to her kitchen.

Wendy made major noise heading up the stairs. She used the bathroom and then tiptoed back down.

Never mind a nap. She needed to go shopping.

Lucky Smith came out of her cramped office at the back of Mid-Kootenay Adventure Vacations. It was past four o'clock and the sun had dipped behind Koola Glacier. She zipped up her bulky winter coat and wrapped her beloved hand-woven blue scarf twice around her neck. Lucky didn't normally indulge in luxuries, but she'd fallen so in love with a scarf she'd seen being created on an old wooden loom in Crawford Bay that, after months of agonizing about the cost, she'd gone back to buy one.

The shop was busy. Andy, her husband and partner in the business, was helping a young woman, an outsider, choose a ski jacket. Flower, their employee, was ringing up a pair of gloves and woolen socks for a local.

A man examined snowshoes hanging on the back wall, and a young mother held her toddler up to see the display of nature and eco-adventure books. The child pointed to one; his mom took it off the shelf, and without checking the price, carried it to the counter. It was the 28th of December and, so far, they hadn't had too many Christmas returns.

In years past the company had offered guided snowmobile tours and cross-country ski trips into the mountains, but as Andy got older and the children, Samwise and Moonlight, grew up and left home, they'd given up that part of the business and concentrated on the shop in the winter. The rest of the year, they offered guided hourly and multi-day hiking and kayaking trips.

The bell over the door tinkled as a group of vacationers came in. Laughing, they shook heads full of fresh snow and stamped slush-covered boots.

Lucky waved her fingers at Flower, and smiled good-bye to Andy. He gave her a wink so suggestive Lucky felt the color rising into her cheeks. Since Moonlight had moved out Andy's libido seemed to have gone into overdrive. And Lucky didn't mind one bit.

She wouldn't be at all surprised if he told Flower he was going for coffee and hurried home after his wife. Even Flower might think an hour's coffee break was a bit much. It had been easier when they were young and operated a shoe-string operation. Not having to worry about employees or inquisitive children, Andy would toss the sign on the door to closed and take Lucky into the broom closet.

Those had been good days for sure.

The glove-and-sock-purchasing local said hi to Lucky and left the store. She prepared to follow.

"Lucky," Flower said. "Can I speak to you for a minute?" Her face was drawn into serious lines.

"Sure." Lucky rounded the counter. "What's the matter?"

Flower lowered her voice. Lucky leaned closer in order to hear. "I think we've been robbed."

"What?"

"See those goggles over there? End of the table beside the helmets?"

Lucky looked. The table featured a display of ski accessories. Helmets, gloves, a pair of very expensive goggles.

"Half hour ago, there were two goggles."

Lucky looked around the store. The outsider had decided that white wasn't what she wanted and asked Andy to find her a colorful jacket in the same size. She carried a shoulder bag not large enough to conceal anything bigger than a deck of cards. The man looking at snowshoes took a pair down from the wall. Unless he'd stuffed them into his coat pocket he didn't have the goggles.

The snow-covered group picked their way through the goods. Just browsing.

"Are you sure?" Lucky asked Flower. "Maybe Andy sold it."

"I've been the only one on cash for the last couple of hours. It didn't go through me, Lucky. There were three of them sitting there when I got back from lunch. Andy sold one about an hour ago. Half-hour or so ago, I noticed that the goggles—both of them—had been knocked askew. I was about to go and adjust them, when we got busy. Next time I looked up, one was left and no one around who might have picked them up while thinking about buying them."

Andy escorted his customer to the check out. She'd chosen a tight-fitting pink ski jacket that, in Lucky's opinion, did absolutely nothing for a woman in her fifties with hair dyed as red as a rotting tomato.

Flower smiled at her and accepted the garment. "I've had my eyes on this myself," she said. "It looks fabulous on you."

The woman beamed and pulled out a credit card.

Lucky drew Andy to the side and told him what Flower had told her.

He sighed heavily. "Can you do a quick search of the store? Look under tables and check the change room. If nothing, I'll call the cops, although that'll be a waste of time."

He looked so dejected Lucky knew she'd been right—he'd been planning on following her home.

Chapter Ten

Molly Smith worked her shift in robot mode. She guided traffic around the mess of cars on George Street. A car with Florida plates and no winter tires slid off the road into a ditch. A fight broke out at the Bishop and Nun, apparently over a girl who decided that she'd found someone more to her liking. She answered a call of a theft from, of all places, her parents' store. An expensive pair of ski goggles, allegedly snatched in the middle of the day in the middle of a crowed shop.

She'd seen Lorraine LeBlanc wandering down Front Street, her face white and her gaze blank. Smith hadn't spoken to her since Christmas Eve so she pulled up to ask how the girl was doing. Lorraine had tugged at the straps of her big bag and basically told Smith to take up sex and traveling.

She had not been called to report to the Chief Constable. Her fellow officers continued to speak to her without sneers or smothered laughter or looks of pity.

Shortly before six o'clock, she headed back to the station ready to close out her shift. Jim Denton smiled at her as she unzipped her jacket and pulled off her gloves. "Plans for tonight, Molly?"

Plans? Other than finding a redirection for her life?

"Nothing. Uh, has the CC left?"

"Long ago. Meeting at city council. Must be as boring as all hell."

"You got that right." Barb rounded the corner. "Hi, Molly. I saw your mom and dad at the fundraiser for the environmental coalition the other night. I talked to your dad for a while. He'll never say so, of course, but he's so proud of you." Barb smiled at Denton. "Remember what it was like to be young, Jim? When our parents cared about what we did?"

"I was never that young," he said. "My kids would rather die than admit their old man's a cop."

Barb laughed. Everyone knew that Jim Denton's two children doted on their dad.

Smith searched around for a mouse hole to crawl into. Finding nothing suitable, she said to Barb, "Anything of importance happening? Say between the Chief and Sergeant Winters?"

"Steam was almost pouring from the top of John's head, he was in such a fever to speak to the boss. You know I wouldn't tell you anything they talked about, Molly, but it doesn't matter as they shut the door. See you tomorrow, guys."

Tomorrow. Would she still be working here tomorrow?

"Are you okay, Molly?" Denton said, as the door closed behind Barb. "You don't look too well."

"Just the cold. It always makes my face red."

"I'd say you're the opposite, very pale."

Dawn Solway came in, stomping snow off her boots. "One more shift, should I live so long, and I'm outa here. Hawaii here I come."

Molly Smith had never been to tropical climes. She liked the winter too much. At this moment, however, Hawaii was looking like a promising destination. Although Outer Mongolia might be even better.

"Going by yourself, Dawn?" Denton asked.

Solway winked. "Top secret. I'd tell you, but then I'd have to kill you." They could hear her laughing as she headed down the corridor.

"Someone's in a good mood," Denton said. "Unlike the thundercloud standing in front of me."

Smith walked around the desk to stand beside the dispatcher. She leaned over and whispered, "Jim, if you hear anything about, well about me, in the next couple of days, I'd appreciate it if you'd let me know."

"What are you going on about, Molly? Are you in some kind of trouble?"

"I'd like a heads up, that's all." She straightened. "Now I'm going to get drunk."

"Molly, wait."

Waving over her shoulder she went to the constable's office to close off her shift. They couldn't fire her outright; she could take her case to the Union. She didn't know if she'd do that—it would all be just too embarrassing.

She stepped out the back door into the street. A light snow was falling, and the weather report on the radio had told her to expect close to twenty centimeters overnight. That was almost ten inches. It would be a great day on the mountain.

Her heart lifted a bit at the thought of going skiing. She was off tomorrow; she'd come in today in the middle of her four days off as a favor to Brad Noseworthy, who wanted to watch his fifteen-year-old daughter play an important hockey game. According to Brad, the girl was so good she was on track to make the Women's Olympic team.

She took the short cut down the alley toward her apartment, watching her footing as she walked. The path hadn't been cleared and it would turn to ice soon enough. She'd told Jim Denton she was going to get drunk. Sounded like a great idea, but she didn't have anywhere to go. She was so well known in this town, both as Moonlight Smith and Constable Smith, that if she pulled up a stool in some low-life bar, or even some high-end bar, everyone would be discussing it over their morning coffee. She could call her friend, Christa. But their relationship had been strained almost to the breaking point—perhaps beyond it— when Christa had been beaten up by a stalker. At least Charlie Bassing was doing well-deserved time in the lockup. Smith did some arithmetic and realized that he'd be eligible for parole any day now. Unlikely he'd come back to Trafalgar: too much would have happened to him in court and in prison for him to maintain his strange obsession with Christa. It wasn't as if she'd been his girlfriend, or even a close friend. He had no ties to Trafalgar, and no ties to Christa. She'd be free of him, Smith was sure, but it was unlikely the two women would ever again share that casual friendship which had made them as close as sisters.

She waited for traffic to clear and watched an elderly lady on the other side of the street picking her way through the snow with only a cane for support. The light turned green and Smith crossed. She was about to ask the woman if she needed help when she turned into a shop doorway.

Light and laughter spilled out the back of *Feuilles de Menthe*, the restaurant next door to Molly's apartment. She walked past, feeling nothing but sad and lonely. In any anonymous city, she'd go to the restaurant, after changing out of uniform, take a quiet table in the back and settle in with a good book, a glass of wine, and the day's special. But here someone was almost sure to ask her to join them, and be offended if she refused.

As much as she loved it here, it might be time to get out of Trafalgar.

Alphonse's Bakery was closed, all the lights off, save for a single low-wattage bulb over the door. No welcoming scents drifted into the alley. Smith approached the door to her apartment. A dark shape walked toward her. The weak light at the rear of the convenience store on the other side of the bakery was at his back and the glow from the light across the street didn't reach him. He stood in a black hole.

"Moonlight Smith. Fancy that."

His voice was deep and he was tall and, as far as she could tell beneath the bulky winter jacket, heavily muscled. A woman alone in a dark alley at night, Molly Smith wasn't afraid. Her jacket was tucked up around her belt. She felt the truncheon at her hip, the solid weight of the Glock, the radio at her shoulder.

"Do I know you?" she said.

With one step he was in the light. "I heard you'd become a cop."

He looked familiar. Close enough to her in age to have been in school with her. He ran his eyes down her body, but there weren't any sexual overtones. He was checking out the snow-covered hat, the jacket with the shoulder patches (Trafalgar City Police. Since 1895), the pants with the blue stripe running down the leg, and, probably most importantly, the equipment belt.

"Don't tell me you don't recognize me, Moonlight? Gary LeBlanc."

She remembered. Gary LeBlanc. Much older than his half-sister Lorraine, he'd been in some of Smith's classes in school. Always the clown, always the fool. Always under detention. Gone as soon as he turned sixteen. Either expelled or dropped out.

"Gary, it's been a while. Back for a visit?" In and out of minor trouble before and after he left school. Then something about a prison sentence. It had happened while she'd been in Victoria at University; she didn't know the details. Next time she was in the office, she'd pull his file.

"Nice family Christmas. Real Charles Dickens stuff. Too bad Mom and Dad spent it in the slammer."

She was standing by the door to her apartment. She'd already started to dig out her keys. It might not, she decided, be a good idea to let Gary LeBlanc know where she lived. Not that everyone in town didn't.

"You're looking good, Moonlight. Real good." He sighed, and passed into the light from above the bakery. Not as handsome as she remembered, now that his nose had been broken more than once and a scar crossed his left cheek. "Happy New Year, eh?"

"Happy New Year."

He passed her, heading toward Monroe Street. She thought she heard him say, "I always liked you, Moon." But his words were caught by the falling snow and she was probably mistaken.

◇◇◇

Mrs. Carmine handed Wendy a piece of paper the moment she came through the front door. Did the woman never leave her post? "Your mother called, dear. In case you'd forgotten, I took down the number of your parents' hotel."

Wendy took the paper. She walked up the stairs and opened the door to her room. It was a Victorian nightmare, hideous pink with fluffy cushions on the bed and swooping curtains over the windows and pink towels and shell-shaped pink soap in the bathroom. A porcelain doll wearing a pink skirt and a teddy bear with a pink bow around its neck were standing on the dresser. But at least, amongst all this pinkness, rather like living inside a Pepto Bismo bottle, Wendy had a room of her own. Being the one single woman in the group, she had a private room. Alan and Sophie shared, of course, and their room was next to hers. Much to her annoyance when the bed began to bounce. Which it did an obscene amount: the man must have superhuman powers. Jason had shared with Ewan—Ewan-Jason, Jason-Ewan—and Jeremy bunked in with Rob.

Wendy tossed her shopping bags onto the floor and wondered if Mrs. Carmine would hang a Vacancy sign out front, now that Jason and Ewan's room was empty. She stood at the window and let the tears fall. Her room looked down the hill, across the city, to the river and the mountain beyond. Lights sparked against the solid black of river, mountains and sky. She wiped her eyes on the sleeve of her sweater.

She was expected to meet her parents for dinner. They'd have to wait: she needed a toke to get ready for it. Wendy pulled open the bottom drawer of the dresser. She'd hid her personal supply of marijuana beneath her underwear. She reached to push the garments aside and her hand stopped. Wendy had been raised to be meticulous in the organization of her possessions. The scraps of silk and lace lay in perfect piles in the drawer. As well they should. Wendy's underwear cost close to a hundred dollars a set. Before leaving for this vacation, she'd shopped on Bloor Street in Toronto, looking for something special. Unable to resist their sexual beauty, she'd splurged on a lavender bra and panty set costing over five hundred.

Bras to the left and panties to the right, the way she always arranged things. Except that when she'd been getting dressed this morning, trying not to listen to the sounds coming from

Sophie and Alan's room, she'd picked up the lavender pieces and caressed them, thinking about the plans she'd had for them, and how it had all gone wrong. It seemed a shame that Sophie, who probably wore sturdy reinforced bras and white cotton panties purchased at Wal Mart, was getting action whereas the lavender bit was lying in this dark drawer. She'd put the bra back down, not on the bra pile but on top of its mate. Wendy wasn't a fanciful girl, but she'd thought that the expensive pieces might as well be together, as no one else would be appreciating them.

They'd been moved. Her bras were stacked together, one on top of the other. Panties in a neat pile beside. Each color layered properly. Even the lavender ones.

Wendy sat back on the bed.

Someone had been in her drawer. Rooting through her stuff. Rage boiled up: some miserable lowlife had been rubbing their filthy fingers over her silk and lace and satin underwear. No way would she ever put those clothes on again. Might as well burn them. Better than donating them to a charity clothing shop, where some old bag would toss the lavender bra into her cart beside white underpants that could fit an elephant.

Five hundred and twenty five bucks for a padded push-up bra and a scrap of lace to fit between her legs. Even her mother wouldn't pay a quarter that. Lorraine, it had to be that miserable Lorraine. God knew why Mrs. Carmine insisted on being nice to the girl. It would be just like Mrs. Carmine to let Lorraine roam around the house without being watched.

Wendy had been given a key for her room, but she hadn't thought it worth bothering to lock the door.

She reached for the phone. The police would get an earful about this. She got as far as punching in 9-1, before dropping the phone back into the cradle. Someone had been rooting through her drawers looking for what? She fell to her knees and pushed her undies aside. Her stash of marijuana looked to be as she'd left it. Far as she could tell, not a flake was missing.

No way could she call the cops and have them search through her things, asking questions. More questions.

Chapter Eleven

Street prostitution wasn't a problem in Trafalgar, but if it was the Mountainside Inn would be the sort of place that could be expected to rent rooms out by the hour.

Doctor Jack Wyatt-Yarmouth met Sergeant John Winters in the hotel lobby. What there was in the way of a lobby: a single couch decorated in cheap tartan fabric; an arm chair, more arm than chair. A teenaged desk clerk, chewing gum and not bothering to pretend he wasn't staring at them.

"I apologize for disturbing you, Dr. Wyatt-Yarmouth," Winters said, holding out his hand.

"Call me Jack, please."

"Jack. Perhaps we could go somewhere a bit more private." Winters threw a look toward the clerk. He didn't even have the grace to look away.

Jack Wyatt-Yarmouth chuckled without humor. He was a small man, about five-seven and underweight. Beneath his round rimless glasses his dark eyes were empty and grief dragged at his thin cheeks. "Our room isn't quite the Royal Suite at the Ritz, but it will do for lack of anything better. We could have stayed at the same B&B as my daughter and her friends, but my wife balked at the idea of taking the room because our son wasn't needing it." He swallowed and looked away. "Come on up."

"Will your wife be joining us?" Winters asked.

Wyatt-Yarmouth punched the button to call the elevator, and, like a good servant, the doors opened immediately. They stepped inside and he pushed another button for the second floor. He waited for the doors to close before answering. "I suggested that an afternoon at the spa would do her some good." He checked his watch. "She's running late, probably poking around the stores to keep her mind occupied, but if she does arrive while we're talking, I'd prefer we continue this conversation at a later time."

Winters made no comment. He'd wait and see whether a conversation with Mrs. Wyatt-Yarmouth was required.

The elevator might have been obedient, but it was certainly slow. Time ticked away as it crawled toward the second floor, but eventually it did arrive. The hotel room was as badly decorated as the lobby, and the heating unit under the window groaned with the effort of emitting air that was far too warm. Jack gestured to his guest to take the single chair. He placed his leather jacket on the bed to the left, after neatly tucking the arms in, and sat on the second of the twin beds. He was dressed in expensive jeans and a good wool sweater in shades of brown and orange, pulled over a crisp white collar.

Winters took the chair.

"Sorry," Wyatt-Yarmouth said with a shrug of bony shoulders, "but I can't offer you a drink."

"This isn't a social call."

"I guessed not. Perhaps you'll tell me why a detective Sergeant wants to speak with me? I'm sure you're aware that my wife and I met with another officer when we arrived. He took us to the hospital. We're only still here," he waved his hand, taking in the room, "in these inadequate accommodations while waiting for our son...our son's body...to be released so we can take him back to Ontario. We met with the coroner when we arrived, and everything seemed to be in order." Jack's eyes were clear, but his voice broke.

Jason's sister, Wendy Wyatt-Yarmouth, in the company of two of her friends, had identified not only her brother, but also the other body as that of his friend, Ewan Williams. Nevertheless, as soon as they arrived, delayed by the weather, Mr. and Mrs. Wyatt-Yarmouth insisted on seeing them both.

"I'm sorry about this, sir," Winters said, "but there's been a complication. What can you tell me about your son's friend, Ewan Williams?"

"Ewan? He and Jason have been friends for a long time, since kindergarten. When they were young, Ewan was in and out of our house all the time. We have a swimming pool, and our house was pretty much the center of the neighborhood back in those days. Then the boys grew up, got drivers' licenses and girlfriends and part-time jobs, lost interest in the pool, and didn't need parents ferrying them about. They went away to university, so I can't say we've seen much of Ewan for the last couple of years. Heard he went to McMaster University, in Hamilton, to study Archeology. Patricia, my wife, told me the police are having trouble contacting his parents. Can't say I know them well. We met at school sports events or on occasions when Mrs. Williams came to collect the boy at our house, or visa versa. But we never socialized. Why are you asking?"

Winters ignored the question. "Once they grew up, became adults, Jason and Ewan, did they stay close?"

"Hard for a father to say. They went separate ways into university. Natural enough, I'd say. Come to think of it, it's probably been a couple of years since I've seen Ewan. Not since the boys finished high school." The man's eyes opened wide. "For God's sake! Look here, man, if you're suggesting there was more than friendship between my son and his friend, any…unnatural relationship…you're seriously mistaken. Jason's had a long string of girlfriends, and I believe Ewan was almost legendary in his pursuit of what we men might call nookie."

John Winters didn't think he'd ever called it nookie. Interesting, however, that Jack Wyatt-Yarmouth used the phrase 'unnatural relationship' in response to something Winters hadn't even been suggesting.

"Have you heard of Ewan Williams being in any trouble? Trouble in school, trouble with the police?"

"No."

"Even rumors? Suspicions?"

"No. The boy was welcome in our home, which he would not have been if he was trouble, or if I'd had reason to suspect he had designs on my boy. I repeat, why are you asking these questions?"

"I'm sorry, Mr. Wyatt-Yarmouth, but the coroner will be keeping your son's body for a few more days."

The man jumped to his feet. "This is outrageous. We've already had to sit in this miserable hotel waiting for the autopsy, and we were told only yesterday that we could take him home. My wife made the arrangements this morning."

"I realize this is a shock, but we do have our reasons."

"And what reasons might those be?"

"Ewan Williams died sometime before the car Jason was driving went into the river."

Wyatt-Yarmouth dropped back onto the bed. The springs squeaked in protest. "What on earth?"

"That's what I'm trying to find out. Your son had a dead man in his car."

"Surely, you're not implying that my son was responsible for Ewan's death."

"I'm implying nothing. I'm telling you the situation. What do you do for a living, Jack?"

"As you probably know, if you're any sort of a detective, I am a full professor of Sociology at the University of Toronto. I happen to specialize in issues of policing in democratic societies and have written extensively on matters regarding the abuse of police powers. I'm also on the police board at home in Oakville."

All of which means Jack-shit to me, Jack.

"Then you'll be aware that the circumstances of your son's death are now a matter for police investigation."

Jack got to his feet once again. He almost visibly stretched in an attempt to make his short frame taller. He clenched his fists. "My son had nothing to do with the death of Ewan. It should be easy to explain, even for officers on a police department as small as yours. Jason wasn't aware Ewan was dead, and was taking him to the hospital." He cracked a smile, stiff and frozen. "My son was, I'll thank you to remember, young and highly impulsive. He should have called 911, I won't argue with that. But waiting for someone else to arrive and take charge wasn't in Jason's nature. I have no trouble believing he decided to act and get Ewan to the hospital by himself. Sadly, that decision cost my son his life." Wyatt-Yarmouth rubbed at his face for a long time. When he took his hands away, his eyes were very red. "If you have no other questions, Sergeant, I'd like you to leave. My wife will be here shortly and I'd rather not see her disturbed any more than she is already."

Winters stood. "I'm truly sorry for your loss. I wanted you to know how the situation stands. The pathologist will have to re-examine your son in light of what she found with Mr. Williams. I'm afraid it can't be helped."

Jack Wyatt-Yarmouth reached the door before John Winters, and pulled it open. "Thank you for your time," he said, not at all meaning it. "I'm sure we won't meet again before my family leaves your pleasant town."

Winters paused half-way out the door and turned back to the room. Of all the police dramas on TV, most of which he couldn't bear to watch, he'd liked *Colombo* the most. "One more thing. What was Jason studying at university?"

"Medicine. Like his mother, Jason intended to be a surgeon."

All Kathy Carmine wanted in this life was to get out of Trafalgar. Her mother's idea of travel was the monthly drive to Nelson to shop at Wal-Mart. Kathy had been to Vancouver once, on a Grade Ten school trip. She'd been awed by the size of the buildings, the panorama of the open ocean, the huge old trees in Stanley Park, the glittering stores, the glamorous people shopping in those stores. Ever since, she'd realized just how small, how confining, how *provincial*, Trafalgar, surrounded by mountains on all sides, was.

Kathy got average marks at school, and she wasn't any kind of an athlete. She'd always had to help her mom run the B&B, cooking, cleaning, and so, unlike her friends, she'd never had the chance to make some money from an after school job.

She was in Grade Twelve, and had applied to Trafalgar College for a diploma in business in the fall—her mom's idea, not hers. Mrs. Carmine had her eye on a small house across the street that she always said would be perfect for a cozy catered vacation home. Something very high end, she'd said, that she could charge an arm and a leg for. The home owners, the McNeils, were elderly, getting close to having to sell up and move into assisted living. Mr. McNeil had broken his hip in the spring, and Mrs. Carmine hovered like a vulture, encouraging Mrs. McNeil to consider moving to someplace that would be "easier for you to manage, dear." To her consternation, Mr. McNeil recovered fairly well, and by mid-summer Mrs. McNeil was back caring for the fifty-year old perennial gardens that accentuated the old home's appeal.

Kathy no longer wondered why, if her mom had enough money to consider buying another property, she wasn't going to use it to send Kathy to University, as she wanted. But that subject wasn't up for discussion. Kathy would get a diploma in business, help her mother run the B&B, and eventually take it over when the cozy catered vacation property became Mrs. Carmine's to manage.

Kathy Carmine's worst nightmare was that she would grow old without ever again seeing the world on the other side of these mountains.

And it would all be her mother's fault.

She'd never had a real boyfriend, just a bit of awkward groping in someone's father's car or in the darkened movie theater. Kathy'd decided after the Grade Ten trip to Vancouver that getting involved with a Trafalgar boy would only tie her even tighter to the town.

She wasn't a brave girl, Kathy, and she'd been waiting, hesitating, afraid to make her move.

It would have to be tonight.

The guests had come in as Kathy had been putting sheets into the washing machine. She'd abandoned the wash and grabbed the fresh flowers she'd left sitting in a couple of inches of water in the sink. She took the flowers up to the second-floor landing. The group had gathered in Wendy's room, and the door was open.

"My parents expect us all to be there," Wendy said, in that hideous nasal whine that she no doubt thought made her sound upper class.

"Look, Wendy, I'm sorry for your parents. I really am. But Jason was my friend too, and I'll thank you to remember that. If I don't want to go out to dinner, then I don't. And so I won't."

"You think I want to go? And be forced to drag out every story about what a nice little boy Jason was, and what a nice young man he grew up to be, and what a nice big man he was intended to be, before being tragically struck down in his prime?"

"Wendy," Sophie said, in her soft Québécoise accent.

"What the hell are you doing here anyway? You hadn't even met my brother before last week."

"Come on Wendy, Sophie's only trying to help."

"Like I care. Do what you want, Rob, okay? But don't think I won't remember that you wouldn't come."

"Listen to yourself, will you, Wendy? I'm not exactly breaking out in hives worrying that you're going to cut me out of your will. I'd rather not go to dinner with your parents, that's all."

"Puh," Sophie said in that absolutely French way. "Do as you want. I am going to prepare for dinner *en famille. Alain?*"

"What?"

"Dinner, *Alain.* Are you coming to dress?"

"Yeah, right."

Alan and Sophie came out of Wendy's room. Kathy was standing in the landing, flowers in hand. She forced a smile. But, as usual, they were so wrapped up in each other they couldn't spare a moment for anyone else. By the time they reached their room, Alan had his hand up Sophie's shirt, reaching for the clips of her bra, and she was unfastening the zipper on her pants.

Dressing for dinner meant something different to Alan and Sophie than it did to most people.

"Don't be in such a rush, Alan," Wendy shouted. "The police want to talk to you guys. I'm calling them. You don't want to be having a *nap* when they get here."

Kathy dropped the flowers onto the table and ran downstairs. She'd heard what she needed to. They would all be going out for dinner tonight. Except for Rob.

She threw open the door leading to the family's private area, and sprinted down the hall to her own room.

"Yes?" A woman answered the phone. Her voice thick and drowsy.

"I'm looking for Dave Evans."

"Who wants to know?"

"Tell him it's Sergeant Winters of the Trafalgar City Police."

"Okay, hold on."

"Sweetie," she said through a big yawn. "You wanna take a call?"

A noise in the background.

"That Winters guy," the woman said. "Didn't he come around to ask Rosemary about her stolen bike last summer?" She giggled. "That was when we met."

"Fuck," a man said. Static, and then: "Sarge, what can I do for you?"

"Not leave your cell phone with anyone inclined to blow me off for one thing."

"Well, yeah, you see…"

Winters pulled on his drug store glasses, size 1.25, to read the fine print on the computer. He hated those glasses. Another step and it was a wheelchair and a bladder bag. He'd interviewed Wendy Wyatt-Yarmouth, a third-class liar if he'd ever seen one, and then her prickly father, and then her friends. The latter had been a quick conversation, as they needed to get ready for a formal dinner with the Wyatt-Yarmouths. Winters didn't much care if the W-Y's dinner plans had to be put back, but the boys didn't have much to say other than echo Wendy. Some of them had gone for dinner on Sunday, some had done other things. No one knew where Ewan Williams had gone, although Rob and Jeremy both said he'd told them he was going out on his own for the night. He'd been eying a girl at the ski resort for a couple of days, a short, attractive dark-haired girl wearing a white ski outfit, and had taken a break for an early lunch saying he was going to track her down. Jeremy gave a rough description of the girl, but they had no idea who she was, or if Ewan had made plans to meet up with her later. Ewan had shared a room with Jason, but Winters couldn't ask Jason what he knew about his friend's movements that night.

Winters had spent his evening here, at the office. Eliza's long time agent, the formidable Barney, who, at age sixty-five, and still an avid skier, was in town combining business with pleasure. They'd been supposed to meet for dinner to discuss some wonderful plan Barney had for Eliza's next job. Which was necessary considering that Eliza's last project had fallen to earth in a spectacular flameout. Dinner would be on Barney's tab, which would, of course, be tax-deductible. He'd called Eliza to say he wouldn't be able to make it. After twenty-five years of marriage to a cop, Eliza said she'd eat his portion. Winters turned to his computer and tried to dig up the dirt on Jason Wyatt-Yarmouth, Ewan Williams, and the rest of their crowd: Wendy Wyatt-Yarmouth, Jeremy Wozenack, Rob Fitzgerald, Alan Robertson, and Sophie Dion.

Wozenack had a couple of drunk charges in Toronto, brawls outside of bars, but nothing serious enough to have caused injury. Dion had several traffic tickets to her name, and was perilously close to earning enough points to have her license suspended. Wendy Wyatt-Yarmouth's file was the interesting one. Juvenile records. Closed. Which told him that there was something to tell him, but they weren't going to. *Na, Na, Na. I know something you don't.* He started the paperwork necessary to try to pry open her juvie file.

"Save it," Winters said over the phone to Dave Evans. "I want to ask you about a fight at the Bishop a couple of nights before Christmas. The twenty-second. You were there, tell me what you remember." While telling him that they didn't know what Ewan Williams had been up to Sunday evening, his friends had mentioned, in that way that people who have something to hide manage to accidentally let you know far more than you'd been hoping for, that Williams had gotten himself into a street fight on Saturday night. Winters had checked the shift report for the night before William's death.

"Same old shit we get all the time," Evans said. "By the time we arrived a full scale punch up was going on outside. Two guys taking swings at each other. The sidewalk was icy and they were having trouble staying upright. They looked like a couple of bloody fools. That's probably what kept them from landing any serious blows on the other guy."

"You recognize either of them?"

"One of them, yes. Don't know his name, but a local guy. The other was probably an outsider, a skier."

"Why do you think that?"

Evans let out a puff of air, and Winters let him think. "The outsider was dressed well, clean jeans, thick wool sweater, good boots. He was small, but knew how to throw a punch. Hard to say, Sarge. Just my impression."

"Impressions count, Dave. You didn't bring them in?"

Evans' voice turned hard, as he moved onto the defensive. "Both guys stepped back, soon as we pulled up. They apologized; said there'd be no more trouble. I thought we should bring them in, but…Molly didn't agree. And that was it."

"Sounds okay with me," Winters said. He had plenty of doubts about Constable Dave Evans. Always too much on the defensive. Winters had run into the Evans type before. One day Evans would toss someone to the wolves to save his own butt. Hopefully at that time he would no longer be in the employ of the Trafalgar City Police.

Evans thought it was his little secret, but Barb knew, and thus everyone else knew, the Chief Constable most of all, that Evans' goal in life was to join the RCMP. Counter-terrorism was his aim: not petty crime or no-account deaths in small mountain towns.

Which, today, was of no consequence.

"What was the fight about?"

Evans snorted. "The same thing it always is. A woman. Mr. Wool Sweater had moved in on Mr. Local's girl while he spent time with his friends and ignored her. This is what I heard outside, Sarge, you follow?"

"I do."

"They'd been leaving…"

"Who'd been leaving?"

"The girl and the outsider guy."

"Continue."

"The girl had, far as I could figure out, been quite happy to be moved in on. But when she got up to leave, the boyfriend noticed and took exception."

Winters got the picture. Local girl, abandoned in a low-level bar while her boyfriend watched Sport TV with his pals. Soon the boyfriend pulls his head out of the brown bottle and, hey, his woman is making friendly with another guy.

"You and Smith were at the car in the river on Monday. Recognize anyone brought out?"

"No. Neither of them. Outsiders probably." Even over the phone it was almost possible to see the light dawning behind Evans' eyes. "Hey. Didn't occur to me before, but, now that I'm putting them together, one of the guys in the river was the outsider in the fight we've just been talking about. It was him all right."

Hardly a positive identification. But it didn't matter, Winters only needed clarification on what he'd been told earlier.

"Same guy," Evans said. "I'm sure of it."

The B&B was dark and quiet by eight. The guests had gone out to dinner with Wendy's and Jason's parents. As they trooped out the door, it was easy to see that none of them seemed happy about it, and who could blame them. Whether they talked about it or not, the deaths of Ewan and Jason would lie over the dinner table like a shroud.

Upstairs, a toilet flushed.

Kathy took a deep breath. Her mother had gone to a movie. There were only two people in the Glacier Chalet B&B. Kathy had gone shopping earlier and found a purple blouse, much more daring than anything she owned. Shoulder straps the thickness of a strand of spaghetti and a deeply plunging neckline. She'd left the store without trying it on, and hadn't thought about a bra. Only when she got home did she realize that her bras, white things with thick straps and multiple clips, would make the purple blouse look ridiculous.

She'd have to go without a bra.

The satin felt wicked and delicious against her bare breasts. Kathy shivered. *So this is what rich feels like.*

She walked up the stairs breathing heavily—and not from exertion: she must climb these steps twenty times a day. She carried a bottle of cheap bubbly wine, stolen from the stash her mother kept to help guests celebrate anniversaries or weddings, a carton of orange juice she'd bought this afternoon, and two crystal flutes.

Her heart was beating so hard, she thought he'd hear it before the knock on his door.

"Come on in," Rob shouted. "It's open."

She had to wedge the bottle of champagne under her arm to get a hand free to open the door.

He was sitting at the desk in front of the window hunched over his computer. He wore baggy track suit pants and a red cardigan over a gray T-shirt advertising a brand of beer. Glasses were perched on his nose. He didn't look up from the screen. "You're back early. Forget something, or just too much misery around the table?"

Kathy cleared her throat.

Rob looked up. Under the round glasses, his eyes were equally round with surprise.

"Hi, Rob. I thought." She cleared her throat again. "You might like a treat." Heat flew up her face and across her exposed chest. "I mean something tasty." She grabbed the bottle and held it up.

One of the crystal flutes fell from her hand. She lunged for it and dropped the carton of juice, which she'd opened in the kitchen. It squirted orange liquid across the beige carpet.

"Oh, dear," Rob said.

Chapter Twelve

No one had been offered cocktails. Instead Dad told the waiter they would have Champagne. *Presumably*, he'd said in his hoity-toity voice, they'd have the *real* thing.

Certainly, the waitress said. She went to fetch it.

Mom looked strained. The delicate skin under her eyes was blue and puffy. Strands of hair had escaped from the knot at the back of her neck. Wendy couldn't remember ever seeing her mother with escaping hair. It made her seem a bit more human. Wendy reached under the table and touched her mother's hand. Mom almost jumped out of her skin, but when she'd settled down she gave her daughter a small smile and pressed her hand in return.

The Champagne arrived; a bottle was presented to Dad and the cork popped. Dad tasted, nodded, and one waitress began to pour, while another placed flutes in front of everyone.

And Wendy knew that this was going to be perfectly horrible.

After they'd all been served, Dad raised his glass. Wendy glanced around the table. Not one of the friends looked as if they wanted to be here. Rob, she thought, was the only sensible one.

"My son," Dad said, taking a sip. The others followed. Even Jeremy, who knew how to knock a drink back faster than anyone Wendy knew, barely touched the wine to his lips.

Another toast, another drink. "Ewan," Dad said.

Mom let out a small sob.

Dad always did like the theatrical. Mom was sitting so low in her chair she was almost under the table. He absolutely hated the fact that his wife was a Member of the Order of Canada and he was not, and to cover up how much he resented it, he felt compelled to mention it at every opportunity.

Sophie put her glass down and opened her menu. "What do you think looks good?" she said to no one in particular.

"My daughter tells me you're taking theater at McGill," Mom said to Alan, sitting on her right at the round table. The restaurant was full, silver gleamed, candlelight flickered, crystal sparkled. The curtains were drawn back, and outside snow fell heavily. "It's a wonderful school. I applied there for my undergrad, but they rejected me."

"Which they've been regretting ever since, I've no doubt," Alan said with his boyish-charm grin. He was handsome enough, with deep brown eyes underneath long lashes, a mop of artfully tossed black curls, and a dimpled smile, to be a movie star. Whether he had any real talent, Wendy didn't know.

Mom put her company façade back on, laughed lightly, and took a sip of Champagne.

"Do you think the salmon's any good?" Sophie said. "I can't stand dry fish."

Time was catching up with Eliza Winters. Designers in Paris and Milan had stopped calling long ago; the big magazines shortly after. That she still got any work at all, she knew, was due to the contacts and skills of her agent, Bernadette McLaughlin, who everyone in the business called Barney. Eliza had been so pleased last summer when she'd landed a job in Trafalgar—big budget, mega-star photographer, national exposure, and to top it all off she wouldn't have to leave home. But the client company folded before the first picture was even snapped. Nothing suitable had come up since.

Barney told the hostess they would require a table for two, not three, as reserved. Flavours was the best restaurant in Trafalgar. It was also the most expensive. In Eliza's experience, those two adjectives were not always complementary, but in this case they were. The room was full, but the noise level not too high. People laughed while black and white clad waiters maneuvered heavy trays.

"A moment, Barney," Eliza said. "I see someone I know." She leaned close to the older woman. "Just lost her son."

Barney followed the long-haired hostess with the thin hips to a table set into a private alcove at the back. It was prepared for a party of three, and the woman whipped the unneeded place-setting away as quickly as if a dog had passed and left its calling card. "Jonathan will be your waiter tonight," she said.

Barney couldn't possibly have cared less what their waiter's name was. As long as he brought the wine list.

Eliza approached the large round table in the center of the main room. "Patricia. Lovely to see you."

The look of sheer pleasure that crossed Patricia Wyatt-Yarmouth's face was, Eliza thought, rather frightening.

"Eliza! How wonderful. Please, won't you join us? As you can see, we haven't ordered our food yet. We're having a glass of champagne in honor of my son and his friend." She turned to the man across the table. "Ask them to bring another chair, dear."

The man half-rose.

"No, thank you," Eliza said. "I'm with a friend. Just the two of us tonight, I'm afraid. My husband's working late."

"That's perfect," Patricia said. "You and your friend can join us. We've had a cancellation ourselves, so there's plenty of room." They were six at a table for eight. Menus were still on the table.

"Thank you, but we have business...."

Patricia Wyatt-Yarmouth was on her feet. She waived to the hostess. "Two more to join us," she said.

The young woman ran for chairs and cutlery.

Oh, dear.

"You're being most presumptions, Pat. This lady has plans." The man was Patricia's age; her husband probably. The rest of their group was much younger. The daughter, small and dark and scowling, was easy to identify, as short and lightly-boned as her mother. The others, one young woman and two men, must be friends as they bore no resemblance to the family.

"Nonsense," Patricia said to her husband. She hailed the hostess once again. "Ask my friend's companion to join us."

Mr. Wyatt-Yarmouth sat down. Two more chairs and matching place settings arrived. Along with a rather startled looking Barney, clutching her linen napkin.

Eliza had no choice. She took the offered seat.

"Hi," said the young man to her left. "I'm Jeremy. Nice to meet you."

"Eliza. My pleasure. This is my friend Bernadette."

Introductions were made. Another bottle of champagne ordered.

Eliza sat between Patricia's daughter and Jeremy. The daughter, Wendy, would have been plain, with her large nose and weak bone structure, except that her teeth were straight and white and perfect and her skin glowed with youth and health. Her hair, light brown streaked with blond, was cut into a highly attractive, and no-doubt highly expensive, chin-length bob. Her earrings were giant silver hoops, which suited her haircut perfectly. A long silver pendant dipped into the cleft between her small breasts.

Wyatt-Yarmouth glared at his wife, and she kept her eyes demurely downcast, as a proper Victorian maiden should in company. Eliza tried to catch Barney's eyes, to signal an apology, but at the first sign of the accent in the "'allo," of the girl she was seated beside, Barney had launched into rapid-fire French. The girl's face lit up and they chattered away.

"Pardon us," Barney said at last. "Dreadfully rude, I know, but now I'm living in Vancouver I so rarely get the chance to practice my French, I simply couldn't resist."

It wasn't as if anyone else at the table had anything to talk about. Eliza and Barney expressed their sympathies to Jack Wyatt-Yarmouth.

He thanked them.

Barney asked when they'd be going home.

That was a mistake.

"We should have been out of here tomorrow," he snarled. "But the police are saying they need to keep Jason for a while longer. Let me tell you, I put in a call to the Chief of Police PDQ. I won't have some two-bit, hick town cop sticking his nose into my son's death and trying to score points by making a tragic car accident out to be something out of an episode of *CSI*."

"Eliza's husband…" Barney began.

Eliza silenced her with a look.

"Please, dear." Patricia said, her voice low and calm. "People are looking."

And they were. Chairs might have scratched the golden hardwood floor as diners at adjoining tables tried to eavesdrop without appearing to be rude.

The young people shifted in their seats. Wendy, the daughter, bristled with anger. She opened her mouth to say something. And it would not have been polite.

Eliza gathered her bag from the back of her chair and reached into a front pocket. "I think it best if we don't interfere in your evening." She got to her feet. Barney scrambled to follow. "Thank you for the champagne. It was a pleasure to meet you, Jack. My condolences again." She touched Patricia on the shoulder and slipped her card into the woman's hand. A bit pretentious, having a calling card in a town like Trafalgar. She rarely used them any more, and only for business. But she didn't want to take the time to scramble for paper and pen. "If you're going to be here for a few days, perhaps we can have lunch, or another day at the spa. That would be fun. Call me, if you're free."

Patricia Wyatt-Yarmouth smiled at Eliza. "Thank you," she whispered.

The waitress hovered to take their order.

"Is the salmon dry?" Sophie asked.

Eliza and Barney turned toward their table, only to find that it had been given to another party in the interim. They turned again, back toward the hostess table.

"Having a nice *family* dinner, are you?"

Eliza blinked. "I'm sorry?"

The girl didn't look much older than fifteen. She was dressed in a patched winter coat and a long scarf full of holes. Black mascara ran down her cheeks, mixed with melting snow or tears, it was impossible to tell.

Incongruously, she wore a small pair of, if Eliza's judgment hadn't completely failed her, 14-carat gold hoop earrings.

"Thought you could have your dinner without me, did you? We'll I'm here, and I'm in mourning too, not that any you gives a fuck. But I'm going to tell you one thing, Mrs. Wyatt-Yarmouth…"

"I'm afraid you've made a mistake," Eliza said.

The patrons were no longer trying not to appear to be eavesdropping. The dining room was so silent that noise from the kitchen, clattering crockery, shouted orders, someone bellowing for carrots, *goddamn it*, could be heard.

The head waiter hurried over, wiping his hands on his white apron. "Is there a problem?"

"Apparently there is." Jack Wyatt-Yarmouth was on his feet. "Now I don't know who you are, girl, but I'd suggest that you leave."

"Sit down, Jack," Patricia said in quiet voice, "and shut up. If you are looking for Mrs. Wyatt-Yarmouth, I am she."

"Oh, you are *she*, are you," the girl took a step toward the table. She faltered and Eliza reached out a hand to steady her. The girl shrugged her off. Her breath was rancid with the sour scent of beer. "Well, I'm an even better she."

"Lorraine, get out of here." Wendy's chair sounded like a gun shot as it crashed to the floor behind her. "This is a private dinner and you haven't been invited."

The girl, Lorraine, turned toward Wendy. "You think I don't know that, you stuck-up rich bitch." She dropped into the chair recently vacated by Eliza. "I've as much right to be here as he does." She pointed at Jeremy. "More." She bared her teeth at Patricia. "I'm Jason's girlfriend, see. We were going to be engaged but before that could happen he...then he...died." She burst into tears.

The head waiter stood beside her, not at all sure of what to do.

Eliza glanced at Patricia. All the blood had drained from the woman's face, leaving it stark white. She might have been a ghost, except for the red in her eyes.

Lorraine picked up a menu. "I'm going to have dinner. Dinner with the family what shoulda been my in-laws. What's the most expensive thing?"

"As you appear to know this person," Jack yelled at his daughter, "do something." He had resumed his seat at Patricia's order.

Wendy tugged ineffectually at the sleeve of Lorraine's heavy coat.

"Shall we go to the powder room, Patricia?" Eliza placed her hand on her friend's shoulder.

Patricia didn't move.

"What a good idea," Barney said. "What do you think you're you looking at, buddy?

The man at the next table began sawing at his steak.

A man ran into the dining room, shedding snow, looking around him as if he quite desperately needed to find something he'd lost. A waitress tried to stop him, but he stepped around her. He walked to the table that was the centre of the room, figuratively as well as literally.

Eliza's hand was on Patricia's arm, guiding the woman to standing. Her legs wobbled and Eliza gripped harder. Barney took the other arm.

"Come on, Lorraine. Let's go home," the new arrival said. The girl reached across the table and grabbed Patricia's unfinished glass of champagne. The man plucked it from her fingers. "Let's go."

The head waiter signaled to the hostess, who picked up the phone.

"I haven't ordered my dinner," Lorraine said.

"I'll take you to dinner. Anyplace you like."

"I want to have dinner here." Lorraine's eyes were red and puffy and her nose ran. She swallowed a sob, and wiped her nose on the sleeve of her coat.

"Please come with me."

The girl looked around. Her eyes fastened on Eliza, who was handing Patricia to Barney.

"Tell them I belong here," she said, her voice a weak whisper.

Barney half-dragged Patricia Wyatt-Yarmouth toward the back.

"Christ, as if," Wendy said in a laugh that was more like a bark. "You're pathetic. We might as well have invited Geronimo to dinner. Jason cared more about that cat than he did about you."

"You," Eliza said, "are not helping."

"Fuck off, lady."

"Will someone get this person out of here," Jack bellowed.

The door opened, bringing in a blast of drifting snow, wind and cold, and a figure dressed in dark blue.

The head waiter, almost jumping up and down with excitement, spoke to the police officer. By now most of the restaurant patrons were standing to see better, the kitchen staff had emerged from the back, and the wait staff lined the walls, twisting fingers in white aprons.

The cop crossed the room. She was young, pretty, blond. Her cheeks glowed red with cold, and fresh snow sprinkled the top of her flat blue hat with the light blue band.

"Hi, Lorraine," she said, in a warm and friendly voice. "Let's go outside and talk. Gary can come with us."

"That's a great idea," Gary said.

"No. I'm here to have dinner with my family. They should have been my family. They would have been. They would have, Molly. It's not fair."

So, Eliza thought, this was Constable Molly Smith, who had driven John to distraction more than once over the summer.

"Life's not fair, Lorraine." Smith dropped her voice so only the people immediately around her, which happened to include

Eliza, could hear. "Gary, can you get her up? I don't want to make a scene, but I've been called to get her out of here. How much has she had? And what?"

"Just beer, I think. When I got home, Lorraine was in the kitchen. She had a couple bottles in front of her and was crying. I tried to talk to her, but I had to go to the can, and when I got back, she was gone."

"What's the matter with this police department?" Jack Wyatt-Yarmouth yelled. His face was almost as red as Smith's. But not from the cold, and the effect was not nearly as attractive. "I demand you remove this person."

"Shut up, Dad," Wendy said, unexpectedly. "She isn't going to shoot her, you know, even if you demand her to."

Jack spluttered.

Sophie let out a burst of embarrassed laughter. Alan studied the tines of his fork. Jeremy leaned back in his chair, looking as though he were enjoying every minute of the other people's misery.

Gary managed to lift a wobbly Lorraine to her feet. Constable Smith talked to her in a quiet voice. Together they guided the crying girl toward the door.

Eliza let out a soft sigh. Patricia had gone to the ladies with Barney and missed the scene. Jack was huffing and puffing and threatening to blow the straw house down. His daughter, Wendy, after throwing Lorraine a look that would freeze lava, resumed her seat.

"I hope we're going to eat now," Sophie said.

Only Eliza saw Gary hand Lorraine to Smith. "What?" the young constable's lips said.

Gary walked back to the table.

"Pardon me, Ma'am," he said to Eliza as he brushed up against her to reach the table. He put two big, hairy hands on a tablecloth as snowy white as the night outside. His nails were torn, the cuticles ragged, dirt trapped in the folds of skin. His eyes passed over Wendy, then Sophie, and settled down to flick between Alan and Jeremy.

Eliza glanced toward the door. Clearly Constable Smith didn't know what to do. She was trying to keep Lorraine standing while watching Gary.

"You guys. You come to our town and throw around your money and show off your flash cars and skis. You fuck our girls, and then you leave. Back to Mommy and Daddy and the trust fund."

"I scarcely think," Wendy said.

"I scarcely care what you think, kid. Get this straight, all of you. Your precious Jason was a whoremonger and a cradle snatcher. And, outside of this table, there aren't many people bothered that he, or his friend, is dead."

He glanced out of the side of his eyes. Eliza followed, to see Constable Smith, still trying to hold Lorraine upright, coming back their way.

"Gotta go," Gary said. "Have a nice evening folks."

He straightened up, and pointed one finger toward Jack Wyatt-Yarmouth. "If you're a religious sort, old man, you'd better pray my sister isn't knocked up. Otherwise, you'll be seeing my ugly mug again."

He crossed the room in several strides. "Ready to leave, Moon?" he said in a booming voice. "I sense we're no longer welcome here. Enjoy your dinner, folks." Gary waved at the crowd, watching him as if he were tonight's floorshow.

"I want to know what all that was about, and I want to know now," Jack Wyatt-Yarmouth shouted at his daughter.

Wendy didn't resume her seat. "I don't think so," she said, heading for the door. She grabbed her coat from the rack by the exit.

"How about we grab a pizza?" Alan said. "Pizza'd be good, eh, Sophie."

"Pardon?"

"We're going for pizza. Thanks for the champagne, sir." Alan and Sophie followed Wendy at nothing much short of the speed of light. Jeremy followed at a more leisurely pace.

Eliza was still standing in the middle of the floor. Thank heavens Barney had gotten Patricia out of here before that hideous scene.

Jack Wyatt-Yarmouth was the only one remaining at the table. He stared at Eliza across the detritus of champagne bottles, crystal flutes, menus, and untouched plates. "Who the hell are you anyway?"

"Wife of a two-bit, hick-town cop. Good night, Jack."

Eliza headed for the back to check on Patricia and Barney.

Chapter Thirteen

The bedside clock radio sprang to life at seven a.m. Molly Smith rolled over and for once didn't punch the snooze button. With a glance at the picture of Graham on the night table, she reached for her cell phone and flipped it open. In the dim light cast by the face of the instrument, she hit a stored number.

After listening to the brief message, she jumped out of bed.

Twenty centimeters of snow at Big Sky last night. Almost ten inches of fresh—untouched—powder. The nearest thing to heaven on this earth. She ran for the bathroom. It had snowed on the mountain for days, and so the conditions would be good. Good wasn't worth getting up at seven o'clock after a long shift for, but new powder—that was worth it.

By seven-fifteen she was carrying her equipment downstairs.

Alphonse was at work and the day's bread was baking. The back door to the bakery opened as Molly reached the landing. A hand passed out a brown bag. She accepted it and the door closed, without a word. The bag was warm and smelled wonderful.

She stuffed it into her pack and headed out into the cold morning. She turned her face to the black sky. Big fat snowflakes drifted down. A lot of big fat snowflakes.

When she moved out of her parents' house, she no longer had the use of their cars whenever she wanted, so she bought herself a vehicle. An eight-year-old Ford Focus in a rather unattractive shade of green. The seats and armrests had been chewed up a bit, hopefully by a dog not a person, but the engine was in good shape and she'd put on new winter tires.

She owned several pairs of skis that she alternated depending on the environment and where she was, but for Blue Sky under these conditions only her newest powder skis would do. She fastened them to the roof rack and drove to Big Eddie's Coffee Emporium. Patrons were streaming in, adding to the line-up that was almost at the door. Soon it would be. Eddie and Jolene and their two helpers moved to the beat of loud dance music. Everyone in line was dressed for a day on the slopes. They came into the shop stomping snow off boots, shaking colorful woolen hats and scarves. Packs were tossed over shoulders and ski passes hung from zippers.

The line edged forward. People chatted and laughed. Locals leaned across the counter and gave the staff hugs or pecks on the cheek. Jolene toasted bagels and made breakfast sandwiches. Her helpers made mochas and lattes, and Eddie poured coffee and took money.

The seating area was empty. At this time of the morning the customers, like Smith, were here only to fuel up and head out to the mountain before the lifts started and the hills got busy.

As Alphonse had kindly provided her breakfast, Smith bypassed the bagel line and ordered her usual extra-large mocha, with full fat milk and whipped cream. She asked, very politely, for an extra dribble of chocolate syrup on the top.

"Sure, Moon," the clerk said.

It was about half an hour to Blue Sky. She munched on warm croissants and drank hot mocha on the way. There was no sunrise, just a gradual lightening of the sky. Except for the pure white snow, the whole world was gray. Gray clouds, gray deciduous trees—gray bark and gray branches—gray-green evergreens, and brief glimpses of gray mountains.

The morning's skiing was as great as she'd hoped it would be. In the early morning, the snow was deep and untouched. The air was so cold and crisp she could almost crunch it between her teeth. Snow continued to fall. The trees were covered in the stuff until it was a wonder some of them didn't topple over.

Shortly before noon she was lucky enough to find an untouched section of powder, and used it to take her down to the lodge. The croissants and mocha had been a long time ago. Skiing in deep powder is difficult, but Molly was very good. She'd dreamt at one time of going to the Olympics, but she wasn't that good, and once she realized it she gave up competition. Although her muscles ached from the morning's exertions, it was a good ache. She headed down the mountain, planting her poles with a light, quick flick of the wrist, accompanied by a flick of the arm that helped to turn the skis in the deep snow. The movement of the skis was gradual, much slower than on groomed slopes, and she barely had to turn to keep herself upright and moving. There was no feeling of friction under her feet; instead, she almost literally floated down the mountain, as if she were soaring on clouds, moving in slow motion, surrounded by nothing by snow and silence. The air was cold on her face, fresh and smelling of pine and ice.

She reached the bottom and rotated her feet into a hockey stop, driving the sides of her skis into the packed snow. Snow flew and she punched the air in sheer joy.

She headed for the lodge, debating between the giant veggie burrito and the wild salmon burger.

Her radio crackled. As a police officer, she could ski for free, provided she wore her uniform jacket over her usual ski clothes, carried a radio, and helped out if needed. *Altercation in the dining area of the lodge. Respond immediately.*

She snapped off her skis and left them and the poles in a ski rest. She ran, as fast as she could in ski boots, up the wooden steps into the building. People, many of them with small children, were hurrying down the steps.

The room was warm and damp and smelled of good food cooking, wet clothes, sweat-soaked socks exposed to the air, and steaming bodies.

She had no trouble locating the problem.

People lined the walls, some of them still gripping plates or cups. A long wooden table had been overturned, bowls of food and mugs of coffee spilled onto the floor. Two men were taking wild punches at each other, yelling and swearing all the while. Blood streamed from the nose of the larger man. In their inflexible ski boots they moved as if they were performing a ballet at the bottom of the Upper Kootenay River. The police officer trying to get through the crowd to reach them walked with no less difficulty.

A resort security guard, all of about sixty-five and weighing a good hundred pounds, soaking wet, jumped from one foot to the other, suggesting that the fighters stop this *right now!*

A girl was screaming at the top of her lungs. She didn't look at all frightened, more like she was enjoying the excitement and happy to add her own contribution.

"Trafalgar City Police," Smith shouted. People in front of her looked over their shoulders and scurried out of the way. The screaming girl toned it down a notch.

There wasn't a lot Smith could do in these damned boots. Fortunately the fighters wore similar footwear and thus couldn't do a lot either.

"Break it up," she said.

They did the opposite, and crashed together, all wild punches and kicks that barely left the ground. They were both young, not a surprise. The heavier one was clean-shaven and short-haired. The other had a scraggly beard and hair that touched the back of his neck.

The bigger guy was closest to her. As he pulled his arm back to aim a punch at his opponent, Smith jumped forward, grabbed the wrist, and twisted. She jerked him back. "Police. I said break it up here."

He resisted for a brief moment before the fight drained out of him. "Okay, okay," he said. "No problem, officer."

Another security guard arrived, running and breathing hard. At least this one was young and looked reasonably fit.

He sized up the scene and launched himself toward the smaller of the fighters, who turned and swung a punch that got the young security guard in the face. He fell back, blood pouring from his nose like lava rushing from an exploding volcano. The girl began screaming again.

"Hey," the older guard yelled. "You can't do that."

The fighter turned toward his opponent. Conveniently restrained by Constable Smith. She read his eyes. "Back off, buddy. Fight's over."

He took a step forward into a pile of rice and tofu and curry sauce. He slipped. The old guy stuck his boot under the fighter's feet to help him to the floor.

Nice.

Smith spoke into her radio. "Request a car. Two to transport."

"Hey," the guy Smith was holding said, "I gave in, didn't I?"

"We'll wait in the office," she said. The younger security guard got to his feet. He wiped blood onto his jacket sleeve, but didn't seem too badly hurt. "Take this one," she said to him. While the taller fighter had given in as soon as the police arrived, the other one had kept on fighting—she'd better take control of him. The old guard was standing over the man on the floor, trying to look threatening.

"Help me get him up," Smith said. They pulled the man to his feet, and she wrenched his arm behind him.

"Hey," he yelled. "That hurts. You're gonna break my arm."

"Then don't make me. Let's go." Smith headed for the stairs, aware that they must make a strange procession indeed. The arresting officer and the two fighters stomped in ski boots that afforded no flexibility of movement whatsoever. The younger security guard's face was streaked with blood, and the older one seemed quite pleased with his prize. The crowd parted in front of them. Smith looked for someone who might get it into his head to free his friend, but no one approached them. The man she was holding took a half-step toward the girl who'd been screaming. Smith jerked him back into line.

It got a bit tricky on the steps to the basement, as ski boots were even more difficult to manage on stairs than on flat surfaces.

Behind them, noise flowed across the main room with the force of water bursting through a broken dam.

Five people just about filled the security office. Smith ordered the two offenders to sit down. The bleeding guard grabbed a handful of tissues off the desk and held them to his face.

"I know you," said the guy who'd given up when the police arrived.

Didn't everyone in a town this size?

"Last night. You were there last night. At the restaurant."

Smith looked properly at the guy for the first time. Last time she'd seen him, he'd been enjoying that scene between Lorraine and the Wyatt-Yarmouth family at Flavours. "Name?"

"Huh?"

"What's your name?"

"Sorry, Ma'am. Sir, Miss."

"Your name?"

"Jeremy. Jeremy Wozenack. I came here with Jason and Ewan, you know, the ones who..."

"I know."

He held out his hand, as if offering to shake.

She ignored it.

"Get out your I.D." She turned to the other man. "You too buddy, I.D."

"What?"

"I said, I.D. Do you have any on you?"

The man dug under his ski jacket and pulled out a worn wallet. He handed her his driver's license.

"Mr. D'Angelo." She handed the license to the older security guard.

"You too, Mr. Wozenack."

"Sorry, but I've got nothing on me. My friend drove so I only brought what cash I'd need."

"Call dispatch with that I.D.," Smith said to the guard. "Spell your name, Mr. Wozenack, and give us your address." He did so and the guard wrote it down.

"Step outside," she said.

Jeremy leapt to his feet.

"What the fuck?" the other guy yelled, half-rising from his chair. The younger guard pushed him down. "You're going to let him go because he eats at Flavours, is that it? How much does it take to buy you? Not much, I'd guess."

"Oh, shut up. No one's going anywhere. Other than into town when that patrol car gets here."

Smith and Jeremy stepped into the corridor. She left the door open, but spoke softly.

"What was all that about?"

"Like I know. Guy launches himself out of nowhere, sort of like Superman or something, across the table. All that was missing was the red cape."

"Let me tell you something for nothing, Jeremy. You've ruined my day's skiing and sent me back to work on my day off. I'm hardly in the mood to hear your flights of fantasy. You have to know what he was mad about."

"A girl."

"A girl?"

Jeremy shrugged. "Isn't it always a girl?"

"No, it isn't."

It would keep until they got to the station. But she wanted to know. She'd disgraced herself, totally and completely, when she'd been allowed to step one hesitant foot into this investigation. Perhaps she could learn something worthwhile and salvage a bit of her reputation from talking to the dead men's friend.

"Are you really taking us to the police station?"

"A car's been called, your I.D. radioed in for a warrant check. Your pal hit a security guard. People, including children, were fleeing left and right. Yeah, you're going to town, Jeremy. You can tell your side of the story to a judge."

"You seem like a nice lady."

Smith considered spitting on the snow-soaked wooden floor. Sometimes she'd rather be called a pig bitch than a nice lady.

"I planned to meet up with my friends for lunch. They weren't here so I got my food and sat down. Was it my fault I sat beside a cute girl? Well, yeah, that might have been my fault, but it sure wasn't when she came over all friendly, was it?"

"You met this girl before?"

"Nice town you've got here. Great skiing, happening bar scene after. You see someone in the bars, you see them again on the slopes. What's your name?"

"Smith. Constable Smith."

"You must have a first name."

"I do not."

"Sorry, sorry, bad line. Yeah, I'd seen the girl before." He coughed and looked around. The security office was in the bottom level of the lodge. The walls were wood, the floor wood. Outside snow was piled so high it covered the windows. It was cold and damp. "I ran into her a couple of nights ago in a bar in Trafalgar. The Potato Famine, stupid name. The food was about what you'd expect from a name like that. Her boyfriend, who you've had the pleasure of meeting, was drunk out of his tiny skull. She was lonely, you know how it is?"

Smith said nothing. Sometimes there were advantages to being a woman on the job. She wouldn't be taking sides here. The drunken boyfriend and the privileged frat boy; most women would know two assholes when she saw them.

"So we left," Jeremy continued. "She didn't want to hang around with nothing to do but watch him get drunk with his buddies, and I," he looked away from her, "suggested we go to the B&B for a bit. She was game." He gave Smith a knowing smile. "No undue pressure going on, you got that, right?"

Smith said nothing.

"And she was certainly of age." He barked out a laugh.

Smith still said nothing.

"We had a pleasant…uh…time." Once again he looked to one side. "And then she left."

"What day was that?"

Jeremy shrugged. "Sorry, Constable Smith, but I'm on vacation, right. One day just runs into another."

"Yeah, I know how it is. I've done it myself. Days on the slopes. Nights in the bar around a big roaring fireplace. Big glasses full of red wine. Someone throws another log on."

He nodded.

"Two friends dead in the frozen river. Happens to us all. Right, Jeremy?"

"Fuck you, cop lady."

"Enough chat. Let's go back inside."

"Okay, okay. It was a couple of days before Christmas when I met this girl. Friday, maybe. I didn't even remember her name until I saw her upstairs just now. We were drinking in this low-life bar. Jason and Ewan and me. Alan's so pussy-whipped he wouldn't dare step foot into a joint like that one. And Rob spends most of his time checking the Internet to see how his stock portfolio's doing.

"And that was it. Stuff happens right? She went her way and I went mine. It matters to me, you know, that Jason and Ewan died."

"Bring me up to today."

"She was sitting with a group of girls. I thought they were her girlfriends, right? So I sat down with my lunch and said hi. She seemed happy to see me, giving me the smile and tossing the hair. I hadn't even had a bite of my food when that guy, the boyfriend, came out of nowhere and started yelling and laying into me. My mistake, she didn't know the girls she was sitting with, but was waiting for him to get back with her tofu surprise."

No doubt the woman in question was the screaming girl. Loving being the center of attention and having two guys fight over her.

Smith flashed back to the previous night and the trouble at Flavours. Gary's rage at Jason Wyatt-Yarmouth, the late Jason Wyatt-Yarmouth, for seducing Lorraine. What had he said to the boys at the table? Something about rich guys coming to town and flashing their money and taking the local girls.

An old story. Plenty of young people came to Trafalgar on vacation; it was not a destination for the blue-rinse, name-badge wearing, bus-tour type. Tourists came here for the hiking and kayaking in summer, skiing and snowmobiling in winter. Some of her friends in high-school had had brief romances with guys in Trafalgar on vacation. Usually the guys left with promises to write, to keep in touch. Never to be heard from again.

She pushed the door open and gestured to Jeremy Wozenack to go back inside.

The old guy was putting down the phone. "Your ride's here, Constable."

◇◇◇

John Winters needed a drink. Toward the end of his career with Vancouver City Police that would have meant a quick visit to a bar, but these days Big Eddie would have what he needed. He'd been in a meeting with the Chief Constable, and Keller was getting pressure from the politically connected Dr. Wyatt-Yarmouth. Like a kettle, when the pressure got too much Keller believed in spreading the steam around the room so he didn't explode.

Molly Smith was standing by the dispatch desk, dressed in the blue standard-issue police winter jacket over shiny white ski pants and clumsy white ski boots. She wore a red helmet with large goggles pushed on top.

"Bad enough that I've spent half my day off here, and now you're telling me I can't get a ride for my car and my stuff?"

"Everyone's out, Molly," Denton told her. "I can't call them in to take you to Blue Sky. You're just going to have to cool your heels. Go home and get your car tomorrow, why don't you?"

"Suppose I can't get a ride up tomorrow? In the meantime my car, with my purse stuffed under the front seat, I might add, is sitting all night in the parking lot. And my skis; I didn't even stop to lock them into the rack." She threw her hands up in the air and half turned.

Color flooded into her cheeks as she saw him standing there.

"Sergeant," she said.

"This is convenient. I was about to give you a call. What's with the uniform? Some sort of undercover operation on the mountainside?"

Denton chuckled. "They've invented a strain of marijuana that grows all through a Kootenay winter. Thrives on deep snow and heavy cloud cover. We're looking for the green tops sticking their heads out from the snow." He stopped chuckling as he answered the phone.

"You remember I told you we get free skiing if we agree to help out with security?" Smith said. "Sometimes it isn't worth saving the fifty bucks." Her eyes narrowed and some of the color drained from her face. "Why'd you want me?"

"You were at an incident last night at Flavours Restaurant."

She snorted. "I certainly was."

"Doctor Wyatt-Yarmouth phoned the CC with a complaint first thing this morning. Paul was in meetings until now so I've just heard about it."

The remaining blood fled from her face, leaving it almost as white as her pants.

"Not a complaint about you," he said. She let out a long breath. His displeasure over the fireplace incident had her spooked.

Good.

"It was to the effect that in our failure to release the bodies promptly we're setting the family up for ridicule."

"No one needs to set that guy up for ridicule. He manages it all by himself."

"The CC suggested that I might want to hear what happened, so I'm asking you."

"The story continues. I have more than even the Chief knows. I've just arrested Jeremy Wozenack, a friend of Jason and Ewan, who was also at Flavours last night."

"What's this about your car?"

"I came back to town with my prisoners in the patrol car. Didn't think it through carefully enough." Her face changed color again. "Well, that is, sure I thought it through, I just, well, I figured…"

"In your eagerness to complete the arrest you left your own vehicle at the scene. And now you can't get a ride back and it's almost dark. Let's take the van, and you can tell me both stories on the way. But first, Molly, we need to stop at Eddies and get me a coffee."

Smith talked most of the way to the ski resort. It was getting late and a steady stream of traffic passed them, heading down the mountain toward town. Yellow headlights broke through the dusk and high snow banks and snow-laden black trees closed in around them. He'd heard from Dave Evans that Ewan Williams had been in a brawl on Saturday night, the night before he disappeared. This morning he'd interviewed the other participant in the fight, and the guy insisted that he'd gone home after the police broke it up and never thought about it again. He'd had more than a few beers on board, he told Winters with an easy laugh, and doubted he'd recognize the other guy if he saw him again. The object of the fight in question had been at the apartment, stretching and preening. She hadn't bothered to put a robe on over her lacy red teddy (with food stains down the front, and a tear at the left hip) in the presence of company. Winters' opinion of Ewan Williams' taste went down a considerable amount, and he wondered if the guy was just out to cause trouble.

The woman also insisted that she hadn't seen Williams since that night. She looked honest enough when she said it, slightly bored at the conversation, but a bit titillated at being involved, however peripherally, in a police investigation.

The skin around her right eye was the color of a tropical sunset. Almost a perfect match for an injury sustained oh, approximately a week ago. About the night she'd dared to flirt with some other guy.

Winters had thanked them for their time and left. He'd started a check on the boyfriend's record, but nothing had come up so far.

And now, according to Smith, it would appear that not only had Ewan Williams been causing trouble over local girls, but Jeremy Wozenack and Jason Wyatt-Yarmouth were playing the game as well.

Fun for some.

Never for the police.

"Tell me about Gary LeBlanc," he asked Smith. "Every town's blessed with a family like that, it seems."

"I knew him in school. He was a trouble maker back then, but never anything serious. He's been away, a guest, as they say, of the government of Canada, for several years. He had a nice little grow-op on Crown land outside of town. Nothing much, from what I've heard. Less than a hundred plants."

"He got several years for that?" Surprising that he got any jail time at all.

"Unfortunately, that wasn't the whole story. The horsemen came across it by accident, looking for a ten-year-old boy who'd gone missing from the family campsite. Gary was watering his garden. A Mountie caught the working end of a spade in the face and needed a heck of a lot of stitches. People in town said it was an accident, the officer tripped and fell into the edge of the spade Gary was holding."

"Is that what happened?"

"I wasn't with the police then, John. I was away at University. I remembered my mom talking about it, so I pulled the file the other day, just out of interest. Gary was put away for assault P.O."

"What about the kid?"

"Kid?"

"The child they were searching for?"

"Found eating chocolate while dipping his toes in a creek and enjoying his great adventure."

"At least part of the story has a happy ending."

"This is one situation in which everyone would have been better off if justice had not been served."

Winters turned his head. "Go on."

"Gary looked after Lorraine, best as he could. My mom knows them. When Gary was around, Mom took a personal interest in the both of them. You know my mom."

"That I do."

"Lorraine's Gary's half-sister, same mother, and he's a lot older than her. When Gary was sent away Lorraine was left in the tender care of her parents. Neither of whom has ever met a bottle they didn't love more than her. My mom tried to help, but she was rebuffed continually so she pretty much stopped coming around."

"Doesn't sound like Lucky."

Smith laughed, without humor. "Doesn't, does it? But even Mom knows to stop when she's beating her head against a brick wall. Well, sometimes she does. And Lorraine, at sixteen years old, is now the town sled."

"The what?"

"Sled. Available for anyone to ride."

"Isn't that a bit insensitive, Molly?"

"It's the way she's seen, even by some of our officers. I feel for the girl, I really do. But she doesn't want my help. Not that that's worth much, but she doesn't want Mom's help or anyone else's. Now Gary's back, maybe he can do something."

The lodge came into view. There weren't many vehicles left in the parking lot. The yellow lights of the lodge and outbuildings looked very small and insignificant against the dark bulk of the surrounding mountains. The moon was lifting above the crest of the mountain to the east. It was waxing, and the light was cold and very white. It made him think of Molly's proper first name.

"That's mine, over there."

A green car was parked close to the building, all alone. He pulled to a halt beside it. "I asked the security guys to keep an eye on my skis," Smith said. A single pair of skis remained in the racks at the back of the lodge. She climbed out of the car, unzipped her jacket pocket and pulled out her keys.

"Thanks for the ride, John. I appreciate it." Her blue eyes said a lot more before she slammed the door shut. He watched her walk in that duck-like gait people in ski boots did. She found her skis and equipment and fastened them to the roof, then climbed into the driver's seat and burrowed into the passenger seat foot-well. She came up with a pair of winter boots and waved them at him. She turned the key in the ignition and the engine roared to life.

Winters made a wide circle, and set off down the dark mountain road.

He'd been in homicide in Vancouver for many years. Most murders consisted of a victim. Victim was found in a certain place. A few people, family members mostly, were the suspects. But in this case there was nothing he could put his finger on. He didn't even know if he had a murder.

He had a victim, or did he? Was there one victim, or none, or maybe two? No place of death that he'd yet found. And no suspects to speak of. He'd found nothing in Ewan's room at the B&B that would necessitate a forensic search, and he'd accepted Ellie Carmine's word that she hadn't had any blood spills to mop up. Not that he would necessarily accept her, or anyone else's, word about anything, but the Glacier Chalet was a crowded, busy place. Even in the middle of the night, he reflected, people seemed to be coming and going. He was pretty sure Ewan hadn't died there.

Jason and Ewan had been a couple of fun-loving rich boys on vacation. Them and their friend Jeremy, who'd been released with a promise to return tomorrow. Local guys were upset because outsiders, dripping with money and good looks and educated voices, were moving in on their girlfriends.

Plenty of fodder for bar brawls. But for murder? Unlikely, although stranger, much stranger, things had happened over the course of his career.

Gary LeBlanc made an attractive candidate. Except for the fact that he'd been angry at Jason, not Ewan.

And Ewan, Winters had to remember, was the one who'd died first.

Jason had died in a car accident. There was not the slightest doubt about that. It was Ewan's death that was the strange one.

Nevertheless, Winters knew deep in his cop's gut that if he could find out why Jason had the dead body of his friend in his car, he'd be a long way toward finding out why Ewan Williams had died.

It wasn't helping that the Wyatt-Yarmouth family were making phone calls and stamping their feet demanding attention. He could only hope the national media wouldn't pick this story up.

Williams had last been seen by his friends on Sunday the twenty-third. They spent the day skiing before returning to the B&B. Around five-thirty, Ewan had gone out alone, on foot, and had never been seen again.

Had something happened at the ski hill that day? His friends thought he'd met a girl. But they hadn't seen her. Did Ewan run into trouble in town? Did he even make it to town?

His headlights picked out the sharp curves and steep banks of the mountain road. This police-issue mini-van was not the ideal vehicle for driving down treacherous mountain roads.

He turned a corner and came into a straightway. The lights of Smith's car behind him flooded the van.

Meredith Morgenstern had been calling, leaving messages hinting that she knew why he was keeping the bodies and why he was showing so much interest in a car accident. John Winters knew lots of good reporters. Men and women who did their jobs and let the police do theirs. Meredith Morgenstern wasn't one of them, and he wouldn't normally give her the time of day. But he might be able to toss her enough of a crumb that she'd write a story asking anyone who'd seen Ewan to come forward.

No one seemed to know where Ewan Williams had gone that night. But he had to have gone somewhere, and seen someone. If only the person who'd last seen him alive.

If that person was Jason Wyatt-Yarmouth, Winters might never find out what happened.

◇◇◇

Lucky Smith bit into a piece of shortbread. She didn't even chew, just let the buttery dough dissolve in her mouth.

"Perfect," she said to Ellie Carmine.

"Thanks." Ellie sipped at her tea. She looked troubled.

"What's happening about your guests?" Lucky asked. "I'm surprised they're still here, after…Well, after what happened to their two friends."

"The sister, Wendy, is waiting to leave with her parents and the boy's body. I've no idea what's going on but apparently the coroner isn't releasing the bodies yet, and won't say when."

"That seems strange."

"Perhaps you could ask Moonlight…"

"No."

"I haven't even said what I want to know."

"I don't ask my daughter anything to do with police business." Lucky would happily ask anything at all, but Moonlight wouldn't tell her more than was available to all in the pages of the *Trafalgar Daily Gazette*. She'd confided a few things to her mother in her early days with the department, but that had stopped.

"Having the police poking around, questioning the guests, it's upsetting for everyone. It was just a car accident, for heaven's sake. He is rather attractive, that Sergeant Winters, isn't he?"

"I hadn't noticed," Lucky said, as her hand hovered over the plate of treats before settling upon a cookie formed into the shape of candy cane. Bands of pink and white dough wound through the cookie. She took an exploratory bite. Not as good as the shortbread.

The kitchen door flew open.

"Robbed. I 'ave been robbed." It was a young woman, with long black hair and full lips. She would have been pretty if not for a much too prominent nose. She was dressed in leather ankle boots, form-fitting jeans, and a tight red T-shirt with Quebec printed across her chest in silver glitter.

Mrs. Carmine jumped to her feet. "Sophie, what on earth?"

"My money. I 'id my money in the drawer. Beneath my clothes. It is gone. All gone."

A strikingly handsome young man stood behind her. "She's right, Mrs. C. Sophie doesn't like to carry too much money when she's skiing, so she hides it in the dresser. It isn't there."

Ellie placed one hand to her chest. "There must be a mistake."

"No mistake, *certainement*. Phone the *Sûreté*."

"The what?"

"She means the police, Mrs. Carmine. Call the police."

"I'm sure that's not necessary. Did you look carefully?"

"What am I, an *imbécile?*" The young woman threw up her hands, turned to the young man, and let loose a stream of French.

He lifted his hands. "Calm down, Sophie. I'll sort it out. She says her cash and credit card are gone."

"She must be mistaken. Nothing can have been stolen. Not from my establishment. Why, why, no one's been here today."

"Lorraine was." Wendy Wyatt-Yarmouth stood at the door. She pushed Sophie aside. "She was here wasn't she? This morning, around noon. I wasn't up to skiing today. Just stayed in my room mostly. But I went into town for lunch and some shopping, and I saw her. She was in the kitchen, eating soup."

"Lorraine was here as my guest," Ellie said. "She's upset about the death of your brother, it seems she was quite fond of him..."

"Fond," Wendy snorted. "Fond of his money."

"I don't know about that, but she came to the door, and she was sad, and I was about to sit down with my lunch. I'd made enough for Kathy, but I hadn't seen hide nor hair of her since she did a pretty poor job at her chores. So I gave her soup to Lorraine."

"Who are we talking about?" Lucky asked, although she could guess. Lorraine LeBlanc. Sixteen years old and already a disaster looking for a place to happen.

"That miserable Lorraine creature. My brother smiled at her sideways, and she seems to think that meant they were about to be married."

"More than smiled at," Alan said with an unpleasant chuckle.

"Who the hell asked for your opinion?"

"Lest you forget, Wendy, I am the complainant here."

"Sorry, I thought that was Sophie. And Sophie wants to call the police, don't you Sophie? People can't be allowed to just walk into a private home and poke around looking for anything they want, right?"

"Yes, I said so, didn't I?"

"Hold on," Lucky said. "So Lorraine was here, having soup in the kitchen. You were with her the entire time, weren't you, Ellie?"

Thoughts raced across the woman's face as she struggled to find the right answer.

Lorraine. Poor Lorraine. Left alone in the B&B, the girl might well be tempted to walk up the stairs, to peek into the two hundred dollar a night rooms and see what sort of stuff the rich carried around with them. And even help herself to what she thought no one would miss.

"Ellie," Lucky said. "Did you leave Lorraine alone for a length of time?"

"I might have gone to the bathroom. I don't remember."

"There you have it," Wendy shouted. "It takes no *length of time* to run upstairs, open a drawer, and snatch the money."

"No," Lucky said. "But it does to find the right room, and the right location, without turning the place over. Was anything in your room disturbed, Sophie?"

Sophie looked at Alan.

He shook his head. "Not so as I noticed. Sophie went into her drawer to get money for dinner and noticed it was gone."

"Lorraine obviously cased the place earlier," Wendy said. "That explains it."

"Explains what?"

The girl's eyes shifted to one side. "Nothing. Just thinking. Are you going to call the cops, Mrs. C?"

Ellie twisted her apron in her hands. She looked perilously close to sheer panic. Lucky touched her friend's arm. "This won't reflect on you."

"It most certainly will," Wendy said. Her voice was rising. "I can't imagine who'll want to stay here after this gets out. In fact, we all should get a sizeable discount, if not our entire stay for free. This place isn't at all the quality it's advertised to be."

"We need to calm down," Lucky said. "We have plenty of time to discuss this. It isn't an emergency." Wendy was over-reacting to a considerable degree, and Lucky suspected it had nothing to do with the loss of Sophie's money, or even with Lorraine, but with the young woman's own all-encompassing grief.

Wendy pulled a cell phone out of her pocket. "If you won't call the cops, I'll have to do it." She punched in three numbers, and went into the hall to make the call.

"This is dreadful, simply dreadful," Ellie said. "I didn't leave Lorraine alone for more than a couple of minutes. Well, perhaps I did, I don't quite remember every detail."

Wendy came back. "The police," she said, very haughty, "will be here shortly."

Ellie groaned.

The small procession pulled into town. John Winters turned into the police station, and Molly Smith drove past. He'd heard she'd taken the apartment above Alphonse's bakery.

He made a quick decision, and turned the van around. There was no traffic on Monroe Street and he caught up to the Focus as it made the next corner.

The Ford climbed over dirty packed snow and ice to reach its parking slot on the other side of the alley. He pulled up behind her, opened the window and waited.

"Everything, okay?" she asked, coming up to the driver's window, ski boots in hand. She'd pulled a knitted red cap over her head.

"I don't know what Jason Wyatt-Yarmouth was doing the day his pal was missing. I need to find out. I know you're not working today, but thought you might want to come with me."

She grinned. "Thanks, John, thanks. Do you want me to put on my uniform?"

"You'll do."

She tossed her ski boots back into her car, locked it, ran around the van and jumped into the passenger seat. As eager as a puppy at play time.

It was almost six. A good time to find skiers resting between the day on the slopes and heading out to dinner. The Wyatt-Yarmouth family and friends were a prickly bunch, and he'd decided, on the spur of the moment, that it would be a good idea to have someone else on hand. Even if only to observe and pick up on unspoken communication.

He backed the van into the alley. The radio crackled. Reported theft at 1894 Victoria Street. Winters turned to Smith. "Isn't that the Glacier Chalet?"

"Yeah, it is."

"What a coincidence." He grabbed the radio. "Winters. I'll take that call."

"You got it, Sarge."

◇◇◇

Molly Smith was not pleased to see her mother, once again, standing in the hallway of the Glacier Chalet B&B. But she knew that Lucky and Ellie Carmine were friends, so her mom did have the right to be here. Although the hotels and B&Bs in town did a lot of mutually-beneficial business with the outfitting and tour companies, Lucky and Ellie hadn't become friends until recently. While Molly was away at University there was something about Ellie having trouble with the police over guests using hard drugs in her B&B. How that would bring her into Lucky Smith's circle, Molly didn't want to know.

"That was quick," Mrs. Carmine said, opening the door. Looking like Mrs. Claus no longer, her face was set in hard, tight lines.

"Constable Smith and I were passing," Winters explained.

Mrs. Carmine hesitated and then stepped back to let them in.

A good-sized crowd was gathered in the entrance hall. Not only Ellie Carmine and Lucky Smith, but Wendy Wyatt-Yarmouth, and two of her friends, the Quebec girl and her boyfriend.

Wendy looked at Smith, sizing up the police jacket and ski pants, red wool gloves, and matching red hat. She didn't bother to contain a sneer. "Are you the only cop they have in this miserable town? Every time I turn around you're standing there. Nice uniform though."

Not that Smith cared much about Wendy Wyatt-Yarmouth's opinions. In her short career she'd already run into plenty of rich types who considered themselves to be above the law, and plenty of young women who wanted to have the female equivalent of a pissing contest with a woman cop. Smith reminded herself to be charitable, that Wendy had just lost her brother, and wasn't handling it all that well.

"You should be pleased Constable Smith is so dedicated," Winters said. "Perhaps someone can explain the problem before we go any further."

"All my money and my credit card 'ave been stolen," the Quebec girl shouted. "From my room."

"We're not entirely sure about that." Mrs. Carmine's face was very pale.

"I am sure, *Madame*."

Lucky avoided her daughter's eyes and put her arm around her friend's shoulder.

Winters asked the standard questions. Smith should be taking notes, but not being in uniform she didn't have a notebook with her.

"Is it possible you misplaced the items, Sophie?" Mrs. Carmine asked.

"*Non*."

"Did you make a thorough search, sir?" Winters said to the young man. "Alan Robertson isn't it?"

"Yes. No. Yes, I'm Alan and no we didn't search. Sophie said her money was missing and we came downstairs."

"This is ridiculous." Wendy almost stamped her foot. "That girl is obviously up to no good and I for one refuse to stand here chattering about it"—Smith dearly hoped that Wendy Wyatt-Yarmouth would insist on leaving the scene—"while she spends every penny of poor Sophie's money. God, Sophie, you'd better cancel your credit cards right away."

Sophie gasped.

"Who is 'she'?" Winters asked. "Do you suspect someone of taking the money?"

"No," said Alan and Mrs. Carmine and Lucky Smith.

"Yes," said Wendy.

"Go on," Winters said to Wendy.

"Lorraine what's her name, of course."

"She means Lorraine LeBlanc," Lucky said.

"You think Lorraine LeBlanc was responsible." Winters said. "Why?"

"Why? It's perfectly obvious," Wendy shouted. She turned to Smith. "You saw the state she was in last night. Demanding to be included in my family."

"I don't see…"

"She was in the house. I saw her myself. I demand you arrest her."

"Is everyone who was in this house today to be arrested?" Winters asked pointedly.

Wendy flushed.

"Before this goes any further," Lucky said, "I'd suggest we have another search of the room. Sophie, you're sharing the room with Alan, right?"

The girl nodded.

"When two people share close accommodations and a strange room, it's easy for things to get misplaced. And Alan," she smiled sweetly, "you did say that you only watched Sophie look in the place she *thought* she'd left the money. You didn't actually search."

Smith glanced at Sergeant Winters. The left edge of his mouth twitched. It was the only sign of a smile he would allow himself.

"Can't hurt," Alan said to Sophie.

"That's a perfectly wonderful idea," Mrs. Carmine said.

"If we must," Wendy said. She began to turn.

"While I'm here, Ms. Wyatt-Yarmouth," Winters said. "I'd like to speak to you about your brother and Ewan Williams. Perhaps Mrs. Carmine would allow us to talk in the common room."

Wendy shot daggers at him with her eyes.

"If it's okay with Alan and Sophie, Constable Smith will go with them. You won't assist with the search in any way, Constable. Just observe."

"Yes, sir," she said.

The front door opened and Jeremy walked in. He stopped so abruptly that Rob crashed into the back of him.

"Hey," Rob said. "What's all this? Has something happened?"

"Yes," Wendy's thin chest rose with indignation. "There has been a theft and these cops refuse to do anything about it. I'm going to make a complaint."

"Oh, put a sock in it, Wendy," Alan said in a tired voice. "Hard as it is to believe, this isn't about you."

Wendy sputtered.

"Where the hell'd you get to anyway?" Alan said. "We couldn't find you when it was time to leave."

"I got a ride back." Jeremy Wozenack smirked at Smith.

"Coulda told us," Alan mumbled. He led the way to the stairs. Smith and Sophie followed.

The upstairs corridor was wide enough to have a thin-legged mahogany table up against the wall, holding magazines and tourist brochures. The wallpaper was stripped pink and cream above the wainscoting. Paintings of historical scenes lined the walls. Whiskered men in suits and ties or overalls and women in long dresses and big hats.

Alan and Sophie's room was at the top of the stairs. Alan opened the door and allowed Sophie and Smith to enter. "Do you normally lock the door, sir?" Smith had not failed to notice that, this time at least, it hadn't been.

"In a respectable place like this? I didn't think it necessary. Maybe I was wrong."

The room was spacious and tastefully decorated. A beautiful quilt made out of interlocking blocks of cream and blue covered the king-sized bed. Large pillows in matching colors were piled against the headboard. A small table beside the window held a single-serving coffee pot, kettle, and a basket overflowing with coffee, tea bags, condiments, and individual-sized packets of cookies.

Smith stood in the doorway. "Does someone come to tidy up and make the bed every day?"

Sophie plopped her plump behind onto the bed. The headboard hit the wall. "They'd better, for what this place is costing us."

"Does Mrs. Carmine do the cleaning?"

"Her or her daughter, Kathy."

There was a wide chest of drawers, matching night tables on each side of the bed, and a cabinet underneath the flat-screen TV. Smith stuffed her hands into her jacket pocket, and watched Alan pull out the drawers, starting at the bottom. He hadn't closed the door and sound travelled quite well up the stairs. Wendy's voice was steadily rising. *That girl needs some serious help before she goes right over the edge*, Smith thought. It seemed, from the little Smith had seen, that her parents were too wrapped up in their own grief over Jason's death to pay Wendy much attention.

Easy to spot the place where they kept their drugs. Alan maneuvered his body to block Smith's view, and Sophie jumped off the bed and made a big fuss of checking out the bedside table, presumably to distract the police's attention.

Not Smith's concern.

Not now.

Downstairs Wendy was saying something about Ewan's taste in women. She really didn't like the guy. Reminded Smith of when they'd been in school and her brother, Sam, had been friends with Doug Whiteside, one of the star baseball players. A real piece of work he was. Lucky despised him, but Sam wouldn't hear a word against him. Smith wondered what had happened to the baseball player. Wouldn't be surprised if he'd gone into politics.

"Hell, Sophie." Alan's hand came up from the right side of the top drawer. "It's here."

She ran over and he handed her a wad of colored bills. She flicked through it, counting. Alan held a silver credit card in his hand. "Is it all there, Sophie?"

"*Oui.*"

He turned toward Smith, his embarrassed grin beneath tousled black curls making him look a lot like the actor Hugh Grant. "I'm really sorry about all this. I guess with what happened to Jason and Ewan we're all on edge."

"Not a problem. It's happened before. Like Mom…I mean Mrs. Smith, said people get things mixed up. Your friend Wendy seemed somewhat quick on the draw to pin it on Lorraine though."

"Wendy's upset, you know. Her brother just died."

"I understand."

"Him and Ewan…"

"What?"

"Nothing. Wendy loved her brother, that's all." But Alan's face was flushed, and Smith knew there was more behind the statement than he was prepared to reveal.

"Let's go downstairs and let everyone know the good news. You should both come, Sergeant Winters has some questions."

"Sure," he said.

Sophie stuffed her money into the pocket of her long wool sweater.

They trooped out of the room. Alan shut the door behind them.

"Sophie has the top two drawers," he said to Smith, in that distant tone a person takes on when they're really talking to themselves. "It wasn't me who moved things." He raised his voice. "You need to be more careful, Sophie, your carelessness could have caused a lot of trouble."

She turned, her dark eyes full of Gaelic fury. "Me, I always place my money under my socks, always. Since I was a little girl." She spoke to Smith. "Always on vacation we went to London or to Paris or Vienna. Always we stayed in the best hotels and always my mother told me to hide my valuables beneath my socks. Thieves, she said, do not think about a woman's socks. I do not put my money under my nightgowns. Never."

She stalked off toward the staircase.

Alan lifted one eyebrow toward Smith. "Sometimes," he said, "we forget what our mommy taught us."

She grinned. "In my experience when criminal masterminds are searching for the loot they rarely avoid a woman's sock drawer."

She settled her face back into serious, professional lines at the sight of the furious woman waiting for them at the top of the stairs.

Chapter Fourteen

The scene might have been plucked directly from a book written in the Golden Age of the mystery novel. The detective, the collection of suspects, the housekeeper wringing her hands on her apron, the fire burning cheerfully in the fireplace, comfortable armchairs, Christmas decorations and a festive tree, outside lights shining on fat snowflakes. The maid bringing in a tray with teapot, cups, milk and sugar, and a plate of cookies. Although in the stories the maid didn't drop the tray onto the table so hard the mugs jumped, collapse into a vacant chair, and say, "I hope, Sergeant Winters, that you are not using the excuse of being called to a crime scene to interrogate these people."

He took a star-shaped cookie sprinkled with red sugar. "Coincidences happen, Lucky. I was headed this way when the request for an officer came over the radio. So I took it. As for interrogating anyone, that's a harsh word for a simple detective asking questions about the death of two men known to these people. If you, Lucky, would prefer not to be *interrogated*, you're free to leave."

Ellie Carmine reached over and patted her friend's knee. "I'd like Lucky to stay."

Lucky Smith was much too polite to smirk.

They had nothing new to say. Ewan Williams went out the evening of December twenty-third and wasn't at breakfast the next morning. No one among his friends considered that to be anything worth worrying about.

"Shacked up with a girl he'd met at the resort, we all assumed," Wendy said, stirring milk into her tea. Her hand was shaking so badly the edges of the spoon rattled against the cup. "When it came to a quick pick-up, Ewan liked to scrape the bottom of the barrel."

John Winters was getting very, very tired of Wendy Wyatt-Yarmouth.

"Come on Wendy, that's unfair," Rob said. "He liked women. Women liked him."

"He did not 'like women'." Wendy crushed a Christmas cookie between her fingers. Pale crumbs fell onto her lap. "He liked sex. There's a difference, you know. That he's dead doesn't change the fact that he was an arrogant bastard."

Jeremy gave a mean laugh, and selected a mince tart. "Way to go, Wendy. Tell it like it is. Ewan didn't give a shit for women. He wanted sex, and he knew how to get it. He was a good looking guy with a deep voice, and a lot of money to throw around."

Winters said nothing.

"And well hung, whew. He was almost as big as me." Jeremy laughed. No one else did. "He was short and skinny, but I guess he thought the size of his prick made up for that. Ewan would have screwed anything that moved on two legs. Although I'm only guessing at the two legs bit. Wouldn't have surprised me if, when supply ran short, he'd gone after the four legged ones as well."

Ellie Carmine sucked in a breath.

"So, Lieutenant or Sergeant or whatever you are, if you're wondering why we weren't all that concerned about our missing pal, we assumed he was warm and comfy in some slut's bed, or, failing that, rutting in a stable somewhere. And, as long as we're talking things out, Jason wasn't..."

A side table, all gold gilt on spindly legs, crashed to the floor. A mug bounced on the rug, spilling tea. "Don't you dare say anything against Jason," Wendy shouted. She was on her feet, her face red and her fists clenched.

"Earth to Wendy. The truth is out there." He stuffed the entire tart into his mouth.

Rob helped Wendy back to her seat. "Never mind him. Jeremy's always been a jealous bugger. Any woman who preferred Ewan or Jason to him obviously had something wrong with her."

"Enough," Winters said, before Jeremy could reply. "I'm not interested in your petty rivalries." Although he definitely was, but it was time to move this on. Ewan Williams left the B&B apparently looking for some action. Until they found the woman, if she existed, that led Winters precisely nowhere.

"I don't see why you're wasting everyone's time with all these questions," Rob said. "In his own crude way, Jeremy's probably right. Ewan spent Sunday night and Monday with a girl he'd picked up. None of your business, unless that's become a crime and no one bothered to tell us. Then he called Jason and they managed to find a bar that was open, had a couple of drinks to give them some Christmas spirit and ended up in the river on the way back here. Sad, but not criminal."

"It's my time to waste," Winters said. "Did Jason get a phone call on Christmas Eve?"

"I don't know! We didn't keep him under armed guard, you know. Can't you check his phone calls or something?"

Everyone knew too much these days, or thought they did, about police methods. Ewan and Jason both had cell phones on them. Completely ruined by their immersion in the icy river. Winters had put in a request for the phone records of the dead men but had yet to hear back. It was a slow week everywhere.

"Tell me about Jason," he said.

"Jason, my brother, was…," Wendy began.

Winters lifted a hand. Bad choice of words. He wasn't here to listen to the virtues, as many as they might be, of Jason Wyatt-Yarmouth. "I mean, tell me about the day after Ewan's disappearance. The…" Wendy was staring at him. Her eyes and nose were red, the skin around her eyes puffy. She lifted a tissue to her face.

Never mind all the doubts he had about this crowd: Wendy Wyatt-Yarmouth was a woman in mourning, and in a precarious mental state.

Footsteps on the stairs.

Sophie first, then Alan, Molly Smith following. No one needed to ask if they'd located the missing goods. Sophie didn't look at anyone, and Alan gave them an embarrassed grin. Smith nodded imperceptibly to Winters.

"Found it," Alan said. "Just a misunderstanding."

"What the hell." Wendy jumped to her feet. "You can't have found it. Someone went through Sophie's stuff."

"Why are you so sure of that, Ms. Wyatt-Yarmouth?"

"Everything's so fucked up." She dropped into her chair. "Can we please get this over with?"

Ellie Carmine gave Lucky Smith a huge smile. The thought of someone's valuables being stolen from her B&B must have been an enormous worry. She selected a gingerbread man and bit his head off.

Lucky picked up the plate and held it out to her daughter. Smith accepted, but she shook her head when Lucky indicated the tea pot.

"We were talking about your brother, Ms. Wyatt-Yarmouth," Winters said, absent-mindedly rubbing his thumb against the face of his watch. "I'm sure this is going to be difficult for you, but I need to know."

She nodded and wiped her eyes.

"You went skiing on the twenty-forth?"

"Yes," Alan answered. "All of us, except Ewan. He wasn't here for breakfast so we left without him."

"Jason was with you?"

"Yes."

"Anything of interest happen at Blue Sky?"

"Nothing I can remember."

"Did Jason seem to be bothered about anything? Something on his mind maybe?"

The friends looked at each other. Sophie shrugged; the boys shook their heads.

"He was just Jason," Alan said, "Same as always."

"Did you come back to town together?"

Rob answered. "Yeah. All of us, except for Ewan. Jason drove. He usually did."

"And when you got back?"

"It was Christmas Eve. I've never seen a town shut down the way this one does. Every bar locked up as tight as if it were a Sunday in Saskatchewan in 1952. The restaurant in the Koola Hotel was about the only thing open, so we went there. Come to think of it, the food was about the same as they'd have served in Saskatchewan in 1952."

No one laughed. Outside, the snow continued to fall.

"We got back around seven."

Wendy rose to her feet. She stood straight and held her head high on a long neck. "If you don't mind," she said. "I'd like to go upstairs now." Her eyes were very wet. "I'm supposed to be having dinner with my parents again tonight. I don't think I can bear it."

Lucky put down her cup. "Can I help you? I've nothing to add to the conversation."

Lucky took Wendy's silence as agreement. She led the girl toward the stairs.

The common room was quiet until their footsteps reached the upper floor.

"Say what you want about Wendy," Rob said. "She and her brother loved each other. I think she relied on him a lot."

"And, despite the way she talks about him now, she had a crush on Ewan," Mrs. Carmine said.

Sophie snorted. "Hardly."

"She's a nut bar," Jeremy said. "Even Jason knew it."

"You ate dinner at the Koola Hotel," Winters tried to get them back on track, "and got back here around seven. What then?"

Alan grinned and Sophie blushed and Winters took a wild guess as to what they'd been doing. Jeremy shrugged. Rob chewed a fingernail.

"I for one," Mrs. Carmine said, "was preparing for our Christmas Eve get together. Jason told me his family always had a light supper at midnight, and everyone opened one special gift. Over the holidays I try to create a home-like atmosphere for my guests."

"We watched a video," Jeremy said. "Wendy and Rob and me."

"Some old Christmas movie Wendy found in the pile under the TV." Rob nodded toward the shelves stocked with video cassettes and DVDs. "What was it called?"

"*It's a Wonderful Life*. Black and white and deadly boring."

"I liked it."

"You would."

"And Jason?" Winters asked, cutting off Rob's reply. "What did he do?"

"Went out," Jeremy said. "Soon as we got back. Took the car."

"Where did he go?"

The three boys exchanged glances.

Smith moved away from the wall.

"Didn't say," Alan said, at last.

"But you can guess," Winters said.

Jeremy spoke first. "He'd picked up a local girl. She was here the previous night, testing out the mattress. I assumed he'd gone to meet her."

"Jason and Ewan were sharing a room, right?"

"Yeah."

"Ewan didn't have a problem with the mattress being tested in his room?"

"I don't know what Ewan had a problem with and what he didn't," Rob said.

"Come on, Rob. I bet this cop's been around the block more than a few times. Probably even with that young constable, eh?" Jeremy leered at Smith.

Smith kept her face impassive; only the veins in her neck moved.

Good thing Lucky Smith had left the room, Winters thought. Otherwise she'd no doubt want to contribute to the conversation at this point.

"Tell me about the relationship between Ewan and Jason, Jeremy."

"They got on well 'cause when it came to girls they were opposites. Ewan liked the prowl. Back alleys, back yard sheds, back bedrooms, back streets. He'd do it anywhere. With anyone. Whereas Jason liked to find a girl and keep her close, for a while. Less work that way. They were never allowed to spend the night, because Ewan would be coming back at some time. Except when he didn't."

"You really are a bastard, aren't you?" Rob said.

"He's telling it like it was," Alan said. His boyish smile had gone and his handsome face had turned dark. He tossed a glance at Sophie, and she studied the polish on her fingernails.

Winters filed that reaction away for later, and spoke before they could start exchanging insults. "We know Jason went out after dinner, in the rented SUV. You assumed he was going to meet a young lady."

"If that's what you want to call her."

"He didn't return?"

"I didn't see him."

Alan leaned up against the fireplace mantel and Sophie'd taken a chair at the other side of the room where she spent her time picking up the Christmas Village ornaments, one at a time, and turning them in her fingers. "*Alain* and I," she said, "came down around half-past eleven. In my family also we celebrate on Christmas Eve. Mrs. Carmine gave us supper. We waited for them for a long time, but Jason and Ewan, they did not come. Only," Sophie pointed at Smith with her chin, "she came. With the bad news."

Mrs. Carmine dabbed her eyes with her handkerchief. Overhead a floorboard creaked. Lucky Smith listening from the top of the stairs.

"This girl Jason had supposedly set up with," Smith said. "Do you know her name?"

"Of course," Jeremy said. "Lorraine. The one Wendy's always in such a kerfuffle about."

◇◇◇

The front door opened with a gentle creak. Light footsteps sounded in the hallway. They hesitated and then went into the kitchen. Winters jerked his head toward Smith, but before she could take a step, Mrs. Carmine shouted. "Kathy, get in here."

The girl's head popped into the common room.

"Hey," Jeremy said, "Come on in. The more the merrier."

She took small, hesitant steps forward, eyes locked on the floor.

"Where have you been?" Mrs. Carmine shouted. "Gone for the whole day. I had to finish all the chores myself. And with my back."

"Sorry," Kathy mumbled into the carpet.

Smith stretched a kink in her neck and happened to look at Rob Fitzgerald. His face was beet red and he also was examining the carpet as if the secret of life were to be found therein.

Kathy Carmine stood in the doorway, shifting from foot to foot, looking like a dog that had peed on the carpet, while Winters asked if she'd seen Jason after he'd left on Christmas Eve. She mumbled something that sounded like "No."

Winters glanced at Smith. She gave him a slight nod to indicate, she hoped, that she knew what was going on. And it didn't have anything to do with the case. Of course, she was a raw recruit to this interrogation and secret signal business; she might have just told him that Kathy was a mass murderer.

Winters got to his feet. "Thank you for your help, everyone. That's all the questions I have at this time. If you think of anything else that happened the nights in question, no matter how minor it appears, I'd appreciate it if you'd let me know."

He placed several business cards on the coffee table and walked out.

Smith followed.

Mrs. Carmine started shouting at her daughter. "I had to make all the beds myself, and with my bad back."

Kathy burst into tears and darted out of the room, almost knocking Smith into the wall. Rob Fitzgerald was heading equally fast for the stairs.

This overly decorated B&B was a proper den of iniquity.

It had snowed while they were inside and the van was covered in the white stuff. Smith switched the wipers on to clear the windows.

"Impressions?" Winters said, as she pulled into the street. "What about the last scene? That girl looked to me like she'd been up to something."

"Kathy Carmine? Up to something with Rob Fitzgerald, all right. I'll take a guess and assume it didn't go well."

"He propositioned her?"

Smith laughed. "The opposite, I'd say. You're a man, John; you can't begin to understand how incredibly humiliating it can be for a girl to offer herself to a guy and be turned down."

"Rejection's pretty rough for us guys too, Ms. Smith."

"Rough, but different. In that house where everyone is thinking about nothing but who they're going to lay next, can you imagine trying to join the game and being rebuffed."

"What makes you think that's what happened? Maybe he tried something and she didn't like it. Maybe she was agreeable at first and then got cold feet."

"Maybe she walked in on him jerking off, I don't know. Anything could have happened, but the attempted seduction and refusal was my initial impression."

"Nothing to do with the Jason and Ewan situation?"

"I'd say not."

"What did you think about that?"

"With all due respect, John, this one makes me glad I'm not a detective."

"Not a clue, you mean?"

"Precisely."

"Except for Lorraine LeBlanc."

"I'd seen her earlier that night, Christmas Eve, on the street. She told me she was going to a party at her boyfriend's place.

I figured she was stringing me a line and was surprised to see her later, at the B&B, when I was there to inform them of the accident."

"She was Jason's girlfriend?"

"Girlfriend is a generous term. If Jeremy was right, and isn't he a charming fellow, Jason had no interest in the chase. He was happy to find a companion to bed down as and when it suited him for the duration of his vacation. Lorraine, I'm sorry to say, fits the bill nicely."

"How old is she again?"

"All of sixteen."

"So this has to be done right. The parents will have to be present."

"It's..." Smith glanced at her watch. "Seven o'clock. They might be half-sober, if we hurry."

"You don't have to come. You're off duty."

"Someone has to watch your back when Mrs. LeBlanc gets a look at you."

The van slipped a few times as it struggled to get up steep streets thick with snow freshly fallen on top of well-packed ice. A group of young people, laughing and happy, wrapped up against the cold, threw snowballs at each other as they walked into town. A Sphinx carved out of snow sat on the front yard of a house at the corner of Aspen street. It was a good four feet tall, the face perfect: strong and proud.

"Cool," Smith said. "Hey, I just thought of something."

She drove past the LeBlanc house. Lights were on in the front rooms. The driveway and sidewalk were unshoveled. "At Flavours last night, Lorraine made a big scene at the Wyatt-Yarmouth dinner party. She wanted to be included among the mourners and they were being all snotty about it. I thought they were darn mean to her, but she'd been told to leave, so I had to get her out. Her brother was there, trying to help her."

"You told me this earlier."

"She'd been wearing these nice earrings. Everything she owns is pretty cheap, lots of it from second hand shops, and she wears the usual teenage junk jewelry. At the time I thought the earrings looked expensive, definitely not her style, but I forgot about them until now. I wonder where she got them."

The gold hoops were just the sort of thing a girl like Lorraine would think she needed to fit in with the family of her, supposed, boyfriend. What a mess.

Winters was thinking along the same lines. "I read in the shift reports," he said, "that there's been a number of thefts in the stores on Front Street lately. Your parents' store amongst them."

"I answered that one. Someone snatched a pair of ski goggles. Two hundred bucks worth. Dad was fit to be tied."

She stopped talking. She turned right. "How relevant is Lorraine, John? No one killed Jason."

"That's about the only hard and fast fact I have to cling to. Unless aliens swooped down and swapped bodies, in which case I'm giving up the job forever, Jason Wyatt-Yarmouth was alive as he drove his rented SUV into the Upper Kootenay River. The driver of the other car is positive the driver was struggling to keep his vehicle under control."

"Any chance the car was tampered with?"

"The inspectors have been over every inch of the vehicle. Nothing wrong with it, they say, other than a crushed roof and broken windows. And a lot of water damage. Ray Gavin and his guys have fingerprinted the whole thing."

"They can do that, through water?" She took a right.

"They can do just about anything these days, Molly. I'm glad I wasn't a detective in the bad old days before ballistics and fingerprinting and such. Water's not a problem. The surface dries and the prints are still there. But they don't even have to wait for it to dry, Ray used a powder suspension, and he had more prints to lift than he'll ever know what to do with. It was a rental car, so it's covered in all sorts of different prints."

She turned right again.

"If anyone's looking out the windows of the LeBlanc home," Winters said, "they'll be calling 911 to report someone casing the joint."

"The LeBlancs would let their house go up in flames before they called the police for help. Unless they could find a way to blame it on us."

"Pull into the driveway, Molly. We're here to ask Lorraine if she saw Jason Wyatt-Yarmouth on the evening of December twenty-forth. All part of a normal inquiry. We're not here to accuse her of anything, so you can put way your truncheon and rubber gloves."

"If you insist." Deciding she couldn't get the van into the snow-choked LeBlanc driveway, she parallel-parked in front of the house. Parking on the unplowed road wasn't all that much easier.

They were scarcely out of the van before the door to the house opened. Harsh yellow light illuminated Gary LeBlanc from behind.

"Always a pleasure, Moonlight," he said. "Sorry, but I don't know your friend."

"Sergeant John Winters, Trafalgar City Police. You are?"

"Here I thought Moonlight was bringing a pal 'round for a party. Something like bishops and hookers, or maybe cops and villains would be more appropriate, considering the state of her uniform."

Smith had almost forgotten that she was still wearing ski pants and the hand-knitted red gloves and hat her maternal grandmother had given her for Christmas.

"I'm Gary LeBlanc, as no doubt Constable Moonlight told you, Sergeant. What can I do for you?" His feet were planted solidly in the doorway, his arms akimbo and his chest puffed out.

Winters glanced at Smith. *Take it.*

She tried to swallow without appearing to be doing so. To get the high-pitched voice that was her curse to drop an octave or two. "Is Lorraine at home?" she asked. That came out well.

"Maybe."

"Gary," she said. "We're attempting to find out what a certain man did recently. We've been told he might have visited Lorraine, and Sergeant Winters would like to ask her about it.

That's all. We're looking for your help, not to accuse Lorraine of anything. Or you either."

She shouldn't have added that last sentence. It implied that she had something to accuse him of. Which she didn't.

"Can I make a confession, Moonlight? I always thought you were the cutest, and definitely the most together, girl in school. I could never get up the nerve to tell you what I thought. Perhaps I should have, maybe things would have worked out differently."

"All that is of no relevance," she said. The night was sharply cold and her coat was unzipped, but suddenly she was boiling hot. Why on earth was Winters not stepping in to give her a hand? He might have turned to stone, for all the help he was.

"Is Lorraine at home?" she said.

"I am." The girl poked her head through the V between her brother's arm and his body.

"Get back inside," he said.

"They know I'm here. Let's get it over with." Lorraine pulled her head back.

Gary stepped to one side. "Sorry Moonlight, cop guy, but I'm not inviting you in. Come here, Lorraine. We can talk on the porch as well as any place else."

"In full view of the neighbors?"

"Shocking, eh? They've probably never seen cops at this door before."

Winters still didn't say anything. Smith cursed him and bumbled on. "Are your parents at home?"

"Strangely enough, no. My dear step-father has been called away on an important business matter to Vancouver, and Mama's visiting her sisters in, shall we say, Toronto."

By which Smith assumed that Gary, fresh out of prison where he'd no doubt learned a thing or two about intimidation, had kicked them out of home and out of town.

No loss to anyone. Least of all to the patrol officers of the Trafalgar City Police.

"What's the matter?" Lorraine asked in her soft voice. She stood at her brother's side clutching a tattered pink robe around her skinny frame. The slippers on her feet had teddy-bear heads. They were clean and looked new. "I'm sorry about last night, Mol. I mean, Constable Smith. But those people...Jason's family, they made me so mad. Are you going to arrest me?"

"No, Lorraine. As I told Gary." She glanced at the brother. All anger and aggression. And, Smith hoped, protection. "We're here about Jason Wyatt-Yarmouth. You knew him?"

"We were engaged." Lorraine pulled a well-used tissue out of her pocket and blew her nose.

"I'm sorry," Smith said. *Why the hell was she conducting this investigation?* "I need you to think back a bit, Lorraine. On Christmas Eve, I was in the police truck outside the convenience store and you were going into town. We talked for a few minutes. Remember?"

"Yeah."

"Think back before that. Like around dinner time. Did you see Jason then?"

She shifted her feet. "Yeah."

"When?"

Lorraine took a quick peek toward her brother. Then she looked so directly at Smith that the officer knew the girl was about to lie, or at least to dissemble. "Jason came here around six o'clock, maybe six-thirty. I was the only one at home, so I invited him in for something to eat. I put a couple of frozen dinners in the microwave and we talked for a while and then we ate." She sniffed. "I'm cold, Gary. Do we have to stand here on the porch?"

"Yes we do. These people are not welcome in our house. Not without a warrant."

"Not a problem," Winters said. "It's a pleasant evening." Somewhere down the street, a snowblower roared to life. At the bottom of the hill a car spun its wheels searching for traction.

"After you had dinner, Lorraine, did you notice what time Jason left?"

She looked everywhere but at the police. "Sure. It was nine o'clock. I went back inside and turned on the TV. The movie was starting. Right, Gary, the movie was on."

"I wouldn't know, Lorraine, I wasn't here."

"Oh, right."

"Where were you, Mr. LeBlanc?" Winters asked.

"I slept on Donnie Bernard's couch. You can check if you want. I'd had a disagreement with my father in the afternoon and decided to spend the night elsewhere. I came by the next morning to check on Lorraine. Found that the parents had been drinking at a friend's place and hadn't even made it home. They were in the drunk tank and Lorraine alone and in a bad way."

"Was Jason driving?" Winters asked the girl.

"I don't know. I didn't look outside."

"Do you know where he went when he left here?"

"Back to the B&B, I guessed. He said he'd phone me later and I could come to their Christmas Eve party. Christmas Eve. Like I was part of a real family."

Chapter Fifteen

"She's lying."

Smith started up the van. "You think so?"

"Yes, I do." *Like a real family. God, but that was sad.* Lorraine had retreated into the house, in a flood of tears after mention of the aborted Christmas Eve party.

"Does it matter?"

"Does it matter that Lorraine's lying to the police in a suspicious death investigation? Don't be stupid, Molly, of course it matters."

Her fingers tightened on the steering wheel and he could hear her take a sharp intake of breath. "I meant Jason's activities that night. He killed his friend, and was taking the body to dispose of it in the wilderness when he went off the road. Lots of wilderness around here. I'm guessing he found Ewan with Lorraine and they got into a fight over her. Both men are dead. Case closed."

"Nothing is obvious here, Molly. Does it matter? Yeah, it does. It matters to the law and it matters to me." He sat in silence as she drove downhill in the direction of town. He'd left her to do most of the questioning of Lorraine because Smith had a rapport, no matter how tenuous it might be, with the girl. Whereas he, obviously, represented authority, Smith, in her handmade red gloves and spiky blond hair, at least knew Lorraine. The brother was another matter. He hadn't needed to say anything out loud to the effect that he liked Molly, it had been written all over his face as soon as he opened the door and saw her coming up the walk. Before the hard guy façade fell back into place.

Winters closed his eyes and thought about what Molly had said. Perhaps he should just write it up as a fight between friends that got out of hand. But suppose there was another reason Jason had been driving around with his friend's dead body in the car. He had to know Ewan was dead. Jason was a medical student, for God's sake. Surely they learned on day one the difference between a dead person and a living one.

Had Jason killed Ewan and been trying to dispose of the body? Or had someone else killed him and Jason was trying to protect him, or her?

Or had Jason, knowing his friend was dead, been taking him to the hospital and gone the wrong way? Why would he do that? To avoid overloading the EMS on a busy night? That sort of consideration wouldn't fit with the impression Winters had gained of Jason Wyatt-Yarmouth.

Smith pulled into the back of the police station. He could tell by the set of her shoulders that she was smarting from his rebuke.

Only eight o'clock and he was dead tired. Barney was a night person, and Eliza said they'd be having dinner around nine. Barney was actually a morning, afternoon, and night person. The woman didn't seem to have low gear. She'd pretty much taken over their computer room. She was on vacation, so she was only working half time—twelve hours a day instead of twenty-four.

Smith backed the van into its parking spot. Winters unfastened his seat belt.

Lorraine LeBlanc was not a bad liar. Considering her family life, she would have learned such a basic survival skill. Sixteen years old. That would throw a good-sized spanner into the works. He couldn't drag her down for further questioning without a parent or guardian present. And considering that the parents appeared to have vacated town without the courtesy of leaving a forwarding address that meant legal complications he most certainly didn't need.

The radio squawked. "Seven-two. 911 call. Disturbance at 1894 Victoria Street."

"Not them again," Smith groaned.

Winters grabbed the radio. "Winters here. I'll meet Seven-two at the scene." He fastened the seat belt. "Enjoying your day off, Molly?"

"As much fun as a day at work." She put the gear into drive.

◇◇◇

Lucky helped Ellie carry the tea things into the kitchen. It was after seven, long past time to be home. Andy would be wanting his dinner. Not that Andy Smith ever expected dinner to be on the table when he walked through the door. Usually he considered himself to be fortunate to be provided with a hot, cooked meal at all. He wasn't incompetent in the kitchen, and when the children were young Andy fed the family about half the time. But somehow, as middle age settled in and Moonlight and Samwise found lives of their own, Andy sort of forgot how to cook. Not that Lucky always took up the slack, but this morning she'd taken a four-bean chili out of the freezer.

"Thank you for being here with me, Lucky," Ellie said as she opened the dishwasher drawer.

"Glad I could be of help."

"This is all so difficult. Those poor boys. And the police poking around. Never thought I'd complain about living in a town with a low crime rate, but I guess if they don't have anything better to keep them occupied they have to make themselves look important. Oh, sorry, I forgot—Moonlight."

"My daughter does her job to the best of her ability." Lucky knew she sounded pompous. It was difficult, sometimes, in the anti-establishment circles in which she moved, to defend her daughter's dedication to her career while at the same time ensuring that she herself still supported the civil rights, environment, and peace activists who might occasionally fall afoul of the police.

"Do you know, Lucky, I'm starting to wonder about letting rooms to these college types."

"People of any age die. You're far more likely to have a sudden death with us of the older crowd, you know."

"All this…going on. Having girls upstairs. Girls like, well, like Lorraine. She's a sorry creature, Lucky. That mother of hers should be horsewhipped."

"I don't think they do that any more." Lucky rinsed the tea pot.

"Well they should. Alan and Sophie aren't married, you know."

Lucky struggled to contain a laugh. She remembered smuggling Andy into her dorm room at the University of Washington. She and her roommate Jane had agreed on the hours Jane was to be in the study hall. Lucky returned the favor. Jane hadn't come back to school after summer break and was dead before Thanksgiving. Lucky was pleased Jane had been able to have some fun in life before cancer chewed through her body.

"They're young, Ellie, what do you expect?"

"Take some baking for Andy," Ellie said. "I've more than I'll use. This business has put the guests off their appetites."

Lucky needed no further prompting to rip a length off a roll of plastic wrap and use to it to bind shortbread, cookies, and squares. Nothing like a touch of chocolate chips or sprinkling of colored sugar to make Andy forget the little wife was late serving his dinner.

She carried her goodies out to the hall and put them on the table by the door while she rooted through the closet for her coat.

The guests were still gathered in the common room. Wendy had come back downstairs to join them. The door was open.

"Ghouls," she said in a voice that could be clearly heard in the hall. "I can't imagine why they're making such a fuss over a car accident. Isn't it bad enough that my brother's dead, without them wanting to drag every little detail out about what happened the day he died?"

"They're just doing their job," Rob said.

Lucky sat on the deacon's bench to pull on her boots.

"He might be, but that female cop. God, have you ever seen such a superior bitch."

Lucky tied her laces, while reminding herself that not everyone in town could be expected to love the beat constable.

"Bet he's screwing her." Jeremy.

"You're the one who's screwed. In the head. What the hell gives you that idea?" Rob.

"She wants to get ahead, doesn't she?" Wendy again. "You can see ambition practically dripping off her."

"Here's an interesting fact, Wendy: ambition doesn't become a dirty word when it's applied to a woman." Rob.

You tell 'em, boy.

"Look at your own mother, Wendy, Order of Canada isn't she?" Rob.

"'Course your mother's quite the screwable piece herself. Despite being, what, fifty years old?" Jeremy.

"What the hell does that mean?" Wendy.

"Will you guys drop it?" Alan, coming down the stairs.

"Sorry, pal. You can't hear yourself when people are talking? That must be a problem. Me, I never much care what I can hear when I'm on the job. Unless she's not breathing, that is." Jeremy. "'Course I might pay attention if that blond cop came banging on my door with her truncheon."

"You are such a jerk." Rob.

"Not that you'd know." Jeremy. "I can see what's going on in the dark, you know, Robbie. You cuddle up to that computer as if she were a whore."

Lucky Smith was certainly not the housemistress of this bunch. But enough was enough. If someone didn't interfere they'd soon be coming to blows. She took a step toward the common room.

"Stop it. Stop it," Wendy yelled. "My brother's dead and you're arguing about who's screwing who. I don't care. I don't care. I don't care." She began to scream. Long and loud, without end.

Lucky took a step toward the girl.

"Well done, Jeremy." Rob took a half-hearted swing at Jeremy, but he missed and tripped over a loose edge of the rug. Rage flooded Jeremy's face, and he pounced and followed Rob to the floor, fists moving.

Kathy, coming out of nowhere, brushed past Lucky. She jumped on Jeremy's back, pummeling him with her fists. Alan grabbed Kathy around the waist and tried to drag her off. She turned, grabbed his arm, lifted it to her mouth. Her jaws closed.

Alan yelled and dropped her. Holding his arm and swearing a blue streak, he leapt backward, knocking into the Christmas tree. The tree swayed and the ornaments rattled.

"*Tabernac*." Sophie grabbed a lamp and swung the base toward Kathy's head.

Lucky grabbed Sophie's arm. "Drop it."

She did and turned to tend to Alan.

Wendy began throwing things. An ornamental blacksmith's shop bounced off the window.

Ellie stood in the doorway, her face as white as her apron. She screamed at the sight of a glass ornament in Wendy's hand. Wendy threw it at her, and Ellie ducked. The piece hit the wall and shattered into pieces.

Jeremy and Rob were well into it. At first Jeremy was on top, his fists moving like pistons on a race car. Then it was Rob. Mild mannered Rob was able to hold his own in a fight. He grabbed Jeremy's head by the ears and smashed it into the floor. Once, twice. Kathy jumped up and down, yelling encouragement.

Lucky ran across the room and dropped to her knees. She touched Rob's shoulder. "No more. Please."

He pulled back. He looked at her, his eyes dull and focused, and for a moment she feared he was about to hit her.

He shoved Jeremy's head down and stood up.

Jeremy jumped to his feet, turned his head and spat blood onto the shiny hardwood floor. The two men faced each other, breathing heavily, fists clenched.

Lucky stepped between them. She put one palm on each chest, and could feel their hearts beating as fast as her own. "This has gone far enough, don't you think?"

Sirens coming down the road. Stopping outside the B&B.

"Will you shut the hell up," Alan yelled at Wendy. "Like we need the cops here again."

She stopped screaming, and her hand froze before it could throw the brightly painted wooden nutcracker soldier she gripped in her right hand.

Fists pounded on the door. "Police."

"Someone get the door," Lucky said. "Or they'll break it down."

Rob and Jeremy glared at each other across her arms. She wasn't sure if she stepped away they wouldn't start the fight up again.

The other combatants began to examine their injuries. "The bitch bit me. I'm going to need a rabies shot."

"*Sacre bleu*, what kind of freaks are you?"

"My late husband gave me that village. You're going to pay for it."

Wendy fell into a chair and began to cry with great heaving sobs.

"I'll let them in," Kathy said.

Dawn Solway was half-way up the path, which was covered with the afternoon's fall of snow, when Smith pulled up behind the patrol car. Winters was out of the van before Smith had brought it to a complete halt.

A pure white Jack Russell barked at him. Fortunately for Winters' ankles, the dog was attached to a leash, held by a woman bundled against the cold. The woman pointed her cell phone toward the B&B. "Someone's screaming in there to beat the band. I thought I'd better call you." A man crossed the street to see what was happening. Next door, the porch light came on.

The B&B looked like Santa's village in the gently falling snow. The roof and doorway were trimmed by tiny white lights;

nets of lights were tossed over the bushes on either side of the porch steps. A big green wreath topped by a white bow graced the front door.

Solway hit the door with her fist. "Police."

She sensed someone behind her and turned around.

Smith came up the path at a trot. Solway took a quick look at her and lifted one eyebrow at the unusual uniform.

Smith shrugged.

"I'll take this," Winters said. "You two follow me." He lifted his hand to knock again, but it wasn't necessary.

Kathy Carmine stood there. "Can I help you?"

"We received a call of a disturbance at this address," Winters said. "Loud enough to be heard on the street."

"It's all sorted out. We're fine, thanks. Just a misunderstanding. Thank you for coming anyway." She began to shut the door. Winters stuck a boot into it.

"I'd like to come in and check for myself."

Smith didn't know why, but Kathy looked at her as if she were asking what she should do. Smith nodded, and Kathy took a step backward, out of the doorway.

Please don't let my mom still be here. Smith entered the house behind Winters and Solway.

But her prayers were not answered. Lucky was in the middle of it all. She stood between two young men, both of them breathing heavily and bleeding from the nose and minor cuts to the face. Lucky wasn't much over five feet tall, a pudgy fifty-six year old woman with graying red hair that refused to keep to its pins; the men were six feet and more, muscular, young and angry. She kept them apart as much by force of will as strength of hand.

The other residents and the owner of the B&B were in various stages of nursing wounds, weeping, crying over broken furniture, and straightening ornaments.

"Who's going to tell me what's going on here?" Winters said. "Mrs. Smith, you can start."

Smith glared at her mother, and Lucky ignored her.

"As you understand, Sergeant Winters," she said, in a voice her daughter knew so well. Her formal, speaking to authority (before cutting them off at the knees) voice. "Emotions are running high around here. Thank you for coming, but it's all over now."

Like an actor who hadn't gotten the changes to the script, Jeremy pointed at Rob, "Bullshit. He came on like a goddamned lunatic." Blood streamed from his nose, and he wiped it on his sleeve. He looked around the room. "You all saw it. He attacked me for no reason."

"No reason," Rob yelled. His lip was split and leaking blood. The skin around his right eye was already changing color. "All you've done since we got the news about Jason and Ewan is make snide insinuations." Kathy slipped behind him and put a hand on the small of his back. He didn't seem to notice.

Jeremy's body stiffened as, despite the presence of three police officers, violence began to creep back in. "Why don't you do us all a favor and go back to your fucking computer?"

It wasn't her place to do anything without orders, but Molly Smith was so tired of this bunch of spoiled brats. And on a day that had started so nicely with a steaming mocha and a bag of fresh croissants and skis on the roof of her car. "Jeremy Wozenack, I'm sick to death of seeing your face. This is the second time in one day I've been called out to find you in a brawl. You're under arrest."

Rob chuckled.

"What the hell, you can't arrest me." Jeremy turned to his friends. "Ask anyone, he attacked me. Didn't he? Didn't he? Tell her, Alan."

Alan was rubbing at his forearm. "From what I saw, he made a fist like a first-grader and you came back like Mohammed Ali. Other than that, I don't much care."

"He started it," Kathy said, pointing at Jeremy. "He attacked Rob with no provocation at all."

"That's a fucking lie. Christ, you weren't even here, kid. Think making up a story's going to get you a date, think again."

"Mr. Wozenack, right now it doesn't matter one whit who started what. A judge will decide that. I'm arresting you because I don't want to be called out any more today. Got it?"

"Think I'm going to be taken away by a blond bitch in an ugly red hat? Think again, *lady*."

Smith felt heat rising into her face. They were all watching her. Particularly her mother. Lucky's lips were pinched. That meant that she was about to explode in righteous indignation. At Molly for acting like a storm trooper or at Jeremy for calling her daughter a bitch. No matter. Molly Smith could only do what she had to do.

"Turn around," she said.

"No."

"Constable Solway." Smith half-turned toward Dawn. She felt as much as heard Jeremy Wozenack exhale and start to relax as he assumed he'd forced her to step down. She whirled around and grabbed his left arm. With a sharp twist she had him facing the wall, struggling to keep his footing.

"Nice." Solway snapped handcuffs on.

Smith let out a puff of breath that meant thanks. Jeremy let out a stream of abuse.

Solway spoke to Jeremy. "Let's go."

"Constable Smith," Winters said. "Help Constable Solway take him to the station. I'll stay for a while longer." He held out his hand. Smith gave him the keys to the vehicle.

Smith and Solway headed for the door. Other than informing the two women of his opinion of their sexual proclivities and those of their parents, Jeremy didn't put up any resistance.

"Now, perhaps someone will tell me what's going on here. And you," Winters said to Rob, "don't start thinking you're in the clear just because you're not being escorted out like your friend."

"That's so unfair," Kathy Carmine said. "It wasn't Rob's fault…"

Smith opened the front door.

A man's hand was raised to knock. Mr. Wyatt-Yarmouth, Wendy and Jason's father. His eyes opened wide and he took a step back. He slipped on the stair and his arms windmilled as he struggled to keep from falling. Solway reached out her free hand to offer support, but he kept his footing without it.

"What on earth?" he said.

"If you'll excuse us, sir," Smith said.

Jeremy, fortunately, didn't say anything.

Wyatt-Yarmouth peered at her. "Didn't I see you the other night at the restaurant?"

"Perhaps. Good evening, sir."

"Wait, just a minute, please, is my wife here?"

"I don't believe so, sir."

"You're with the police?" Mr. Wyatt-Yarmouth said. As if he'd finally understood that two women, one in full uniform, the other wearing a police jacket, escorting a handcuffed prisoner with a bleeding nose, might be real officers and not girls dressed up for a costume party. He coughed. "Perhaps it's fortunate I've run into you…uh…ladies."

"Why's that, sir?" Smith said.

Solway gave Smith a nod around Jeremy and gave him a prod toward the car.

"Well," Wyatt-Yarmouth said. "It's that…Well you see. I mean…"

"Sir, is there a problem?"

"Yes, there is. My wife has gone missing."

Chapter Sixteen

Ellie Carmine had an attack of the vapors. Sophie Dion forgot how to speak English. Alan Robertson insisted that he didn't need to go to the hospital, although no one had offered to take him there. Kathy Carmine wept and moaned over Rob Fitzgerald's minor wounds with as much drama as if he'd been bayoneted in the Charge of the Light Brigade. Lucky Smith walked around the room picking up shards of glass.

Jack Wyatt-Yarmouth walked into a scene of total chaos. His daughter stopped crying, breathed in what bit of fragile strength she still possessed and approached him.

"Hi Dad," she said. "Sorry. I guess I'm late for dinner, eh? I'll run upstairs and tidy up and be right with you." She looked around the room. "Might be just us tonight, though."

"Is your mother here?" Jack said. Without a hug or a kiss or even a question as to why rivers of black mascara scarred her cheeks.

He didn't even seem too concerned at why the Christmas tree was leaning against the wall, Mrs. Carmine keening over broken decorations, Alan trying to get Sophie to come upstairs, Kathy rubbing Rob's face while he swatted at her eager fingers, as if they carried swarms of starving mosquitoes.

"I don't know where Mom is," Wendy said.

Jack Wyatt-Yarmouth turned to Winters. "I'm glad I found you here, Sergeant. My wife has gone missing. This is unusual behavior, and I have to tell you that I fear for her safety."

Wendy fell into a chair. "No more," she moaned, "please no more."

Wendy, Winters thought, alone among this pack of drama kings and queens, truly needs some help.

"When did you see her last, sir?" He stepped into the hallway, willing Jack to follow.

"We had breakfast together, at a restaurant in town, around nine."

Winters checked his watch. "It's eight o'clock. You must realize we can't consider this to be a missing person case with less than twelve hours having passed."

"Look here, Sergeant. My wife and I have come to your *charming* town to collect the body of our son. Since arriving we have been told that the body is not going to be released, pending further investigation. Whatever that means. Our family dinner was interrupted by a street person to such a degree that the police had to be called. And tonight I can not find my wife."

"Careless of you."

Winters turned. Wendy Wyatt-Yarmouth stood in the doorway. Her eyes were red, nose and cheeks matching. She held a crumpled tissue in one hand.

"Go and wash your face," Jack told his daughter.

"Won't help," she said.

Ellie crept past them, heading toward the kitchen. In the common room Alan said something about going home, and Kathy told Rob she'd help him manage the stairs.

Winters had no idea what Lucky Smith was up to, and that worried him.

Wendy blew her nose. "Mom's out of her mind with grief. Can't you let her have some time to herself?"

"For once in your life, you stupid child, will you at least pretend to have a modicum of common sense. My wife will not be allowed to wander the streets by herself."

Wendy turned to John Winters. "So there we have it. Mom *will not be allowed* to grieve or to mourn as she sees fit. I've had it. I'm going to bed. You can expect to see me at your door in the morning, Dad. I don't expect the Glacier Chalet B&B will be all that hospitable tomorrow, at least toward those of us who threw an illumined blacksmith's shop against the wall."

Wyatt-Yarmouth sputtered.

"I haven't met your wife, sir," Winters said. "But I believe Constable Smith, who you just passed, has. I'll stop in at the station and ask her for a description. As I said, we can't issue an alert for an adult this early, but I will ask our officers to contact me if they see her."

"I would have expected, Sergeant Winters, that in light of my wife's state of mind…"

"Shut the hell up, Dad," Wendy said. "You're the last person to know Mom's state of mind. Why don't you just go away?"

Jack Wyatt-Yarmouth gaped at her, and Winters guessed the man didn't normally encounter outright mutiny from his family.

"You're still at the Mountainside Inn?" Winters said, before Jack could reply to his daughter.

"Sadly, yes. It seems the town is full."

"Call here tomorrow. I expect there'll be rooms available." Wendy turned and walked away.

"Children," Wyatt-Yarmouth said, "are not worth the bother."

"Do you have a cell phone?"

"Yes."

"Give me the number. I'll call you if we locate your wife. But be aware we'll first ask her if she wants us to contact you."

"I trust you'll remember that my wife is an important woman. She is a recipient of the Order of Canada. I myself am on the board…"

"Number?" Winters tapped his pen against the notebook he'd pulled out of his pocket.

Wyatt-Yarmouth spat it out.

Winters wrote it down, before looking pointedly toward the door.

Wyatt-Yarmouth didn't take the hint. "My daughter seems to be not herself. I'd better check on her."

"Please, don't worry." A short, chubby red-headed bundle stepped out from the common room, where she'd obviously been listening from behind a wall. She held out her hand. "I'm Lucy Smith. My friends call me Lucky."

Wyatt-Yarmouth took her hand. Lucky folded it into both of hers. "Please don't worry," she repeated. "I'll check on Wendy. I have a daughter of my own that age."

Winters refrained from rolling his eyes. Good thing Lucky's last name was Smith. If it had been something noticeable, like, say, Wyatt-Yarmouth, Jack would have immediately connected it to the police officer and objected to Lucky's interference. Winters knew that it made no difference who, and what, Lucky's daughter was, but not many people would see it that way.

"Thank you," Jack said.

"I'll let you know if I hear anything." Winters edged the man toward the door. It didn't help that Lucky was still holding his hands and looking into his eyes. Finally Wyatt-Yarmouth broke away, turned, and stumbled down the steps.

Winters did, in fact, plan to do something about the absent Mrs. Wyatt-Yarmouth. This wasn't a normal disappearance by any means. The woman's only son had died days ago, and the body wasn't being released so she could make arrangements and try to find some sort of peace. He couldn't do much, yet, to search for her, but he'd ask everyone to be on the lookout. It was Saturday so officers would be in and out of the bars all night. Mrs. Wyatt-Yarmouth was probably sitting in a hotel lounge, in a better bar than anything in the vicinity of the Mountainside Inn, nursing a quiet drink, wanting to be left alone to remember her son when he'd been a laughing, mischievous boy with all the promise of the world ahead of him.

He turned to see Lucky Smith watching him.

"Are you going to tell me what's been going on here tonight?" Winters asked. People were talking in the common room. A woman was crying and a man spoke in a low voice full of anger. "Is there someplace we can talk in private?"

"We'd be best outside, if you're looking for privacy." Lucky was wearing her black winter coat, a lush blue scarf wrapped around her neck. "After you."

They stood on the porch watching the snow fall.

"They're upset about the death of their friends, John."

"A friend of mine died two years ago. I'd say, without reservation, that he was the best friend I ever had. We met the first day on the job, both of us young and keen. We were best men at each other's weddings. I've the honor of being godfather to his oldest son. He was killed in what some would call a car accident."

"What some would call?" she repeated, turning the statement into a question.

"My friend was a patrol officer. All he ever aspired to be. He was standing at the side of a pleasant road in one of the best parts of town, writing out a ticket for a guy going too fast through a school zone when he was sideswiped by a car that was going *much* too fast through a school zone."

"That must have been hard for you to deal with."

"Hard, yes. But you know what, Lucky? I didn't smash up my house, or knock around the next person who walked by. I didn't even stake out the perp's home and vandalize it when he wasn't there."

"What happened to him?"

"For once, justice was done, and the driver, despite being a pillar of the community and a deacon of his church, was found to have been drunk at the time and sent away to a place where he is, even as we speak, considering the evil of his ways."

Lucky Smith reached out her hand, palm turned up. Winters looked at it. For a moment, just a moment, he considered taking the offering. Instead, he continued, "What I'm telling you, Lucky, is that I don't particularly care how much these people are hurting. I need you to tell me what the fight was about."

"John, we've had dealings before."

And wasn't that the truth?

"I will." Her eyes shifted and she looked everywhere but at him. "Never, ever, forget what you did for Moonlight, for my daughter, when she was held in…that place."

"I did," he said, almost choking back the tears himself, "all the job requires. But we're not talking about Molly. This is about the bunch staying in the Glacier Chalet B&B."

There wasn't a great deal she could tell him. Rob and Jeremy had been snapping at each other in such a way that it was almost certain to turn physical. Alan and Sophie wanted to be left alone but found that they couldn't. Wendy was mad at everything and everyone. Her dead brother and her parents most of all. Oh, and Kathy Carmine was besotted with Rob, who was embarrassed to be seen with her. That, Winters reflected, was pretty much what Molly had told him.

He let out a breath, watching it gather shape and form in the cold night air.

"Ewan and Jason," Lucky said. "I never met them. Their friends are mourning, in their own way. Why is this dragging on? Can't you just let them take the boys home?"

He looked into her intelligent green eyes. "This goes no further than this porch? Will you agree, Lucky? Or not?"

"I promise. Not a word."

And he told her what Doctor Lee had found.

She ran her fingers across the top of the railings, scooping up fresh snow. Her hands were bare but she held the snow and crushed it into a ball. "Difficult," she said at last. "For every one. I told her father I'd look after Wendy, and so I should." She pulled at the edges of the blue scarf. "Thank you," she said, and went back into the house.

Finally, Molly Smith went home. Dawn said she'd take care of booking Jeremy Wozenack into one of their best rooms. Once he'd been settled into the back seat of the patrol car, Jeremy had let them know that as soon as his father heard about this *vendetta* Smith seemed to be carrying on, he'd sue her for everything she was worth, and the Trafalgar City Police along with it.

"That's your privilege," Solway said.

Oh, and his nose might be broken; he had to see a doctor immediately.

Smith let herself into her apartment. The room was cold and dark. Perhaps she should get a cat, someone to greet her when she got home. But, she reminded herself, she wasn't much of a cat person. Dogs had always been the Smith family's pets. She couldn't even consider getting a dog with her hours.

She took off her gloves and boots and hung her jacket in the closet before going into the bedroom, undoing her ski pants as she walked. Clothes tossed into a corner, she dug under her pillow for cozy flannel pajamas.

The doorbell rang.

She groaned.

This apartment was rooms over a shop: it didn't come with luxuries like an intercom. If she wanted to know who was calling, she had to walk down the stairs. She was in her bra and panties. She considered not answering: if it was work they would have called first.

The bell rang again. She dug in the closet for a pair of baggy track suit bottoms and a ratty old sweater, and ran down the steps. A peephole was set into the door.

Gary LeBlanc.

Abandoning the bell, he hammered on the door with his fists.

She opened it. "Gary, you can't come to my home. If you need to talk to someone, go to the police station."

"I don't want to talk to *someone*, Moonlight. I want to talk to you. I'm sorry to bother you at home, but, I saw you walking by and knew you weren't asleep or anything."

Meaning he'd either been waiting for her in the shadows or watching the police station and followed her.

"I'm back at work tomorrow at three. You can talk to me then."

"I'd rather this wasn't official."

Oh, God, let him not be wanting a date. "Gary, I only ever work officially. And if you know anything about Lorraine and the Wyatt-Yarmouth/Williams case you need to talk to Sergeant Winters. Not me. Good-night."

She began to shut the door.

He stepped forward.

"Take one more step and you're threatening a police officer."

He lifted both his hands, palms facing out. "Sorry, Moonlight, sorry. Look, it's hard for me. I want to do what I can for Lorraine, but I've been away. Plus I'm a guy. I need a woman's advice."

"Then you've come knocking on the wrong door. I'm not a woman, I'm a police officer. My mom volunteers at the Trafalgar Women's Support Center. Go see them tomorrow morning."

"How about I take you for a coffee? Half-hour of your time, no more."

She didn't want coffee, she wanted dinner. She'd missed lunch due to the fight at the ski lodge and hadn't had a minute to get a bite since.

"I'm going to make it, Moonlight. I learned carpentry in prison, and I've already started getting work. You know what a demand there is around here for tradesmen." She certainly did know: her dad complained constantly that he couldn't get anyone out to fix a leaky pipe or build an extension onto the deck, or lay new ceramic tiles in the kitchen. "And I'm going to take care of Lorraine. See she stops hanging around the streets, and trash like Jason Wyatt-Yarmouth and his high-class buddies, and finishes school. She's smart. Smarter than everyone else in our family for sure. If she can get back to class and work hard and graduate from high school, she could go to university. But she won't be going to university unless I can stop her from wandering the streets."

"I only want a half-hour, Moonlight, and I'll buy the coffee."

She sighed. "No one but my mother calls me Moonlight. I'm Molly. Let me get my coat. Wait here."

She shut the door, and locked it behind her.

At a table in the back of Big Eddie's, Gary skipped around the question of where his parents had gone. What he really wanted to know was when the group staying at the Glacier Chalet B&B

would be leaving, taking their dead with them. Lorraine was insisting she go to Ontario for Jason's funeral. And as he, Gary, had absolutely no intention of paying money he couldn't afford to finance such a trip, he was afraid she'd approach Mr. and Mrs. Wyatt-Yarmouth and, finding them unwilling to provide for her (*no kidding!*) do what she thought she had to do to get there.

"She's..." Gary coughed into his mug of black coffee. "Never, far as I know, taken money for...I mean..."

"You mean she's not a hooker, but you're afraid she'll turn into one trying to get the money to go to Ontario."

"Yeah."

Smith swirled the remains of her hot chocolate around in the bottom of the mug. She knew, and probably Gary did as well, that a last-minute plane trip from remote Trafalgar to Toronto would cost in the region of a thousand bucks. Minimum. If Lorraine started hooking, she'd be lucky to earn a hundred before being busted.

Theft? Where'd she get those nice earrings she seemed so proud of anyway? Did Lorraine have anything to do with the other thefts in town? Such as the two-hundred dollar ski goggles snatched from Mid-Kootenay Adventure Vacations?

Smith eyed Gary across the table. His head was turned toward the door, where Jolene was turning the sign from open to closed. He'd come to her looking for some sort of help, not to put the idea in her head that Lorraine was a thief. But she hadn't asked him to drop in to her home of an evening. She'd ask her mom if Lorraine had been in the store around the time the goggles were snatched. However, Smith knew, Lucky would eat the loss before turning a girl she felt sorry for over to the strong arm of the law.

What a mess.

She got to her feet. "Time to leave. They're closing."

"You'll think about what I said?"

"I will. Look, Gary, if you think Lorraine knows something about the deaths of Jason and Ewan, you need to let Sergeant Winters know, okay?"

"What's to know? They were driving too fast and went off the road into the river. Must have been a shock for a couple of invincible rich boys when they hit the water and knew they were about to die, as if they were mere mortals. I'm not crying any tears for them, Moon, I just want to protect my sister from the fallout. Why's your boss twisting his boxers into a knot worrying about them anyway?"

"Beats me. He doesn't have to confide in a lowly constable such as me." *Was Winters making a mistake keeping what they knew about Ewan's death under wraps?* No one seemed to be all that worried about helping the police with what everyone believed to be a tragic traffic accident.

Jolene held the door open for them. "Good-night," she said, her upper-crust English accent making it sound as if their carriages were waiting.

Smith pulled her collar up against the falling snow and dug into her pockets for her mittens.

They stood at the entrance to the coffee shop as the lights were switched off. "Good-night, Gary." She spoke without a fraction of the class Jolene had put into those two words.

"I'm going your way. I'll walk with you."

"I'm not going home yet."

"Okay. Look Moon…I mean Molly…I was sort of wondering if…well, when all this business is over…if you'd…"

"No." She waited for him to take the first step. Whichever way he went, she'd head in the opposite direction.

"'night," Gary turned right, going uphill.

She stuffed her hands in her pockets and turned left. She was starving. Too hungry to go home and take the time to cook something, she headed for Front Street. A yellow curry from Trafalgar Thai would be good. With spring rolls to start. They could have the appetizers on the table in minutes, which would keep her from dying of starvation while waiting for the curry.

She headed down the hill toward the lights of Front Street shops and restaurants. Dark and black. Cloud shrouded the mountain on the other side of the black river. She shivered and pulled her collar tighter.

Gary. He was so bitter, so angry at Jason and his friends. Perhaps he had a right to be. His father left town when Gary was in primary school, never to be heard from again. His mother married the town drunk and almost immediately joined her new husband in his favorite hobby. Barely twenty, and Gary'd been sent to prison to pay for a minor crime gone wrong.

The Wyatt-Yarmouth crowd. Tossing money around like eighteenth-century nobility visiting the peasants. Exchanging status for sex with local girls who were searching for everything from a fun night on the town to a lifetime commitment with a trust-fund guy.

Might Gary have had something to do with the death of Jason? No, Jason died in a car accident. There appeared to be no doubt about that. Ewan? They hadn't uncovered any link between Lorraine and Ewan.

Smith turned onto Front Street. A bunch of tourists passed her without a glance. Sometimes, in this town where it seemed as if everyone and his dog had either rubbed her head when she'd been a toddler or had been arrested by her, it was nice to be anonymous.

The scent of spices spilled out from Trafalgar Thai. She could almost taste that yellow curry.

A couple came out of the restaurant. They were laughing, their arms wrapped around each other. Light from the streetlamp above them shone on snowflakes drifting to the ground. A car drove by, window down, the stereo playing Sarah Brightman's duet with Paul Stanley: *You will never be alone,* they sang. The woman tilted her head and the man bent to kiss her. She'd managed to get through almost the whole day without thinking of Graham once.

She brushed past the couple, blinking away the tears.

A slow chill crept down her spine. She looked up to see a dark figure standing at the street corner on the other side of the restaurant. The cap was pulled low, the jacket black and bulky, hands stuffed into pockets, boots large.

Inside Trafalgar Thai, wait staff were hurrying with plates filled high with fragrant dishes. Customers talked and laughed and drank green tea and beer.

He, and it was almost certainly a he, wasn't moving. Just standing and watching her.

Cars drove by and people looked into shop windows and read posted restaurant menus. A group of giggling teenage girls came down the sidewalk like a river in flood; they parted around the man as water passes a boulder.

He lifted one black-gloved hand. The index finger moved slowly, beckoning her.

The girls swirled by Smith, a splash of voices like rapids running the narrows.

She couldn't see his face.

She was without uniform, gun, radio. His finger continued to move.

The restaurant door opened, spilling yellow light onto the sidewalk. Smith glanced to her left to see two elderly couples, enveloped in their winter gear.

When she looked back down the street, the corner was empty.

She hadn't seen his face. She hadn't needed to. Size and manner were good enough.

Yellow curry forgotten, she pulled out her cell phone.

"Ingrid, I need a parole check and fast."

"Happy to oblige, Molly, soon as I can. I've got a Canada-wide warrant spotted in Uptown."

"This is bad stuff, Ingrid. Local bad stuff."

"Go ahead."

"I need to know if this one's out of jail. Bassing, Charles F. That's F as in Fucking."

Chapter Seventeen

A late-model SUV, large and black, was parked in his driveway, a rental company logo slapped on the bumper. Not Barney's; she'd been picked up by Eliza at the airport.

Lights were on in his house, but that was no surprise. Nine p.m. and for Barney, all seventy-years old of her, the evening was only beginning. That all John Winters wanted to do was drop into bed, preferably in the soft, perfumed, satin-covered arms of his wife, wouldn't have crossed Barney's mind any more than the idea that he'd want to go out back and perform a human sacrifice.

He opened the front door. Women's voices came from the living room. He plastered on a smile and went to join them.

Nothing in all of John Winters life ever matched the joy he got from a first glimpse of Eliza after a long, hard day. Tonight she was curled up in her favorite leather chair, smiling at something Barney was saying, lifting a glass to her lips. A floorboard creaked and she looked up and saw him standing in the doorway.

"John! How wonderful." She jumped up. She was dressed in loose gray slacks and a sweater of soft pink, without jewelry. Her face was scrubbed clean and her dark hair hung loosely around her chin. She grabbed his face and gave him a lush kiss. "You're earlier than I expected."

"You look like a man in need of a drink," Barney said. "What'll it be? We're drinking mimosas, but I'd guess a man of the world would prefer something stronger."

He smiled. He did like Barney. "A beer would be nice."

"Coming right up." She dashed for the kitchen.

"John," Eliza said, her hand light on his arm, turning him slightly. "This is my new friend Patricia."

A woman was sitting in the wide-winged armchair by the window, draped in shadow. He approached her, hand out-stretched, and she leaned forward. The lamp caught her face. Finely sculpted cheekbones, neat chin, wide brown eyes, soft brown hair, artfully streaked. Perfect make up and expensive hair couldn't hide the pain behind her eyes.

He took her hand. "Pleased to meet you, Patricia. Welcome here."

"Thank you." Her voice was deep and rich.

Barney came back with his drink: golden liquid with a creamy head wrapped in an icy glass.

He took a seat, calculating how long he'd have to make friendly before escaping to bed. But first, he needed to eat. Should have picked up something in town. Eliza's skills did not lie in the kitchen.

"Are you new to Trafalgar, Patricia?" he asked. A husband doing his duty toward his wife's new friend.

"Just visiting. It's beautiful here. Early days yet, but I'm thinking I might want to buy a vacation home."

Barney launched into a discussion of the value of property in the area. Skyrocketing, she put it.

"You've missed your chance," Eliza said. "There were plans to build a major resort outside of town. But that all fell through at the end of the summer, and the developer ran back to the city with his tail between his legs. The property's now for sale."

"Why?" Patricia asked.

"No one, almost no one, knows." Eliza glanced at her husband from underneath dark lashes. Frank Clemmins and M&C Developments had packed up and left as if a posse were after them. Rumor and suspicion swept through town. Someone claimed the site was an ancient alien landing ground with a curse placed against Earthling interlopers.

The reason M&C developments had so abruptly scurried back to Vancouver had nothing to do with space ships or hostile aliens. After being involved in not one, but two, murder cases, Frank Clemmins wanted nothing more than to abandon Trafalgar permanently.

"Resort or no," Barney said. "You couldn't do much better than buying a place in the Kootenays. Heavens, you're not even from Alberta. That'll give you a leg up right there. They do hate anyone from Alberta, isn't that right, John?"

"They produce good beef in Alberta," he said. "Speaking of which, is there anything to eat?"

"We had a late lunch, so didn't worry about supper. There might be a pizza in the freezer," Eliza said, sounding not at all sure of her facts.

He finished his beer. There had to be something he could eat—a hunk of cheese, a can of soup, bread, perhaps even the remains of last week's packaged pot roast. "If you'll excuse me, I've had a hard day. Pleasure to meet you, Patricia." He fought his way out of the deep chair. "Will you be in Trafalgar for long?"

"As long as required," she said.

A strange answer. He glanced at Eliza. She moved one finely-sculpted eyebrow. He looked at Patricia. The woman's eyes were red, the fine skin underneath dark with new strain.

All he wanted was to have something to eat and go to bed. With or without his wife. Instead he sat back down and put his beer on the side table. "Patricia. May I ask your last name?"

Rob sat in the big leather armchair by the fire. He lifted his arm to wipe the blood from the cut on his lip onto his sleeve. Kathy handed him a tissue and placed the box onto the side table close to him.

"You okay?" she asked.

"They really arrested Jer?"

"Off he went to the slammer. Molly Smith grew up in this town. Everyone knows her, so she tries to act real tough, throw being a cop into your face."

"'bout time someone got tough with that jackass. Maybe a night in jail'll give him some perspective on things."

"I bet it will. Molly knows what she's doing."

He dabbed at the cut on his mouth.

Kathy took a deep breath. Okay, so last night hadn't gone exactly as she'd dreamed. But now that she was thinking about it, she realized he hadn't rejected her as she'd thought at the time. "Not now," he'd said. Not here, a sordid groping in the dark in her mother's house.

Later.

He'd said later.

She gave him what she hoped was a flirtatious smile. He looked at the floor.

Sophie clattered down the stairs. She dropped into a chair with such force the springs squeaked. "I want to go 'ome."

"So go," Kathy said. "No one's stopping you."

"*Alain* is *très* difficult. He wants to stay. To be here for Jason, his *ami.*"

"Jason's dead. Time you all got over it."

"Hey," Rob said. "That's a bit harsh, Kathy."

She backtracked quickly. Jason was dead, and she didn't have much time before Rob might decide to end his vacation and go home early. After that fight in the common room, her mother would have been well within her rights to throw them all out onto the street, without a refund. Fortunately, Ellie felt sorry for them because of the death of their friends, and was satisfied at the arrest of Jeremy, who she saw as the troublemaker. "Sorry, that was unkind. I only meant that it's bothering you all so much. I mean it should bother you, but not so…"

"Whatever," Sophie said with a shrug.

Rob said, "Christmas day Alan wanted to leave but you were set on staying. Now you've changed your minds. You're both nuts. You don't have to stay here just because Alan wants to, do you?"

She studied the nails on her right hand. "No, I do not. But Alan, well you know what 'e's like. Jealous."

"Yeah, I know. Come to think of it, didn't Alan and Ewan have a bit of a set to at the Calgary airport? Something about Ewan looking at you?"

Sophie preened. "As I said, Alan is jealous."

"As I remember, there was something about you looking back. You should tell the police about that."

She shot him a sharp look. "Don't be ridiculous. Alan told Ewan I was with 'im, and that ended it. No one *killed* Ewan, you know."

"I wonder. But if you're so unhappy here, go home."

"Alan has the ticket information."

"So stay then. Jeeze, Sophie, I don't care what the hell you do. Just stop complaining about it, will you."

Sophie pouted. It was not, Kathy decided with some satisfaction, an attractive look.

She jumped out of her chair, but, to Kathy's disappointment, didn't head upstairs to pack. Instead she crouched in front of the rack of DVDs and ran a recently manicured finger along the spines.

Rob stood up. "If you're going to watch a movie, I'm going for a walk."

"I'll get my coat," Kathy said.

"I'd rather…" Rob began, but Kathy was heading for the door.

"Pathetic," Sophie said.

Kathy had no idea what the Quebec girl was talking about.

In that strange land between sleep and awake, Smith could see Christa, bloodied and beaten as the paramedics carried her out of her house, then lying pale and bruised against hospital pillows. She could hear Christa's voice: angry and frightened, turning all her rage onto Molly, who should have protected her. She saw Charlie Bassing, leaning into the window of the police van, leering at her, spots of blood dotting the front of his T-shirt.

It was still dark when she gave up any hope of getting to sleep. The bedside clock said six o'clock. She rolled out of bed. She needed to tell Christa Charlie was back in town. But she was afraid to. It was probably too early to call John Winters. There was someone who'd be up, even on a Sunday.

When Molly Smith walked into the kitchen of her family home, her mom was sitting at the big, scarred pine table, eating yogurt topped with Saskatoon berries harvested from the woods around the house over the summer and frozen. A cup of coffee at her elbow, she was reading yesterday's paper, dressed in her tatty old rainbow-colored housecoat, her blue flannel pajama legs sticking out and slippered feet adorned with the fluffy heads of grizzly bears. The slippers had been a Christmas gift from her grandson, Ben.

Lucky gestured to the coffee pot. "Finish it off, and make more for your dad, will you, dear. He's not up yet."

Smith scratched the top of Sylvester's head. "Nice to see you, too, Mom. I'm doing fine, thanks."

Lucky lowered her drug-store reading glasses. "I saw you only yesterday and you are obviously not doing fine or you'd be home in bed. You're on afternoons this week, right?"

Smith poured the last cup of coffee and reached into the cupboard for a fresh filter. "What are you, a mind reader?" she said, pouring coffee beans into the grinder.

"Just a mother. Leave that, your dad can make it. Come and sit down." Lucky waited until her daughter was seated and sipping coffee. "What's the problem?"

"Charlie Bassing's in town."

"Oh, no." Lucky put her cup down. "I thought he was in jail."

"Out on parole. For good behavior."

"Are you sure he's back here?"

"I saw him myself." She neglected to mention that his actions toward her could have been interpreted as threatening.

"Does Christa know?"

"That's why I'm here, Mom. I'm going to have to tell her, but, frankly, I'm afraid to."

Lucky let out a long breath. "She won't take it well. Can you do something about keeping him away from her?"

Smith smiled for the first time since she'd seen the bastard in the street, mocking her. It was unlikely Lucky even noticed that she'd referred to the forces of law and order as 'you'.

"A condition of parole is that he have no contact with Christa and not come within two hundred meters of her or her place of residence or employment."

"That's good, isn't it?"

"If he abides by the parole order. But we won't know if he doesn't until he...well...doesn't."

Lucky swirled her mug and glanced into its depths. Sylvester, who loved Lucky above all, put his head onto her lap and whined.

"You couldn't order him out of town?"

"No. This is where he lives, Mom. He probably told them he had a job to come back to. I think he does some odd-job sort of work now and again, when he runs out of beer money."

"I'm not going into the store today. I'll come with you to talk to Christa."

Which was what Smith wanted to hear, although she didn't like to admit it. She was a police officer, and good officers rarely took their mother along to break bad news. But Christa wasn't just a citizen, she was Molly's friend. And probably soon to be her ex-friend.

"I don't like to ask you, but, thanks, Mom."

Lucky glanced at her watch. "Not even seven yet. Too early to call on Christa. Around nine would be best. I don't want to phone ahead and tell her I'm coming over. She'd worry about what I want to talk about.

"You might as well have some breakfast. You're looking a bit thin. When did you last eat?"

"I'm doing fine, Mom." Smith didn't say that her last meal had been yesterday's breakfast in the car. Seeing Charlie had killed her appetite for spring rolls and yellow curry.

Lucky went to the fridge. Without asking she pulled out sausages and eggs and put a frying pan onto the stove.

"Thought I heard your voice." Andy Smith came into the kitchen. He kissed the top of his daughter's head. "Early for a visit, isn't it?"

Lucky explained the situation. Andy said something about rearranging Charlie's anatomy before asking, "Is that for me?" He cast an eager eye on the cooking sausages.

Lucky cracked eggs into a bowl. "I could probably be persuaded to give you some."

"I left my car at the bottom of the driveway," Smith said. "Too much snow to try to get up. I'll give you a hand with it after we eat, Dad."

"Always happy to have help. That old snowblower's on its last legs. We'll have to get a new one for next year. I'll look for something on sale in the spring."

"You don't usually go into work on Sunday, Dad."

"It'll be busy with Boxing Day sales and Christmas returns. I remember when it *was* just Boxing Day. Now they call it Boxing Week. Next all of January will be Boxing Month."

Andy finished preparing a second pot of coffee and Lucky served them a hearty breakfast of sausages, scrambled eggs, and piles of toast with homemade raspberry jam. After they ate, Smith and her father struggled into their heaviest winter clothes and went outside. Six inches of snow had fallen in the night, and the morning sky was heavy with the threat of more to come. Andy started up his snowblower and worked on the driveway while Molly shoveled the front path and cleared a route into the woods at the back of the property for Sylvester. Not even New Year, and the snowbanks along the driveway were almost three feet tall.

Faces glowing with cold and exercise, Andy and his daughter put their equipment into the shed and walked back to the house as Sylvester ran around in circles in the cleared driveway.

"You doing okay, Molly?"

"Yeah, Dad. I'm great. Why?"

"Just wondering. Your mother misses you, you know."

She felt a warm, comfortable glow in her chest. That was Andy's way of telling her that *he* was missing her. She reached out and touched his arm as they climbed the steps and stamped their boots free of snow.

Lucky was in the kitchen, reading a political magazine. "Moonlight and I are going to drop in on Christa."

Andy shook his head. "Good luck with that." He kissed his wife, smiled at his daughter, grabbed his keys from the hook by the door and left.

Smith stood on the mat, still wearing coat and boots.

"Before we go," Lucky said. "Tell me about Lorraine."

"Lorraine who?"

"Don't be silly, dear. You know very well who. What's her involvement with these people staying at Ellie's place?"

"Mom, that's an ongoing police investigation. I can't tell you anything."

"Of course you can. I know, for example, that one of those boys didn't die in the car accident. Oh, don't look at me like that. I'm not going to tell anyone else. I am concerned about Lorraine. She refuses to let anyone help her, but she needs help nonetheless."

Smith sputtered for a while. She could only wonder at how her mom knew the results of an autopsy that hadn't been released to the public. Somehow Lucky always knew everything that went on in Trafalgar.

"She considers herself to have been in love with Jason Wyatt-Yarmouth. He probably led her to think that she was more than a vacation pick-up."

"I find it hard to believe he could have been attracted to her. He was, what twenty-two, twenty-three? A university student. Lots of money, well traveled, influential parents. Yet he took up with a sixteen-year-old girl who's never been out of these mountains, daughter of the talk of the town."

Smith shifted her feet as she remembered something she'd heard someone say about the late Jason Wyatt-Yarmouth. "He was lazy. Liked sex served up like a Big Mac. I doubt there was any need to woo Lorraine."

"Bastard." As she passed, Lucky slammed the dishwasher door so hard the dishes rattled.

Chapter Eighteen

Doctor Lee's official report was waiting in the in-basket when John Winters opened his e-mail.

He skimmed it quickly. A detailed reading would wait.

Then he leaned back in his chair and swiveled to look past Ray Lopez's desk and out the window. The clouds were weighty and the mountains obscured. *Sort of like this case,* he thought in a rare moment of fancy. A young woman strolled down the hill, wearing a purple hat topped with three drooping spikes, each of which ended in a yellow pom-pom. That, and her matching yellow mittens, gave the only bit of color outside the window, and he watched the ends of the hat bounce as the woman walked on.

Ewan Williams. His last meal had been a mixed-up concoction of salmon, curried tofu, and hamburger and fries, eaten five to six hours prior to death. No alcohol in his system. Winters made a note to ask the friends if they knew what he'd had for lunch. If it had been that strange meal, that would give them some idea of the time of his death. Provided, of course, he hadn't gone out later and had another burger. Because it was mid-winter there was very little insect activity on the body that might help Lee establish time of death. She estimated between twelve to thirty-six hours prior to the body being fished out of the car and the river. Cause of death: hypothermia. A recent blow to the head had done enough damage to cause confusion and unconsciousness, and he'd died of the cold. The report backpedaled a bit on the trace evidence found in the boy's head: bits of wood, yes, traces of ash on the wood, but not necessary indicating he'd been struck by a length of wood. He had a bruised cheekbone and scrapes on the right knuckles, but the injuries were partially healed, meaning not fresh enough to have been caused at the time of death. Almost certainly obtained, Winters thought, during the altercation outside the bar on the Saturday before he died. Lee found no more recent injuries, just the blow to the back of the head that probably brought him down, leading to his death. It was, therefore, unlikely he'd been fighting when he died.

Jason Wyatt-Yarmouth: Death by drowning. Marijuana and alcohol, although not in significant quantities, consumed some hours before death.

All of which did little to help him with the two major questions: who killed Ewan, and what was Jason doing in the hours before he went into the river, taking his friend's dead body with him?

With a reluctant sigh, he looked up a phone number, and dialed.

An answering machine picked it up.

"This is Sergeant John Winters of the Trafalgar City Police," he said, as if she wouldn't know who he was. "Returning Ms. Morgenstern's call."

The phone was picked up. "I'm here, Sergeant." Her voice was thick with sleep but she soon shook it off. "Thank you for returning my call. People are wondering why the bodies of Jason and Ewan are not being released, even though it's been almost a week since the accident, and Jason's parents are here to take him home."

By *people* Winters knew that Meredith meant *she* was wondering.

"I'm interested in speaking to anyone who saw or spoke with Ewan Williams on the evening of December twenty-third or anytime on the twenty-forth. A picture would help. Do you have one?"

"One of his friends sent me a couple."

So Meredith had been talking to the friends. No one had told him that.

"Are you confirming, Sergeant, the rumors that Ewan Williams was killed prior to the accident on Christmas morning?"

She was uncomfortably well informed about the results of the autopsy. Someone in the morgue had a big mouth. The *Gazette* had run a story the day following the accident, with a picture of the car being pulled out of the river, and a brief mention that the dead men were university students in Trafalgar on a skiing vacation. Tipped off by her contact, Meredith must have continued digging.

He tried to remind himself that digging was what good reporters did.

Too bad Meredith Morgenstern wasn't a good reporter.

"In order to complete our investigation, we would like to confirm Mr. Williams' activities during the time in question. You can run a story repeating the details of the accident and the emphasizing that the police would like the public's help."

"I don't need you to advise me on how to write a story."

"A pleasure talking to you, Ms. Morgenstern."

He hung up as she shouted 'wait'.

He'd given her the opening she needed to put what was so far only rumor and unauthorized information into print. He hoped the results would be worth it.

<><><>

Molly Smith phoned Christa as Lucky drove across the big black bridge into town. She could tell by the muffled voice that Christa had been asleep.

"Hey, Chris." Smith tried, and failed, to sound cheerful. "It's me. Mom and I are in town and Mom said she'd like to drop in for a visit."

"When?"

"How about now?"

"Now? I'm in bed."

"Then get up."

Lucky grabbed the phone and drove with one hand. "Christa, Lucky here."

"I'm still in bed, Lucky. Can you come back later?"

"We need to talk. I'm parking the car right now. If you look out, you'll see us."

"What's this about?"

"Come down and open the door." Lucky spotted a parking spot, threw the phone into Molly's lap, and did a U turn in the narrow street, forcing a pick-up truck to come to a halt. The driver leaned on the horn. Lucky completed her turn in a stately manner. The pick-up sped past as the driver lifted a finger to them.

"You do know that a U-turn is illegal, Mom? Not to mention dangerous. Suppose that guy hadn't seen you in time to stop?"

Lucky parked with the front tire on the sidewalk. "I calculated precisely how long it would take for him to see me and to bring his vehicle to a complete halt and decided I had sufficient time."

"Yeah, right. Next time, drive around the block, eh? Or I'll give you a ticket myself."

Blinking back sleep, Christa met them at the door. She grunted once in greeting and they climbed the narrow staircase to her second story apartment.

She looked good, although much of the old sparkle was gone from her eyes and she needed to regain some of the weight she'd lost in the bout of depression after the attack. She'd required a lot of dentistry, and although her relationship with her father had always been tense and they rarely saw each other, he paid for the work. The new, straighter teeth suited her.

Once they were inside the small living room, she turned to face them, her skin very pale. "Is it my dad, Lucky?" Her eyes filled. "What's happened?"

"Your father's fine. Everyone's fine. Why don't we have a seat?"

Christa turned to Smith. "Charlie?"

Smith nodded.

"How about a cup of tea?" Lucky said.

"He's out?"

"'Fraid so." Smith said.

"I thought he got six months."

"Parole. For good behavior."

"Good behavior! Are you freaking kidding me?" Christa turned, grabbed a glass candleholder off the table and moved to throw it against the wall. Lucky touched her arm. "Tea," she said, taking the object and putting it back in place. "Moonlight will explain what parole means."

Smith and Christa followed Lucky into the kitchen. It was barely large enough for the three women. There were only two chairs. Lucky set about putting the kettle on and rooting through the cupboards for mugs and spoons, tea bags and sugar.

Christa dropped into a chair. "So explain."

Smith leaned her butt up against the kitchen counter. "His parole has conditions, Chris. He's not allowed to contact you or to come within two hundred meters of you. If you see him, or if he calls you, you've got to call us…the police…right away."

"And he'll be sent back to jail?"

"Well, uh, the parole board will take it under consideration."

"By which time I'll be dead, right Molly?"

Lucky dropped a mug. It hit the cracked linoleum floor and shattered.

It was the morning of December thirtieth. Ray Lopez was still on leave, as were the two most senior constables and Staff-Sergeant Peterson. Tonight and tomorrow night there would be a full complement of officers working, but they'd be kept busy on the streets. Winters had dragged Molly Smith half-way around town yesterday, on her day off, and she was on duty tonight. She'd be sound asleep this morning. He couldn't call her up and ask for help.

He pushed back his chair. He'd have to pound the pavement himself.

At least it was a Sunday: people would be at home.

Driving through the snow-covered streets, he thought about last night. Doctor Patricia Wyatt-Yarmouth sipping mimosas in his own living room. Earlier, he'd decided to visit Jason's parents this morning to explain why he wasn't releasing their son's body.

Instead, realizing that Eliza and Barney would offer her more support than she was likely to get from her own husband, he'd carefully told Patricia about the strange circumstances of Ewan's death. She'd remained calm, although she finished her drink quickly and asked Barney for another. She asked medical questions that Winters had been unable to answer. She was an intelligent woman, a surgeon of international reputation after all, and instantly realized that the circumstances of Ewan's death, and where his body had been found, raised questions about Jason's conduct on the night in question. And, although no one mentioned it, the boys' friends and Jason's sister as well.

He offered to drive her back to her hotel, but she insisted on calling a taxi. Somehow Eliza and Barney ended up in the cab with her, and he was glad Patricia had the company.

He hadn't heard his wife climbing into bed beside him.

Aspen Street was steep and narrow and difficult to negotiate at the best of times. The day after a heavy snowfall was not the best of times. In the older parts of town many houses didn't have garages or even driveways, so cars parked on both sides of the street year round. The snowplow had been unable to do much other than scrape off the middle of the road. Parking was haphazard; cars scattered across snow packed into ice. Several vehicles hadn't been moved in days and resembled car-shaped snow sculptures.

The neighborhood was an eclectic mix of modern structures of brick and glass and wood, heritage houses restored to early twentieth-century glory, and heritage houses that couldn't remember their glory days, if ever they'd had such a time.

The LeBlanc home was one of the worst. The neighbors on the left had erected a tall fence: stiff, varnished wooden planks standing like soldiers protecting their owner from sight of the run-down property.

But Winters wasn't here to call on the LeBlanc family.

He went up and down the street, knocking on doors, considering himself lucky to find most people at home. At each house he asked if anyone had noticed a yellow SUV on the street on Christmas Eve. Fortunately that was an easy day for most people to remember.

Unfortunately no one had noticed much of anything. A few of the neighbors gave him their uncensored opinion of the LeBlanc family. He thanked them and moved on.

He was heading back to the van, dreaming of a mug of Eddie's strongest coffee, when a blue Toyota stopped in the middle of the road. The woman behind the wheel rolled down the window and gestured to him. He'd spoken to her at the first house he'd called upon, but she had nothing to tell him.

He crossed the street.

"I've picked up my mom from Church," she said. "I mentioned you'd been asking about Christmas Eve and she said she might have something to tell you."

A fragile, white-haired lady smiled at him from the passenger seat.

"Follow me," the driver said.

He did so.

He was invited in for tea. Outside, the house was warm wood and glass. The inside was modern and sparse, painted neutral colors with lots of mirrors and pale hardwood floors topped by what real estate agents called cathedral ceilings.

He was led into a small room overlooking the street, crammed with heavy, dark, old-fashioned furniture. Black-and-white and faded color photographs sat on round white doilies, covering every surface. The last time he'd been in air this warm, he'd been in a sauna.

Winters was offered tea, which he accepted only because he suspected that the elderly lady liked a cup after church.

The daughter left to get the tea, and the older woman, introduced to him as Mrs. Frances James, sat on a stiff-backed, wooden-armed chair covered in brown and orange print. She placed her large black patent leather handbag on the floor beside her. Feeling like the Detective Inspector in a mystery novel of the classic age, Winters leaned against the fireplace—electric, unlike those of the classic novels.

"I do wish Ruth would at least allow the children to accompany me to mass on occasion," Mrs. James said. "But she sees fit not to. Except for Christmas Eve and Easter Sunday.

"Speaking of which, when Ruth picked me up at Church she mentioned you were asking about events on this street on Christmas Eve." Mrs. James waved her left hand. The diamond on her third finger wasn't much smaller than the Koh-I-Noor.

"That's right. I..."

"When my husband died, my daughter and her husband were kind enough to invite me to come and live with their family here in your lovely town." Mrs. James' thin lips were outlined in deep red lipstick and pinched in disapproval. Winters guessed that she wasn't all that happy living at her daughters' invitation, but she'd die before admitting it. "I accepted, realizing they need help with the children. It is difficult these days, what with families requiring *two* incomes." If Mrs. James hadn't been such a lady, she would have spat on the floor. "It was understood from the beginning I'd need my private space." Another twist of the lips. "They arranged this room for my use. Isn't it lovely?"

It wasn't lovely at all, at least not to John Winters' eyes. But it did sit at the front of the house, with a big bay window and a clear view of Aspen Street. And the LeBlanc home. Which was all that mattered.

The door opened and a tea tray came in, followed by Mrs. James' daughter. She placed the tray on a glass-topped wooden table with ornate legs. "Thank you, dear," Mrs. James said. "It's rather cool in here. Turn on the fire, will you."

"Sure, Mom." Ruth grimaced at Winters, but she flicked the switch to start the electric fire.

He took a seat by the window.

Mrs. James poured the tea. "Sugar?"

"Please."

She placed two slices of shortbread on the saucer and handed the cup to her daughter. Ruth gave it to Winters.

"This is my mom's sitting room," Ruth said. "She spends a good part of her day in here. She might have seen something on Christmas Eve, right, Mom?"

Mrs. James touched her cup to her lips. Winters nibbled at a cookie and repressed a sigh. Mrs. James, he thought, only wanted to be entertained.

But she surprised him. "I must confess to an officer of the law that I find the goings on across the street to be as entertaining as the television, if not more so. However, I won't go on too much. You're interested in Christmas Eve and the day before, Ruth tells me."

"Yes ma'am."

"My name is Frances. In my youth people called me Franny. Not at all dignified, was it? Never mind. Back to Aspen Street. I don't sleep at all well these days. Old bones can't quite settle. I often get out of bed and sit here where I can look out on the street and read for a while." Two books were on the table beside her chair. The one on top had a picture of a statue of Beethoven on the cover. *Cemetery of the Nameless*, it was called. *Nice title.*

"It was the night before Christmas Eve. Christmas Eve Eve the children call it. They were getting most excited. Supper was long over. The children had gone to bed. I'd watched a movie with Ruth and Joe and came in here to read before turning in. When I sat down, I happened to glance out onto the street. Ruth said you've been asking about a yellow vehicle, what I believe you call an SUV. I saw one parked outside number 484. Two men came out of the house. I can tell you, Mr. Winters, they were in a most dreadful state of agitation. Yelling and waving their arms and generally carrying on. As I watched, one of them struck the other." Her pale blue eyes shifted and she looked at Winters to judge his reaction.

He kept his face impassive. Hard to tell, sometimes, if a witness was telling you what they saw or what they thought you wanted them to have seen. Or even what they thought would make them sound the most important.

"Can you describe the men?" he asked.

She shrugged thin shoulders. "One of them was the boy who's been living there the past few weeks." Gary. "The other was tall, dark haired, quite nice looking."

"Come on, Mom, you couldn't see his features from here."

Mrs. James huffed. "I am an excellent observer. You'll note, Sergeant, that despite my daughter's sarcasm, I have not mentioned the color of his eyes, or that he had a dueling scar running down his left cheek. I am merely reporting what I observed. The street light is located at the end of their path, remember. You," she glared at her daughter, "can believe what you will. Or not.

"They punched at each other, but I suspect they had some trouble keeping their footing in the snow. They never shovel the walk over there, you know. It's quite a hazard. I've a mind to call the city about that."

"The fight, Mom. You saw a fight."

"Yes, I did. She was there, that girl who lives there."

"Lorraine?" Winters asked.

"I've no idea as to what her name might be. In my day she'd have been driven out of town, but these days we look past her behavior to the life the poor girl's had to live. Well, most of us do." Mrs. James sniffed toward her daughter.

"If you're referring to the time we…"

"What happened with the fight?" Winters interrupted.

"They pushed and shoved at each other. The girl stood on the stoop yelling at them. And that was about it. The tall one, the one I didn't recognize, pushed the other man into a snowbank and got into his car. The girl joined him, and they drove away, leaving the man sitting in the snow." Mrs. James threw back her head and laughed, showing teeth yellow and misshapen. "He did look rather comical trying to stand up.

"More tea, Sergeant?"

"Tea? No, uh, no thank you."

Mrs. James talked for a bit longer, but she had nothing more to report about the fight she'd witnessed on Christmas Eve Eve.

So Gary and Jason had a fight on the steps of the LeBlanc home the night Ewan disappeared. Presumably the fight had been over Lorraine. And Lorraine had then left with Jason.

Winters snatched another piece of the excellent shortbread and finished his tea before saying good-bye and thanking Mrs. James for her help. He left his card on the table beside the chair overlooking the street. He considered signing the old lady up as a police informer, but decided that the daughter might have some objections.

He was in the van, turning the key in the ignition when the thought struck him.

A tall, dark man had fought with Gary LeBlanc, while Lorraine (and Mrs. James) watched. He'd assumed the man had been Jason. Jason who was involved, apparently, with Lorraine.

A white man, tall, dark, brown hair. A yellow SUV.

The description suited Jason.

It didn't fit Ewan, who was a good bit shorter, and slimmer, than his friend. Mrs. James wasn't much taller than a garden gnome; to her almost everyone must look tall.

Other than being white, young, short haired, and physically fit, the two men didn't look much alike.

Did the similarities count for more than the differences?

Could Ewan have been killed in mistake for Jason?

And did Jason, realizing that, panic?

Chapter Nineteen

Wendy Wyatt-Yarmouth was still staying at the Glacier Chalet Bed and Breakfast. When she'd phoned her parents' hotel looking for a room, the receptionist had almost laughed out loud. As Mrs. Carmine hadn't pushed her bill under her door, she decided to stay put.

She'd listened at the top of the stairs, checking that all was quiet, and peeked over the railing into the common room to ensure it was empty. She snuck out of the house and walked into town to meet her parents at George's for breakfast.

It had not been a pleasant meal. Her mother obviously wanted to talk but her father kept shushing her as he threw dirty looks at passing waiters and the occupants of nearby tables as if they were all here only to listen in on the family's troubles.

They left half-finished plates and no tip and went out to the street. Wendy wrapped her scarf around her neck. Her mother touched the wool. "Is this new, Wendy?"

"Nice, eh?"

"I saw one almost exactly like it in the craft store yesterday. Handmade. It was lovely, but very expensive."

Wendy lied. "Got it at a second hand place on Queen West."

"Never mind the goddamned scarf," Doctor Wyatt-Yarmouth Number One snapped. "I want to know what the hell we're going to do now."

"We can do nothing," Doctor Wyatt-Yarmouth Number Two replied, as she took Wendy's arm and began to walk. Her husband followed. "The news isn't good, honey," she had said.

The front door closed behind her. Wendy stood to one side and peered through the etched glass. Her parents were heading back to town. They walked together, but so far apart that her father was almost stepping into the road and her mother had one foot in the snowbanks. Wendy twisted her hands.

She'd managed to stay calm while her mother told her that the police had doubts about Ewan's and Jason's deaths. Doubts, Wendy'd asked, how can they have doubts? They're dead.

Patricia explained what she'd learned from Sergeant Winters while Jack puffed and fumed.

Wendy listened quietly and told her parents that she'd be perfectly fine and planned on joining the others at the ski hill later. Her parents had walked her back to the B&B.

From behind the front door, she watched them round the corner, turning left, toward their hotel. Wendy left the B&B and marched down the street. She went right, into town. When she'd bought the red and gold scarf at the craft gallery she'd seen a fabulous necklace of beaten gold set with stones so blue you could imagine swimming in them. It would be perfect for a blue summer dress.

She couldn't afford the necklace, but right now she deserved a dose of retail therapy.

Murdered. The police thought Ewan had been murdered.

Lucky Smith drove Moonlight to her apartment.

They didn't say much.

A snow plow was coming down the alley, and Lucky pulled over to the side of the street.

Moonlight didn't get out. Lucky reached over and patted her hand.

"That didn't go well," Moonlight said.

"Christa's got a right to be worried."

"I don't see Charlie coming after her. He has to know what'll happen if he breaches his parole order. And, even more, what'll happen if he…well, if he attacks her again."

"Unfortunately these men with their obsessions and their power complexes don't always see reason, Moonlight. Is there anything you can do? I mean the police?"

"Probably. This is a small town. A disadvantage when it comes to keeping Charlie away from Christa but an advantage when it comes to keeping an eye on him. I'll give John Winters a call and mention it. This is important to him, Mom. He's the one who found her, after all. Catch you later."

Moonlight got out of the car and slammed the door. She crossed the street, and gave her mother a wave as she ducked into the alley that led to the back of Alphonse's Bakery. It was snowing again; fat flakes fell onto Moonlight's golden head.

Children. You never do stop worrying about them. And even about those that aren't yours.

Lucky drove up hill to Aspen Street.

Moonlight would not be at all pleased to know her mother was planning to make a call on Lorraine LeBlanc. But Lucky knew Lorraine from the years when the girl had hung out at the youth center where Lucky volunteered. Lorraine hadn't been seen at the center for years, but as far as Lucky was concerned, that was an irrelevant detail.

Parking was difficult on Aspen Street, but making one of her famous U-turns, she found a spot outside a concrete and glass monstrosity that was the very definition of gentrification.

She locked the car and marched down the sidewalk.

The walk had not been cleared so Lucky made her own path by stepping in half-covered footprints.

She pressed the doorbell. She didn't hear anything in response. It was ten o'clock. An unlikely time to find a sixteen-year-old girl awake. Too bad. She was here now.

She looked around. The paint on the door frame was peeling, a section of window set into the door covered with plywood, the cement steps cracked and broken. It was possible the doorbell didn't work. She knocked on the door. That got a response: inside the house a dog barked and something moved. She'd raised her hand to knock again when the door opened. Lorraine was nicely dressed in a long blue sweater over jeans. Gold hoops were through her ears and a gold necklace shone at her throat. She had her hand on the collar of a big mutt. The dog strained at the restraint, but it didn't bark again.

"Yes?"

"Lorraine, I'm glad to find you at home. I was pleased to hear Gary's back in Trafalgar. Hearing about Gary naturally led me to think about you and I thought I'd drop in and see how things are going." Lucky smiled. She never had any qualms about butting in where she might not be wanted. As far as Lucky Smith was concerned, if she wasn't welcome, she soon would be. And if not, there was obviously something wrong and she needed to find out what.

"That's nice of you, Mrs. Smith."

"I'm sorry I haven't been in touch before this," Lucky said. "But we do get busy with our own lives don't we? Tea would be nice."

"Tea?"

"That's if you have time, of course. I wouldn't want to stop you if you're going out." Reverse psychology. Worked every time.

As it did this time.

Lorraine stepped back, releasing the dog. "Sure, I can make tea. Come on in, Mrs. Smith."

Lucky held out her hand to the dog and let it have a good long sniff, knowing that her clothes must be full of the smell of Sylvester. When the dog seemed satisfied, she stepped over the threshold. The house was shabby and desperately in need of paint and a hammer and nails. But it was reasonably clean. She followed Lorraine into the kitchen. The dog followed Lucky.

The dishwasher door was open and the sink was full of white foam from which the handle of a frying pan stuck out.

"I was putting away the dishes," Lorraine said. "Gary says the dishwasher has to be turned on every night before I go to bed whether it's full or not. It's a bother, but it makes Gary happy so I do it."

The dog crouched in front of its water bowl and drank with enthusiasm. Contented, it lifted its head and yawned. Water and drool dripped from the big jaws.

"Never mind him, Mrs. Smith. Rex isn't nearly as tough as he looks."

"I guessed that already. He obviously can smell my dog, Sylvester, and thus knows I'm a dog friend."

Lorraine opened and closed cupboard doors before saying, "I don't think we have any tea, Mrs. Smith, sorry."

"Not a problem. I had coffee with my daughter earlier. You know my daughter?"

Lorraine leaned against the counter and studied the floor. It wasn't so clean you might want to eat off it, but neither was it providing a breeding ground for toxic mould. "Constable Smith, right?"

"Yes." Uninvited, Lucky took a seat at the kitchen table. "Word around town is that your parents left once Gary came back. If you'd like some support, Lorraine, I'd like to give it."

"No thanks." Lorraine watched the dog make circles on the floor before finding a spot to settle. "I'm good."

"Glad to hear it. My daughter tells me you've made friends with some young people here for a skiing vacation."

Lorraine lifted her eyes. They were very wet. "That's right. I'm sure she told you what happened to...to...my...to Jason." She dropped into a chair and her shoulders shook and the tears began to fall.

Lucky stretched her arm across the small table. She rubbed the back of Lorraine's hand with hers until the sobs subsided.

"No one cares. No one. Jason loved me, he really loved me. That rich bitch of a sister of his sticks her nose in the air as if I've brought in a bad smell, and his father has me thrown out of a restaurant, and his friends laugh when they pass me in the street. He loved me, but no one understands. He was sharing a house near the university, and I couldn't move in there, so he was going to move out of the house and get us an apartment. It would be easy for me to find a job and I'd support us while he finished med school."

Lucky's heart almost cracked in two. Better for Lorraine to think that after Jason's death his cold-hearted family shunned her than to be abandoned in Trafalgar, waiting for word as days turned into weeks, and weeks into months. Which would have happened had Jason lived and gone back to Toronto, laughing all the way at how easy it had been to capture the heart, and the body, of a small-town girl. Whenever he bothered to think of her.

"Forget his family," she said. "Let them take Jason home. Only you know they're not taking the truth of his life with him." *Wasn't that a mouthful of trash?*

"You're right, Mrs. Smith. His family would have fought us all the way, wouldn't they, once Jason and I were properly engaged. I was afraid they'd disinherit him, but Jason said not to worry because he had an inheritance from an aunt that would be enough to at least get us settled into our own apartment. And then I could work and he'd stop taking vacations and finish his studies as fast as possible."

Lorraine pulled a tissue, heavily worn with use, out of her pocket and blew her nose. Lucky fished in her bag and found a small package. She pushed it across the table. Lorraine took one and held it to her eyes. "Jason's friends are bad enough, but that Wendy, she's the worst. I know about her. Things Jason told me. She can't afford all the stuff she wants, but she keeps buying them anyway. His dad used to pay her bills, but her mom told him she had to start standing on her own. Once Jason graduated and became a doctor, I'd be able to have nice stuff too, like Wendy has." She touched the gold hoop in her right ear.

"Never mind that, Lorraine. Stuff isn't worth all that much, you know."

"Yeah, right. Tell it to people like Alan and Sophie and Jeremy. The only nice one of all of them is Rob. Have you met Rob?"

"Yes, I have."

"I like Rob. Kathy Carmine's got the hots for him. It's positively pathetic."

Not for the first time, Lucky wondered at the human capacity for self-deception.

"I wasn't sorry to hear Ewan died, Mrs. Smith." The tears had stopped and Lorraine shredded the tissue in her fingers. "Only that he'd taken Jason with him." She gave Lucky a knowing look. "Ewan wasn't a nice man. He had a real problem with women, you know. I'd say he hated them and used them for sex in the same way you use a tissue to blow your nose. Something you throw away after." She tossed her own tissue toward the garbage can in the corner. She missed and the dog picked it up.

Young as she was, Lorraine had learned a thing or two in the back alleys.

"Ewan wasn't like Jason. Jason was a one-woman man. Isn't that a great saying, Mrs. Smith? Once Jason found me, he didn't want anyone else. He and Ewan had been best friends since grade school. Jason didn't like the man Ewan had grown up to be, but what could he do? They were best friends forever, right?"

Lucky swallowed a gag.

"Ewan didn't care about women or their feelings. Why he even went after his friends' girlfriends. Alan and Ewan almost got into a fight over Sophie before they even got to Trafalgar. Some friends, eh?"

Lorraine stopped talking. She rubbed at her face, as if trying to scrub away the memories. She looked at Lucky. "Despite it all, no matter how much Jason disliked the things Ewan did, they were best friends forever. And they stayed best friends as they marched into the face of death. I'd like to find a friend like that. Wouldn't you, Mrs. Smith?"

The romanticism of the very young. Still alive in Lorraine, despite all that the girl had been through. Or perhaps stronger because of it.

Lucky got to her feet. "If you need to talk, Lorraine, any time, please call me." Lucky dug into her bag for her card with her name and contact information at the store. She found a pen and wrote her home number on the back. She pressed the card into Lorraine's hand.

John Winters needed to speak to Gary LeBlanc. According to Mrs. James, Jason had been at the LeBlanc house the night before Christmas Eve, where he and Gary had argued. Presumably Gary had found Jason with his sister and thrown the young man out. According to Lorraine, Jason had been at her home around dinnertime the following day, Christmas Eve. Gary said he hadn't been there. Jason left around nine, telling Lorraine he was going back to the B&B to join his friends, and saying he'd call her when it was time for her to come over.

Had Gary arrived home as Jason was leaving and been angry at him for being in the house after having been thrown out the day before? If so, that might go a long way toward explaining the situation if it had been Jason who'd been killed that night. But it hadn't. Jason had been alive several hours later when his car went into the river. It had been his friend Ewan who'd already been dead.

What had Jason Wyatt-Yarmouth done between leaving the house on Aspen Street and failing to make the turn on Elm Street?

Was it possible Gary had followed the yellow SUV and later mistaken Ewan for Jason and killed him without looking into the boy's face? Ewan had suffered a blow to the back of the skull. No, the timing of that was off—Ewan had, according to Doctor Lee, died before Christmas Eve night.

But that scenario could have happened the previous night.

He needed to have another chat with Gary LeBlanc.

He'd tried the LeBlanc house after leaving Mrs. James, but no one came to the door and there hadn't been a car in the driveway. When he'd visited yesterday with Molly, Gary had been in the house, but there'd been no sign of a vehicle. If Gary was just out of jail he might not have a license or a car. Winters punched a search into the van's computer as he drove toward town. He then called Jim Denton on the dispatch desk and requested that officers keep an eye on 484 Aspen Street and let him know if they saw Gary.

Back in his office, he checked the computer. He needed to find someone, anyone, who'd seen Ewan Williams after he left his friends around 5:30 on Sunday—Christmas Eve Eve, Mrs. James' grandchildren called it. Nothing. Zip. Nada. Ewan had met a girl on the ski hill that day, no one his friends recognized, and ate lunch with her. He'd driven back to town in the yellow SUV with everyone and had gone out, almost immediately. His friends assumed he'd gone to meet the girl. Winters had absolutely no idea of who the ski-girl was. The newspaper story he'd planted with Meredith wouldn't be out at least until tomorrow, and with Monday being New Year's Eve, anyone who could tell him anything might not even read the paper.

An idea came to him. He turned to his computer, looked up a number and picked up the phone.

Chapter Twenty

Molly Smith hadn't liked the gleam in her mother's eyes when Lucky dropped her off. But as she couldn't decipher the gleam, and probably didn't want to, she let it go.

She climbed the stairs to her apartment and let herself in. She'd only been gone for a few hours, but the place seemed cold and empty. When ski season was over and she got some time perhaps she'd start looking for a way to personalize this place.

She sliced a bagel and popped it into the toaster. While it browned, she went to the front window. The street was quiet, the ski tourists all out for the day. She curled up in the single armchair in her living room.

A very angry bee was trying very hard to get out of a glass bottle.

Smith blinked. Not a bee, but her phone.

She fumbled in her pocket and dragged it out.

"Sleeping, Molly?" Sergeant Winters.

Oh, no. She'd fallen asleep and missed showing up for her shift. In a panic she pulled at her sleeve and checked her watch. One o'clock: she wasn't due in until three.

"Just resting. What's up?"

"I know you're on afternoons, but I need you to do something for me earlier. I've run it past the acting Sergeant and he agrees with the overtime. Before you come in for your shift, go up to Blue Sky. Wear your uniform, this is official."

Heads turned as Molly Smith walked into the main lounge of the Blue Sky Ski Resort. Too bad, she thought, it was not because of her style or her beauty but because she was dressed in full uniform. As out of place in this room packed with skiers as if she'd been wearing a sarong and had a hibiscus tucked behind one ear.

She tried not to grin with embarrassment and made her way to the security office.

"Hey, Constable Molly. What's up? You look quite formal."

"I'm here on business, Fred."

The Chief of Security's face darkened. "Trouble?"

"Long over. I need to ask your people about something that happened a week ago. I'm not a detective, but I guess they sent me 'cause I'm known around here. Can I talk to the staff? It's the lodge staff I'm most interested in, not the people outside."

"Sure, Molly. Whatever you need. Want to start with me?"

She pulled Ewan Williams' picture out of her pocket and handed it across the desk. "This guy was here several times before Christmas. I'm particularly interested in December twenty-third. That was a Sunday. I'm looking for a woman he had lunch with. She's dark haired, early twenties, attractive, quite short. She was wearing a white ski suit. That's all I know."

Fred Stockdale leaned back in his chair. He caressed his beer-belly with one hand, reminding Smith of a pregnant woman in deep contemplation, while the other held the photograph. "Means nothing to me," he said at last. "We get so many of these types in here every day, they're all a blur to me." He stood up and gave back the picture. "Let's go talk to the staff. If you're lucky someone will remember serving him. A girl might; he's a good looking guy."

She was lucky. The lunch rush was over and the kitchen staff had time to give the picture a good look. "Oh, yes," the young woman who tossed salads said with a happy sigh. "I remember him, all right. Such a doll. With a smile that would melt my grandmother's frozen heart. And she's been dead for ten years." The two women angling to get a look at the picture laughed.

"Not local," one of the boys said, in a tone that explained it all. "Tourist." He wiped his hands on his once-white apron. "What's he done?"

Reports of Ewan and Jason's deaths had been in the local paper, but no pictures of the dead men.

Smith told the serving line staff she needed to find the woman he might have had lunch with one day. They looked at each other. "I remember him," the salad girl said, "'cause he wasn't the only cute one. His friend was quite the dish as well. But I didn't see him with a girl."

"I did," another woman said. She was a good bit older than the others, almost as round as she was tall with hair more gray than blond. Her apron was streaked with grease. "There was this girl from Quebec. She gave me lip because she didn't think the fries had been cooked long enough. Take it or leave it, I said. The lineup was almost to the door and here she was telling me to prepare her fries just so. He," she gestured to the photograph of Ewan, "told her to go back to Quebec if she wasn't happy with B.C. cuisine. She left her tray right there on the counter and stormed off in a huff. She acted like a bitch, but he wasn't any better, I thought. He'd really goaded her."

The salad woman said, "One day, I can't remember exactly when, he bought a ton of food. We'd just started setting up for lunch and were busy with prep, so I didn't have time to watch what he did with it. Looked like he was feeding an army."

All of which was of no help. There was no doubt Ewan and his friends had spent time at the Blue Sky resort. The group made an impression everywhere they went. Not always for the good.

Unfortunately the serving staff couldn't remember Ewan eating lunch with anyone in particular.

Stockdale accompanied her into the kitchen. Pots boiled and frying pans sizzled. She remembered the salmon burger she'd never had the chance to eat the last time she'd been here. The kitchen staff obediently looked at her picture, but no one recognized Ewan. Not a surprise—he would have been unlikely to venture into the kitchen.

"Lift operators?" Stockdale asked.

"I guess." She wasn't optimistic. All day long, the lift operators saw nothing but the shape of bodies and if they did look at faces, they were likely to see nothing much more than goggles and helmets.

But she asked anyway, and got the answers she expected.

"The glamorous life of a detective," Stockdale said as they walked back to the lodge.

"Let's check ski patrol before I give up," she said. "Someone might have been having lunch at the time in question and seen something."

Stockdale's radio squawked. "Be right there," he said. He turned to Molly. "Someone's remembered something."

The woman who cooked the fries met them as they came through the doors. A young woman in slim white jeans and a white sweater with the Blue Sky logo over the right pocket stood beside her. She was much shorter than Molly and as thin as a ski pole. Her long hair, black highlighted with streaks of copper, swung in a ponytail that reached halfway down her back. Her skin was golden, with high flat cheekbones, and she was exceptionally pretty.

"Show the picture to Marilyn," the woman said.

Smith held it out and the girl took it.

"That's him," she said, almost immediately. "Positive."

"Marilyn's my daughter," the woman explained. "She's a cashier. She was on her break when you came by. I told her about the guy you're looking for and she asked to have a look. Right, dear?"

"I can talk, you know, Mom," Marilyn said.

"You remember seeing this man?" Smith asked.

"Yes, I do." Marilyn glanced at her mother out of the corner of her eyes.

Smith said, "Thank you very much, Mrs...."

"Monroe. I'm Janice Monroe."

That would make her daughter's name…Marilyn Monroe? Marilyn read Smith's face. She was probably used to the expression. "I'm Marilyn Chow. When my parents divorced my mother went back to her maiden name. I chose not to change."

No need to wonder why.

"Thank you for your help, Ms. Monroe. I don't want to keep you any longer," Smith said. A small lineup was forming at the serving counter. Although no one seemed in much of a hurry to be served: they were all watching the police officer question the women.

"You can go back to work now, Janice." Stockdale said, not as politely as Smith had done.

Janice Monroe tilted her chin and returned to her station. Marilyn sighed audibly.

"I'm not actually looking for this man," Smith said. "He… uh…isn't missing. But we would like to speak to a woman he met here, at the resort, on December twenty-third. She was dressed in a white ski suit. They had lunch together. If you can give me any information about the woman, I'd appreciate it."

"Why?" she said. Her dark eyes studied Smith.

"As part of an ongoing police investigation."

"Which doesn't answer my question, but never mind." Marilyn took a step backward and held out her arms. "Not exactly ski clothes. But this might be white enough for you. I had lunch with the guy in the photo that day."

A man was leaning off the edge of his chair, so obviously trying to hear better he was about to drop onto the floor. Smith glanced at Stockdale.

"My office," he said. "Let's go."

Marilyn Chow had met Ewan Williams on December twenty-second when he paid for his lunch. He'd smiled and flirted and she hissed at him that he'd get her fired if he didn't move on. He paid twenty dollars too much for his food. She put the money in the tip jar to share with the rest of the staff.

He took a table close to the checkouts and watched her as he ate his lunch. Meal finished he bought a coffee. Coffee drunk, he went for a slice of blueberry pie. His friends had stopped at his table, and asked why he wasn't sitting with them. 'Because I've found the spot that has the perfect view' he'd said, with one eye on Marilyn. His friends had gone off shaking their heads.

Time came for her break and she'd left her checkout. He stood up as she passed his table. "I'm in a relationship," she said, and ran for the stairs.

He didn't follow.

The next morning he was in the breakfast line. As he paid for his coffee he pulled a fresh red rose out of the inside pocket of his jacket. "What time do you take lunch?" he asked.

Marilyn was in a relationship, but it was getting wobbly. "Eleven," she'd said. "Before the rush."

"I'll reserve a table."

At ten to eleven he walked into the lodge. He gathered up his friends' backpacks and placed them across the seats at a long table in an alcove toward the back, thus reserving the entire area.

He slipped up behind her, as she accepted the money for two hot chocolates, and whispered, "Anything you don't eat, Madame?"

Charmed, she'd laughed. "I eat anything and everything."

He soon was back to pay, pushing two trays along the line. Salmon burger with side salad, spinach salad, sweet potato soup, hamburger and fries, curried chicken and rice, Thai noodle salad, scrambled tofu.

"Anything and everything," he said as she racked up the bill.

Yes, yes. All terribly charming. Smith steered the conversation to the evening in question.

"He didn't show," Marilyn said.

"You were going to meet where?"

"Six o'clock at the Bishop and Nun in Trafalgar. I waited for an hour and left. I don't hang around in bars waiting for men who can't be bothered to show up."

Smith would bet a year's pay that Marilyn was not accustomed to being stood up.

Marilyn had taken the visitor's chair in Stockdale's office. The security chief sat behind his own desk. Molly Smith leaned against the wall. Marilyn was so tiny, so incredibly lovely, that she made Smith, in her heavy boots, uniform and gunbelt, feel like Godzilla.

"And that was the end of that." The girl shrugged. "I gave him my number. He never called."

"You don't seem too upset," Stockdale said.

"His loss."

Molly Smith wondered what it must be like to have that much confidence in yourself. "Did you see him again? Or hear from him?"

"Nope. Look, I figured I'd go out with him that night, check him out, right? What the hell, he was good looking, sure knew how to lay it on, and seemed to be rolling in dough. My boyfriend and I were having problems. I agreed to meet Ewan in town after I got off work. It didn't exactly break my heart when he didn't show. Tell you the truth, Constable Smith, I went home and phoned my boyfriend. We had a long talk and I think that when he gets back after the holidays we'll be okay."

Marilyn fidgeted in her chair. "I need to go back to work now. It's not fair to May for her to be the only one on cash."

"We're done here. Thank you for your time."

Marilyn stood up. "I've seen you before, Constable Smith, skiing. Here's a tip: try the Shanghai noodle bowl. It is to die for."

Smith grinned, liking this young woman very much. "Are you trying to bribe an officer, Ms. Chow?"

"Guaranteed."

Marilyn put her hand on the door.

She turned around. "Hey, I never asked. Why all the questions? I'm guessing Ewan was up to some trouble that night. What happened to him anyway?"

Chapter Twenty-one

Wendy Wyatt-Yarmouth opened her eyes. She'd fallen asleep, fully dressed, draped across the bed. The weak winter sun was slanting through her window, the angle low. She must have slept for hours.

She pushed herself off the bed and went into the tiny bathroom. She stared at herself in the mirror. Hair standing on end, dark circles under her eyes. The necklace she'd bought this morning was draped around her throat. She lifted a hand and fingered it. So beautiful. Blue stones set into silver.

And it hadn't been all that expensive. Hundred and fifty dollars for a piece of handmade jewelry. You'd pay twice that in Toronto, maybe more.

She'd hesitated at the matching earrings, not sure if her credit card could stretch for another fifty bucks.

Wendy eyed her reflection in the mirror. The blue stones did look great against her white throat, and would look even better with the earrings. What was the worst that could happen? Her card would be rejected: she'd act indignant and huff and puff and vow to sort it out. And leave.

Not a problem.

If Doctor Wyatt-Yarmouth Number Two got wind of how much Wendy's credit card was carrying, she'd have a fit, but what did it matter. Jason was dead. Which proved what they said: life was short. Live fast; die young. And then her parents could take care of her bills.

Wendy grabbed her leather coat and left the room. She didn't bother to lock the door behind her. Her suspicions at the room having been broken into were largely forgotten. Besides, what did it matter? She'd tossed her underwear, including the lavender bits, into a trash bin on the street corner and bought more. Who would have thought that in a town the size of Trafalgar one could find an exclusive lingerie shop?

Before selecting what she'd come for, the blue and silver earrings, Wendy wandered through the gallery again. The large spacious room was full of soft winter light, the floor a warm blond wood, the walls aging brick. Items on display, glass and wood, copper and iron, paint on canvas and paper, were arranged with care and without clutter, allowing the beauty of the gallery itself to draw shoppers in. The woman behind the desk wore a hand-painted scarf around her neck and large gold hoops in her ears. She smiled warmly at Wendy in recognition but, with discretion rarely found in sales staff these days, hadn't rushed forward to ask Wendy what she was looking for.

She was studying the prints on the walls when the bell over the front door tinkled. It was that dreadful Lorraine thing. The one who actually thought Jason cared for her. How pitiable was that. The last thing Wendy wanted was to have to speak to the creature. She ducked behind a rack of postcards.

Lorraine drifted through the shop with that slightly crooked gait she had. The buttons on her big black coat were undone and the coat flopped behind her as she walked. Her scarf hung limply around her neck and her boots dripped on the wide-plank floors. She pulled her gloves off and stuffed them into a pocket.

Wendy saw the sales clerk rise to her feet, watching the new customer. Her eyes narrowed and her lips pinched together and the official smile disappeared.

Lorraine lingered over a group of glass balls hanging from hooks in the ceiling. Light shone onto them and the balls shot sparks of color as if from the wand of a magician. She ran her fingers across the surface of one of the balls. Her nails were plain, chewed to the quick.

The sales clerk rounded the desk watching as Lorraine touched the precious things. "Can I help you with something?" she said. Her voice was not welcoming.

Lorraine didn't turn around. "No thanks, just browsing."

"Let me know if you need anything."

Lorraine made her way toward the jewelry display. Another couple of steps and she'd see Wendy hiding behind the wall.

The phone rang. The clerk picked it up, her eyes still on Lorraine. "Good afternoon. This is the Trafalgar Craft Gallery." Her salesperson's voice, as chirpy as a cricket, was turned back on.

"I told you not to call here if it isn't important." The clerk's eyes met Wendy's and she turned to face the wall. "Tell him I said no. Isn't your father home yet?"

Lorraine reached the jewelry display. Eyes on the clerk, whose voice was starting to rise, Lorraine grabbed a gold bracelet. It disappeared into the depths of her coat.

The clerk dropped the phone, letting it swing in the air from the cord, and whirled around. "Hey," she shouted. "I saw that."

"You saw nothing," Lorraine said, jumping back. "You think your store's too good for the likes of me."

"Put that back, right now, or I'm calling the police." The woman gathered the phone, and hung up on the person yelling at her from the other end. A large gilt-framed mirror behind the cash register showed Wendy most of the back end of the shop. Obviously, it was not just there for display.

Lorraine headed across the floor. "Nothing to put back. Screw you, you stuck up old Nazi."

Wendy ran out from the alcove, through the gallery, and jumped in front of Lorraine as the girl reached for the door. "I saw her take it," Wendy shouted to the sales clerk. "It's in her coat."

Lorraine's eyes widened as she recognized Wendy. "You bitch."

"Thought you were good enough for my brother did you?" She pitched her voice too low for the sales clerk to hear. "I wonder what he'd think now."

Lorraine dug into her pocket, and pulled out the bracelet. It wasn't even a particularly good one, just a thin bit of ten-carat gold. She threw it on the floor. "Here, you can have it."

"I've called the police," the clerk said.

"Too late to give it back then," Wendy said, feeling quite smug.

◇◇◇

Molly Smith was also feeling pleased with herself. As ordered, she'd found the woman Ewan Williams met at the ski resort, and the woman had a lot to tell them about Williams' activities the day he died.

Perhaps she'd make a detective yet.

She backed the patrol car into its bay and went into the station. She scratched the back of her arm and said hello to Jim Denton, huddling over his computers and consoles.

"What's up?"

"Shoplifter nabbed in the act. They're bringing her in."

"I'll see if they need a hand."

She went back downstairs. The patrol car would drive into the garage, doors would close, and the officers would take the prisoner out of the vehicle to be processed in the adjoining room. And put in the cells, if necessary.

Smith punched in the code to bring up the computer as she heard the doors open and the car pull in.

The door to the booking room opened. "Jesus, Molly, you have to help me. It was that sister of Jason's. She framed me."

The prisoner was Lorraine LeBlanc.

"You know this young woman, Constable Smith?" Noseworthy asked.

"Yes."

"It was frame-up. You know she hates me. Let me go and we'll forget all about it."

"I'm sorry, Lorraine, but it's not my call. Constable Noseworthy?"

"Clerk at the Craft Gallery saw her pinch a bracelet. We got there and the bracelet was on the floor. Witness, a shopper, says she saw this woman take the item and drop it when she was accused." Lorraine's eyes were round and wild. She was dressed in her winter coat and boots. Noseworthy carried a tattered scarf. He tossed it onto the counter.

"Tell them, Molly," Lorraine pleaded. "Please tell them."

"I'll call Gary," was all Smith could say as Noseworthy went to the computer.

"Full name?" he said.

Lorraine moaned.

Fortunately Gary was home when Smith called. He arrived at the police station red-faced and breathing heavily. He placed his hands on his thighs and gathered his breath for a few moments as Smith explained the situation.

Lorraine was a minor, with a local address, a relative to take care of her, and no prior record. She was released to her brother's care.

Smith walked with them to the door. The air was sharp but the sky clear in the approach of night. A few stars were popping up in the east. "This isn't over, Lorraine. You'll have to appear in court."

The girl avoided her brother's eyes. He put an arm around her and gave her a hug, but his fist was closed tight, knuckles white. "We'll worry about that when the time comes," Gary said. "You understand, Moon, that this is a vendetta by that Wyatt-Whatever bunch."

Smith let out a breath. It turned to mist in the cold air.

"Wait for me at the bottom of the stairs," Gary told his sister.

Lorraine left them. Her head was bent, her coat formed a black shroud around her thin frame.

Gary LeBlanc and Molly Smith watched until Lorraine was standing on the sidewalk, underneath a street lamp. A patrol car pulled out of the station parking lot. Brad Noseworthy glanced at them.

"Wendy Wyatt-Yarmouth was in the shop, Gary," Smith said. "But she only backed up what Mrs. Roberts told Constable Noseworthy. And that was that she saw Lorraine take the bracelet, put it into her coat and head for the door. When she was stopped, at the door, Lorraine dropped the bracelet."

"When she was stopped by Wendy Wyatt-Yarmouth who, as we all know, has a personal animosity toward my sister. Mrs. Roberts didn't see the bracelet emerge from Lorraine's coat. She only says that it was there on the floor."

"I'm not an attorney, Gary. Don't argue your case in front of me."

"They won't be hard on Lorraine, will they, Moon? She's never been in trouble before, you know that."

"I've no idea what the courts will do. But I can tell you one thing: you don't want a repeat of this. Talk to her. Get her some help."

Gary lifted his chin, but his eyes shifted to one side and the slightest touch of color crept into his face. He could afford professional help only if he used the money he was trying to put together for Lorraine's education.

"Call the Trafalgar Women's Support Center. Ask to speak to my mom. She'll know what to do to help."

"Thanks, Moon."

An RCMP car drove past. It signaled a turn into the Trafalgar City Police parking area.

Constable Smith stood on the steps of the police station as Gary LeBlanc wrapped his arms around his sister and guided her up the street toward their home.

Molly turned and headed back inside.

Adam Tocek was talking to Jim Denton. They looked up as Smith punched in the code to let her into the station.

Tocek had deep brown eyes and curly black hair and a five-o'clock shadow no matter the time of day, but his face always seemed to light up from inside when he saw Molly Smith. "Hey," he said. "Haven't seen you for a while. How's it going?"

"Problems. Always problems. Where are you from, Adam?"

"From? My grandparents emigrated from Slovakia in 1950. My father was very premature, born on the ship in the middle of the Atlantic. Lucky, so the story goes, to have lived."

"Sorry, no. I mean where are *you* from? Where did you grow up?"

"Toronto. The Big Smoke." He glanced at Denton. Denton shrugged. "Why are you asking, Molly?"

"To be honest, Adam, I don't know."

"Well, I know that it's almost four and if my replacement doesn't get here in the next two minutes, you'll be short a dispatcher," Denton muttered to no one who cared. "Not again." He took a 911 call.

"Do you have time to grab a coffee, Molly?" Tocek said, in deep contemplation of the floor.

She could feel her heart beating in her chest. A coffee. With Adam Tocek, the big, tough Mountie who turned to mush around Molly Smith. Should she have a coffee? Would that be a betrayal of Graham? Graham would want her to be happy.

She took a deep breath and opened her mouth.

"Vehicle out of control," Denton said. "Corner of Front and Elm. Pedestrian injured. Brad is occupied and can't take it. Sorry to break up this *tête-à-tête*, Mol, but we have work to do here."

"See you, Adam." She ran for the parking lot.

Chapter Twenty-two

Low clouds covered the tops of the mountains and mist rose from the river running through the valley. The trees, thickly covered with fresh white snow, seemed almost to float in the gray air, neither anchored to earth nor reaching to the sky.

Someone might have stolen all the colors from God's crayon box, leaving only black and white, and a stub of brown, to work with. John Winters stood at his kitchen window, drinking strong dark coffee.

"More snow?" Eliza wrapped her arms around him from behind and laid her warm cheek against his back.

"What day is it?"

"December thirty-first, as you know full well. Why do you ask?"

"This much snow I thought it'd be February at least."

He felt her smile. "Let's buy a home in the mountains, I believe I heard you say. Fresh air, great views."

"You could have reminded me that it has been known to snow at higher elevations."

She chuckled, and he felt her move away.

They'd house hunted in November, when the snow was a dusting high on the mountains, and moved into their new home in the middle of March, after two weeks of spring sunshine had gone a long way toward reducing the size of the snow pack.

Winters was from Vancouver. He'd lived most of his life in that coastal city where winter meant thick gray clouds and lots of rain. When the snow did fall, the city ground to a halt for a day or two, then the temperatures rose and it all melted.

"You might have to get the snowblower out," Eliza said.

"The SUV can handle it. That's why we bought it. The plow guy will be here soon." He turned away from the window. "Any chance of a working man getting breakfast around here?"

"I might be able to rummage up an egg or two." Eliza opened the fridge. "You haven't forgotten we're going out tonight, have you, John?"

"New Year's Eve. I haven't forgotten."

Eliza preferred to spend Christmas Eve and Day enjoying a quiet celebration at home, but tonight was a night to party. They always went to one of the best restaurants in Vancouver or to a fashion-industry party. Always, that is, once he'd moved up the police ladder enough to be allowed the night off. This would be their first celebration in Trafalgar, and he'd made a reservation at Flavours.

A thump on the stairs, another thump, then the sound of a body being dragged across the floor. Barney came into the kitchen, having deposited her wheeled suitcase, which was the approximate size of a steamer trunk, at the door. "It doesn't look too promising for my flight."

"In the mountains the weather can change on a dime." Winters desperately hoped such would be the case today. Barney was due to take the one o'clock flight out of Castlegar to Vancouver. If it was cancelled, there was another at three-forty-five. If that one didn't go, she'd be coming with them to Flavours. He liked Barney well enough, but, like fish, after three days her time was up.

Eliza pulled the cast-iron frying pan out of the cupboard. Barney pushed her aside and made bacon (crispy) and eggs (not tough) and toast (unburned) for the hungry working man.

"Did you speak to Patricia yesterday?" Winters asked around a mouthful of bacon as he ran a sliver of toast through the smear of yellow egg yolk on his plate.

"Briefly. She's not doing too well, John."

"I get the feeling," Barney said from the stove, "that her marriage has been a train-wreck for a long time. Instead of bringing them together, this horrible business has driven her and her husband even further apart."

"He's a right prick." Eliza rarely, if ever, used bad language. "Why an educated, wealthy woman, a doctor for heaven's sake, would put up with that sort of emotional detachment, I can't imagine."

Winters said nothing, although he wondered if emotional detachment was a family trait. According to Molly, the police had to notify Wendy Wyatt-Yarmouth of her brother's death although her parents knew about it, and Patricia appeared to be so wrapped up in her own grief that she wasn't much concerned about her daughter's precarious mental state.

"And now she's still sitting around that cheerless hotel," Eliza said.

"I expect to order the release of the bodies today. The Wyatt-Yarmouths have a funeral home ready to accept them and arrange transport to Toronto. Everything will be shut down tomorrow for the holiday, and I don't see any reason to keep them any longer. You're not to say a word, either of you. If something changes, I don't want Patricia's hopes to be up."

Barney and Eliza smiled at him with as much innocence as two puppies in the window of a pet shop.

"Any luck in contacting the other boy's parents?" Barney asked.

"No, but the neighbors who're minding the house say the Williamses are due back from their sailing trip on January third. They'll be met at the airport and given the news."

"Hard." Barney helped herself to more bacon.

"No matter how they hear about it," Eliza said, nibbling at the edges of a slice of unbuttered toast.

He pushed himself away from the table. Breakfast had been great. Regardless of whether or not she could cook, Eliza's idea of a proper morning meal was blueberries and yogurt with a sprinkling of granola, or toast without butter and a scraping of low-sugar preserves.

Ugh.

"Nine o'clock," Eliza said. "The reservation is for nine."

"Yes, dear, I know. You should probably call the snow plow guy and make sure he'll be here before you have to leave for the airport."

Barney got to her feet and held out her arms. Winters gave her a big hug. "Good trip."

"Keep safe," she said.

Ten minutes later, John Winters was trudging back to his house though snow up to his calves. The front of his SUV was half buried in a drift and the big winter tires had dug deep furrows in the driveway.

"Call the snow plow guy," he shouted into the kitchen. "Tell him I'll pay double if he's here within half an hour. If you dare laugh, you're out of my will." He slammed the door and went to the garage for a shovel.

◇◇◇

Lucky Smith didn't normally go into the Trafalgar Women's Support Center on a Monday. Monday was the busiest day of the week in the office, with all the weekend activity to sort out.

But Moonlight had called last night, just as Lucky and Andy sat down to dinner. "If you hear from Lorraine or Gary LeBlanc, Mom, you might want to talk to them."

Now that she'd been given an opening to interfere, Lucky felt she could tell her daughter what Lorraine had told her: the trouble Ewan had apparently caused between Alan and Sophie.

The CBC news was starting when the phone rang again. Gary LeBlanc, asking if Lucky'd mind talking to Lorraine in the morning.

Lucky had returned to the news, not paying much attention to what Peter Mansbridge had to say about the state of the world. It was always depressing anyway.

"What brings you here this morning, sweetie?" Bev Price opened the door with her usual welcoming smile. Bev was even shorter than the five-foot-nothing Lucky Smith, although a heck of a lot thinner. A bundle of positive energy, Bev was the personification of the support center she'd founded and kept afloat by little more than her own heart and soul and skill at begging for funding. Lucky knew, although not many did, that Bev's only daughter, at age seventeen, had died many years ago on the streets of Halifax, her baby at her side. Dead of malnutrition, both of them, because the mother didn't know how to access what government services were available. Bev, not much over thirty at the time, had been in jail, the result of a knife fight arising from a drug deal gone wrong and a vengeful pimp. Once she'd been released from prison, instead of wallowing in despair over the death of her daughter and granddaughter, Bev had thrown all of her formidable energy first of all into getting herself clean, and then into making sure that women down on their luck were able to find the support they needed. Now in her late fifties, she'd arrived in Trafalgar ten years ago and immediately set about coercing the good citizens into funding and staffing the support center.

"I'm meeting someone," Lucky said. "We need a place to talk in private."

"The nutrition-in-pregnancy group's here at nine-thirty. Some of the girls like to get here early." And they were girls, probably not one of them over eighteen. Women with careers, money, supportive families, employed partners, didn't have need of the services of the Trafalgar Women's Support Center.

"We can sit in the living room," Bev said. "So you can close the kitchen door. That okay?"

"Thanks. It's Lorraine LeBlanc. Do you know her?"

Bev's bushy gray eyebrows rose. "Lorraine's never been too keen, shall we say, to come here. Something's happened to change that?"

"Quite a lot." Lucky stopped talking as a burst of laughter announced the arrival of the first class of the day.

Gary accompanied his sister to the meeting. He looked most uncomfortable walking through the living room, full of young women blossoming in all the stages of pregnancy. But Lucky didn't particularly care about Gary's comfort level.

Gary was carrying a plastic supermarket bag. Before he even sat down, he pulled out the contents and put them on the table. Ski-goggles. Lucky flicked over the price tag that was still attached to the strap. Mid-Kootenay Adventure Vacations. She lifted one eyebrow toward Gary.

"Somehow these found their way into our house," he said. "As did these." He placed a thin gold necklace, a jar of face cream and a bottle of bath oil on the table. "Let's leave it at that, okay?"

Lorraine studied the floor.

The meeting did not go well. Lorraine was prickly and defensive. At first, she denied she'd had anything to do with the bracelet that found its way, apparently all by itself, to the floor of the Craft Gallery. Then she was blaming Wendy Wyatt-Yarmouth, saying that Wendy'd planted the jewelry on Lorraine. Finally Lorraine laid her forehead on the table and cried. Gary and Lucky eyed each other over the girl's heaving back. His face was tight with anger. Whether at Lorraine, or Wendy, or the whole world, Lucky couldn't tell. She passed Lorraine a box of tissues.

Eventually the girl lifted her head from the table. Her face was red and puffy, her cheeks streaked with tears. Wendy and Sophie and that crowd had so much. The best ski clothes and equipment, passes for cat-skiing and heli-skiing, good restaurants and lattes and cappuccinos, money for jewelry, clothes, anything they wanted.

She touched the gold hoop that ran through her right ear. "See," she said. "See. He gave me these. He wanted me to have as many good things as his sister had. Why can't I have them now? It shouldn't make a difference 'cause Jason's dead. He wanted me to have everything. He did." She fell onto the table again, her body convulsing with sobs. Gary stroked his sister's back and looked at Lucky as if she would pull her comfortable beige cardigan, the one with roses crawling up the sides of the zipper, aside and reveal a giant S. S for Superwoman, ready to leap into the air and solve the problems of every poor child brought up in an abusive family

Why indeed? Why did Wendy Wyatt-Yarmouth get to go on ski vacations and attend good universities and shop to her heart's content, while Lorraine LeBlanc screwed strangers in dark alleys in a search for love, and her brother tried to scrape together every cent he could find to get her an education.

Why wasn't life fair?

Lucky Smith had given up worrying about that long ago.

"It just isn't," she said.

"What isn't what?" Gary asked, and Lucky realized that she'd spoken that last thought aloud.

"Never mind." She forced herself to smile at the LeBlanc siblings. "If it comes to court, and it might not despite what the police say, I'll be happy to testify on your behalf, Lorraine. I hope you know, dear, that possessions don't buy happiness. Lorraine, look at me."

Obediently the girl lifted her head. Her eyes were red, her face pale.

"Right now, I can't imagine a sadder person than Wendy Wyatt-Yarmouth and that bunch."

Lorraine shrugged.

"They have money, lots of it. And plenty of stuff that money can buy. Do you think they're happy, Lorraine?"

Another shrug.

Lucky and Gary exchanged glances again.

"Tell us what you think about this, Lorraine, please," he said. "Are Jason and Ewan's friends happy people?"

Lorraine jumped to her feet. Her chair toppled over and crashed to the floor. "Happy? Are you freaking kidding? Ask me about happy will you? Jason's dead. There's nothing else that matters."

John Winters visited the Doctors Wyatt-Yarmouth at their hotel, and told them Jason's body would be released today. Jack mumbled something about the incompetence of the Trafalgar City Police, and Patricia smiled her thanks. She had not looked surprised at the news, and Winters suspected Barney had been on the phone even as he uselessly tossed shovelfuls of snow into the woods while waiting for the plow to rescue him.

◇◇◇

Molly Smith came on duty at three o'clock. The weather was supposed to be good—nice and cold to keep the snow frozen, but no new stuff expected to fall.

They had a full complement of officers on duty, ready for anything, and everything, that might happen.

Very little did. A few drunks were taken into custody to sleep it off, a couple of marijuana smokers warned to put it out, and several cans of beer poured into the gutter. At about eleven-thirty Dave Evans had been attacked by an amorous female, and Smith had to pull the woman off him. She was in her forties, at a charitable estimate, with the skeletal body of long-time heroin user.

"Damn it," Evans said, wiping furiously at his mouth with his glove, as they watched the woman walk backward, still blowing kisses to him. "Who knows what diseases she might have?"

"Here's an idea," Smith said. "You stop with the digs against me, and I won't tell everyone Fancy Nancy's got a crush on you. What'd she call you? *The sexiest cop in B.C.?*"

"I've never made a dig against you, Molly."

"Or was it all of North America? I forget."

"Drop it, Smith."

"It's nice sometimes," she said with a laugh, "to be a female officer. We don't have to deal with harassment like that."

Evans growled. Smith doubted he got her point, but it had been fun making it anyway.

They were sitting in the patrol car outside the Potato Famine watching the clock tick toward midnight. The window was rolled down and they could hear pounding music, shouts, and overly-loud laughter coming from inside. The music was cut off in mid-note, and people began to chant. Smith glanced at her watch. "Midnight," she said. "Happy New Year, Dave."

"Same to you, Molly."

Cheers and cries of Happy New Year filled the street. A group of young men ran out of the bar, waving brown bottles over their heads and yelling. A bottle hit the brick wall of the pub and shattered. The red light in the bar window advertising a brand of beer glistened off shards of glass. Smith and Evans got out of the car and went back to work.

Warnings were issued, beer emptied into snow banks, and the broken glass was being picked up, piece by piece, by the miscreants to be deposited into a trash bin when radios crackled. Fight at the Bishop and Nun. Evans took the car and Smith remained behind, to continue walking the beat. "Am I going to hear anything more from you guys tonight?" she asked.

"No, ma'am. Not a peep." They swayed slightly and their words were stirred, but they'd sobered up quickly enough at the sight of Evans and Smith approaching and poured out their beer before being told to do so.

"Make sure of it," she said. "You can go now."

"Happy New Year," they shouted, as they continued on their way.

She watched them go for a few moments before turning to take a walk through the pub, to check that everything was under control. The hair on the back of her neck bristled and she looked around. The light over the entrance of the small office building across the street was burnt out. The streetlamp touched the edges of a black shape standing in the doorway. A red glow from the end of a cigarette did nothing to illuminate the face. It was a man. He was very large and was watching her.

She placed her hand on the butt of her gun. He stepped into the light.

Charlie F. Bassing.

He looked at Smith, his expression unreadable in the light hitting his face from above. Or, perhaps, there wasn't an expression for her to read. He flicked the burning cigarette into the street and walked away with slow, lazy strides.

Smith took a deep breath and watched until he turned at the corner.

She felt a blast of hot, sweat-filled air. The bouncer stepped out and joined her on the sidewalk.

"Everything okay?" she asked.

"So far. But there's some serious drinking going on in there. One or two that might be trouble later." He narrowed his eyes. "Are you okay, Molly?"

"Sure," she moved her hand away from her gun and tried to smile. "I'm fine." She flexed her fingers.

Chapter Twenty-three

Molly Smith was late getting to the ski slopes. Last night's shift had been long and tiring, but other than a handful of arrests for drunk and disorderly, uneventful. She hadn't seen Charlie again, but he played at the back of her mind all night. She could hardly make a complaint against him for standing on the other side of the street and not talking to her. She'd call Christa tomorrow evening and find out if Charlie had been watching her. That Smith could complain about. Christa had promised to contact the police, or Molly, if she saw Charlie, but Christa might decide to 'not make a fuss'. Not wanting to make a fuss was what had gotten her beaten up in the first place.

Smith had made it home at four-thirty, had a quick shower, laid out her ski clothes, and gone to bed, planning to get up at seven. When she opened one eye to peer at the clock, the room was light and it was after nine.

She was on the road before nine-thirty, at the hill by ten. She'd considered paying her money for a lift ticket so she could be sure of spending the day in peace, but New Year's Day should be quiet. The partiers would be sleeping it off, or too subdued to make trouble. It would be mostly families today and those serious enough about their sport to avoid overindulging the night before.

A cheerful yellow sun shone in a pale blue sky. In the meadows, snow sparkled as if ground glass had been sprinkled across the surface.

The parking lot wasn't full, but Smith had to park far away from the lodge. She left her skis and poles on the racks outside and went into the basement to let them know she was here and get a radio. The equipment rental area was next to the security office. Crowds of people were stomping their feet into unfamiliar boots, testing the length of poles and checking out bindings and the surface of skis. The wooden floor was wet with melting snow and the enclosed room smelled of damp wool, human sweat, and excitement.

"Hi, Constable Smith, what are you doing here?" Ellie Carmine's daughter, Kathy, lifted goggles away from her face. Her smile was broad and her eyes shining. Without her habitual hangdog expression, she looked good. One of the guests from the B&B was beside her, although he was not looking quite as pleased with himself. Smith dug around in her memory banks for his name, but couldn't find it.

"Same as you, I'd guess," Smith said. "Out for a day on the slopes."

"Maybe we'll see you out there," the girl said. "I'm so excited. I've never skied before." She lifted her poles as evidence. "Can you believe it? I've lived in Trafalgar my whole life and I've never been here."

"Have fun," Smith said. She always felt uncomfortable when, in her civilian persona, she ran into people she'd met in her professional capacity.

"Rob's going to show me the ropes. Aren't you Rob?" She gave him a big smile.

The boy shrugged and went back to measuring her poles.

"That makes one of us."

"Pardon?"

"One of us who's excited about today's little adventure." Wendy Wyatt-Yarmouth followed Smith toward the security office. Not that she was really following the police officer. More like drifting along in her wake because she couldn't think of anything better to do. Her yellow ski suit was formfitting and expensive. "This morning, Mrs. Carmine asked if Kathy could come skiing with us. What a presumption, as if we're friends or something rather than paying guests. She acts as if we owe her because of that little scuffle at the B&B. I told her my dad would pay for what got broken, but Rob's all embarrassed about it and trying to make nice. Which suits Kathy, you can be sure. Rob's too nice by half. He needs to get some backbone and tell Kathy to get lost. Oh, well, not my problem. I'm not going to waste my time holding her hand."

It might not be Wendy Wyatt-Yarmouth's problem, but she was enjoying talking about it. "Have a nice day," Smith said, putting her hand on the security office door.

"I doubt it. This place is a gigantic bore. You'll be pleased to hear, Officer, that we're getting the hell back to civilization tomorrow."

Won't be sorry about that, Smith thought as she said, "Have a safe trip."

It had snowed the night before and, as she'd expected, the harder runs were relatively empty and the snow pure and untouched. As the morning drew to a close, heavy clouds moved in, promising more new snow. She hoped it would arrive before closing. She loved skiing through a whiteout. Visibility was reduced to nothing, giving her the feeling of being wrapped in a white blanket, only able to see as far as the tips of her skis. That sense of soaring through clouds was unbeatable and it required all of her skill to just let go and allow the texture of the snow beneath her skis to tell her when to turn.

The radio was quiet, and she stopped only once, for a late lunch, peeking around corners and tucking her head down at a table in the back of the room in an attempt to avoid any more encounters with the gang from the Glacier Chalet. She saw Wendy Wyatt-Yarmouth sitting at a table across the room. Wendy was alone, leaning up against the wall, just staring off into space. A group of several families grabbed the table next to hers. They were too many for the big table, and a young woman spoke to Wendy. The girl waved her arm languidly. The parents didn't spare her another glance as they tried to organize the pack of children who, cheeks rosy from the cold and exercise, eyes gleaming with exhilaration, alternatively bounced in their seats or ran around in circles. Moms and dads were young, lean, well-scrubbed, with good hair and nice teeth, and the children laughed with sheer pleasure at being free and alive.

Wendy Wyatt-Yarmouth leaned up against the wall and wrapped her arms tightly around herself. She paid the children no attention, but kept her head down and stared into her lap. Her shoulders shook, and Smith knew she was crying.

Poor Wendy. Smith ate her lunch quickly and went back outside to get her skis.

She was standing in the line for the lift to Bear Cave Run when the man beside her took a double take. "Hey, Moonlight. It's you, right Moonlight? How are you?"

"I'm fine, Doug. You?"

The line stopped moving. A child was yelling something about not wanting to get into the chair. "Just great, Moonlight. Back in town for a visit with the folks over the holidays. You too?"

"Yeah." Just the other day she'd thought of Doug Whiteside for the first time in years, and here he was in real life. She hoped her thoughts hadn't conjured him up. *What the hell was the problem with this line, couldn't they move it up?*

"What's with the jacket?" Doug grabbed her arm and half-turned her to have a look at her back. She wrenched her arm away. "Hey, didn't I hear something about you becoming a cop? I figured that was a joke."

"No joke." she inched forward. Her face burned. After all these years, she was still embarrassed about what had happened between them.

"How's Sam anyway?"

"He's a lawyer. Lives in Calgary."

"Funny, isn't it, how some people grow up exactly like you'd expect them to, and others turn out completely different. Never would have figured you for a cop. I saw Meredith a few days ago. In school all she ever talked about was being a reporter. And she went and did it. Between you and me, I got the feeling she's not too happy being on the staff of the *Gazette*. I think she figured she'd at least be a foreign correspondent for the *Globe and Mail* by now. She looks good, though," he added, almost wistfully.

Doug chatted on while Molly's cheeks burned. Years passed, and they finally got to the front of the line. The next chair had room for just one more person and Smith leapt in, leaving Doug waving and suggesting they go for a drink and talk about 'the old days.' She'd rather spend the night in the Trafalgar jail.

Doug Whiteside had been friends with her brother Samwise when they were in school. Sam was several years older than Moonlight, and so were his friends.

Doug had been a popular guy, good looking, pitcher on the school baseball team. His parents were well off, and he'd been one of the few kids in their school who had a car of his own.

She'd been thirteen the summer Sam and Doug were seventeen. When they weren't chasing girls, or begging rides from sailboats on the lake, the boys liked to go fishing where the Upper Kootenay River broke off a branch and ran through the back of the Smith property.

One warm, lazy day Moonlight was at home alone. Her parents were at the store and Sam had taken a hiking party on a three day wilderness trip. She was on the dock by the river, swinging her long brown legs in the air, reading and daydreaming, and ignoring the chores her mother had left her. Doug drove up and walked over to the dock to say hi. He asked if Sam was ready to go. When Moonlight explained that Sam had gone away for a few days, Doug smacked his head with a laugh and said he'd forgotten. He turned to leave, and Moonlight jumped to her feet.

She asked him if he'd like to go to see a movie tonight.

"I thought Sam didn't get back until Monday?"

"I mean, go with me. Just me. I mean us."

He ran his eyes slowly down her skinny, young body, all long limbs, sharp angles, and knees, making her feel like a slab of meat in the butcher's display counter, and then he began to laugh. It was not a kind laugh. "I don't think so," he said at last. "You're a cute enough kid, but I'm not into robbing the cradle."

Humiliated, embarrassed, she stood rooted to the spot while he sauntered across the lawn back to his car. "Although...," he said, turning.

"Yes!"

"You could do me a favor and set me up with your pal Meredith Morgenstern. She might be the same age as you, but she looks, you know," he made a gesture like he was weighing two coconuts in his hands, "older." He winked and got into his car. He drove away in a cloud of dust, while Jerome, Sylvester's predecessor, ran alongside, barking.

Moonlight wanted to die. From that moment on she'd never had a kind word to say about her brother's friend.

For the rest of the afternoon, the memory of the teenaged Doug's mocking laugh followed Molly Smith around the hills. He didn't seem to have been laughing at her today, though. Perhaps, she told herself, he'd forgotten what had happened and was genuinely interested in talking about the old days. He'd never dated Meredith, far as Smith knew, and he'd probably forgotten all about Moonlight's awkward attempt at asking him out.

But it was still so mortifying.

She remembered the way her mother's eyebrows rose in a question when, from that day on, Moonlight had mocked, ridiculed, slandered, disparaged Doug Whiteside every time his name came up. Even more embarrassing, Lucky probably knew why her attitude had changed so abruptly.

Smith barely missed colliding with a snow-laden Douglas fir. She dug the edges of her skis in and came to a hockey stop in a swirl of cold powder.

Who the hell did all that remind her of?

She took refuge near the tree, getting out of the way of anyone who might be coming down, before pulling her helmet off and rubbing at her face.

Wendy Wyatt-Yarmouth didn't have a good word to say about her brother's friend, Ewan Williams. What was it Smith had overheard Wendy saying about Ewan?

When it came to women, he liked to scrape the bottom of the barrel.

Chapter Twenty-four

John Winters read the e-mail from Doctor Shirley Lee confirming that the body of Jason Wyatt-Yarmouth would be released to the funeral home arranged by his family.

He took his glasses off and rubbed the bridge of his nose. He'd arranged to come in to work later today, thinking that rank had its privileges and he'd take the privilege of enjoying a pleasant, relaxing New Year's morning at home, breakfast on the sun porch, catching up on the newspapers. Perhaps he'd bundle up later and go for a run. A perfect morning following a perfect evening out with his wife.

It hadn't quite worked out that way. Instead, Barney had come with them to dinner, and he'd been woken by the sound of the phone ringing and Barney chattering in the computer room next door as she made calls to re-arrange her schedule, having been unable to get a flight out yesterday. Barney wanted to go to town at noon to see the annual polar bear swim in the Upper Kootenay River. John Winters had absolutely no interest in watching a pack of people without a lick of common sense between them jump into an icy river. But Eliza asked him to drive, and, like a good husband, he'd put the newspapers aside and done so.

Winters swiveled his chair and looked out the window. The sun was shining in Trafalgar, but there were several mountain ridges between here and Castlegar, and that meant a lot of weather. The one o'clock flight had gotten away, but it had been full, and Barney was booked on the later one.

Hopefully tomorrow's planes would leave on time. It would not be good for Patricia Wyatt-Yarmouth if she had to spend hours in the waiting room while the body of her son lay next door in the cargo area.

With the departure of Doctors Wyatt-Yarmouth the friends would also be heading back to Ontario. He had no reason to keep them in Trafalgar, but once they were gone it would be difficult, if not impossible, to continue with the investigation.

Whether Ewan Williams' death was deliberate or accidental, one of his friends had to know a lot more than they were saying.

Winters stared out the window. An old van, the sort of Volkswagen Kombi that had bounced down the road to Woodstock, clattered up the hill, puffing and wheezing as if, like an old timer still trying to keep up with the kids, its age was catching up with it. The inside was loaded with young people and the roof with skis. Ewan Williams had been alone, supposedly, when he left the B&B on Sunday evening after the day's skiing. He was never seen again. At least not by anyone who was prepared to tell the police so. He had met a woman earlier that day at the lodge and arranged to meet her at a bar in the evening. He hadn't arrived. Winters had sent an officer to the bar to check that the woman, Marilyn Chow, had told Smith the truth. Chow was attractive enough that the bartender had no trouble remembering her. He'd watched her sitting in a table in the corner, alone, for about an hour, and then leave, alone, at the time she'd told Smith she had.

Winters mentally checked the hard-to-accept scenarios off on his fingers. The B&B wasn't in the wilderness, and there were only a few blocks of well-travelled and well-lit city streets between it and the Bishop and the Nun. Ewan was on foot: if he'd had an accident on the way into town, someone would have reported it. If he'd been mugged he would have been rumbled and left on the sidewalk for a passer-by to find. If he'd changed his mind and was heading for someplace other than the Bishop, the same rules applied. Ewan didn't have a vehicle except for the rented SUV, which had not gone missing, so he would have been walking.

He might have been picked up. A random or serial-type killing, Winters dismissed off hand. He'd come back to that if necessary, but right now the idea was way out in left field. Someone Ewan knew, one of the men he'd been in a fight with because of paying attention to the guy's girlfriend? Unlikely. Ewan didn't seem to be naive enough to accept a lift from someone he'd offended.

Lucky told Molly she'd heard that Alan and Ewan had sparred over Alan's girlfriend, Sophie. Clearly the incident hadn't been forgotten: Winters remembered the dirty look Alan had given his girlfriend when the discussion had come around to Ewan's sexual habits. He made a note to have a talk with Alan Robertson.

Ewan had stepped out the front door and disappeared for twenty-four hours. It was highly likely he'd never left the grounds of the Glacier Chalet B&B.

Winters thought about the property around the lovely old house. Neat gardens and perfect lawns, now covered in deep snow, backing up against a patch of woodland. No fence, the lawn was outlined by perennial beds.

What do you find in a forest? Lots of wood. Dead branches.

Tomorrow, when everyone was back after the holidays, he'd get the Mounties' forensic team crawling through those woods.

Jason had been at Lorraine LeBlanc's house in the hours before his death; his bright yellow SUV parked on a city street in clear view of any one passing. Highly unlikely he'd left a dead body in the front seat while he went inside for his Christmas Eve supper with Lorraine. So he had to have found, or recovered, the body between leaving Lorraine's and midnight, when he went off the road. Where had Jason told Lorraine he was going when he left her?

Back to the B&B.

Like a movie unraveling in his head, Winters tried to play out the last movements of Jason Wyatt-Yarmouth's life.

He leaves the LeBlanc's around nine, telling Lorraine to join him later at the Glacier Chalet. He gets into the car while Lorraine watches from the door. Jason drives back to the B&B. Does he get there? Winters had sent reserve officers down the street, asking if anyone had seen the yellow SUV parked at the B&B between nine and midnight. A few people said they might have, but they were unsure about the time, or even the day.

For now, Winters would assume it had been there. The movie continued.

Jason parked the car, but didn't go inside. The house was busy with preparations for the midnight celebration, someone would have seen or heard him.

Why didn't he go inside? Did he remember something he had to do? Buy a last minute gift, perhaps? As he drove through town, Jason would have noticed that the stores were all closed.

Winters watched Jason get out of the car. With a flick of his finger on the remote door-lock he takes a step toward the house. It's snowing heavily.

Someone steps out of the shadows. Snow covers head and coat. He or she had been waiting.

Why is someone else involved? Jason could have been coming back to get the body he'd stashed earlier.

Again, unlikely. Jason had, by all accounts, not behaved that day like a man with the death of his best friend on his mind. Like his friends, Jason thought Ewan had met up with his date and it had gone so well he was still with her. Apparently it wasn't out of character for Ewan to instantly drop the company of his friends when he found more pleasing companionship.

In John Winters' private movie, the figure waiting for Jason stepped out of the shadows. The streetlight shone into her face. Wendy Wyatt-Yarmouth's expression was bleak and her face was wet with melting snow and tears.

Winters stopped the movie, and thought about Wendy. A bitter and angry young woman, who appeared to be veering perilously close to the edge of a breakdown. One would think that with all the money and influence her parents had, they'd have taken her to a good therapist. Maybe they had, and it wasn't working.

Or maybe they hadn't. Maybe the depth of Wendy's problems had only started coming to the surface on this vacation.

He glanced at his watch. Almost four. He had one last chance to get Wendy to tell him what she knew before she left tomorrow.

He reached for his coat.

Chapter Twenty-five

The main room of the lodge was full of people changing out of their heavy outerwear, removing boots, stuffing accessories into back packs, talking over the day on the slopes. The kitchen was closed, only the hot beverage and dessert counter still open for last-minute business.

Smith went downstairs to hand in the radio. There was time for another run, but she was no longer in the mood.

The old guy was behind the desk. "Good day?" she asked.

"Wish every day was so quiet."

"Then you'd be out of a job."

He laughed. "Back tomorrow?"

"Wouldn't miss it."

Kathy Carmine was sitting on a bench removing her boots. Her face shone with happiness and cold and exercise. She waved at Smith. Her pleasure was almost infectious, and Smith smiled at her. "Have fun?"

"The best day ever."

"Where's Rob?"

"I'm such a slow-poke that he wanted to spend some time skiing by himself."

"Is the rest of his crowd here?"

"Wendy and Alan and Sophie came with us. Jeremy's still in jail." Kathy giggled. "Sorry, forgot that was your fault."

Smith had been skiing powder all day, and her arms and legs ached. Time to get out of here. As soon as she got in cell phone range, she'd call Christa and ask her around for pizza and a movie. With Charlie back in town, Smith had promised herself she'd keep a close eye on her friend.

She climbed the stairs once more and grabbed her backpack from the hook where she'd left it. She rummaged for her water bottle and took a long drink. Tucked into one corner of the lodge was a small bar with a scattering of seats arranged around a wood-burning fireplace. Flames jumped as the bartender tossed in a fresh log. Every seat was taken and men stood three deep at the bar. As Smith put her water bottle away, the crowd shifted and she could see Wendy Wyatt-Yarmouth, lifting a wine glass to her lips, sitting alone against the far wall. Her yellow ski jacket hung on a hook behind her.

Wendy swallowed the remainder of her wine and waved her glass at the waiter.

Smith went into the bar.

"Not you again," was Wendy's greeting. Her eyes and nose were very red and her words were slurred.

"Mind if I join you?"

"There isn't an empty chair."

"I'll stand."

The waiter put the drink on the table. Someone had carved a pair of initials, surrounded by a heart, in the dark wood.

"Getcha something?" he asked, picking up the empty wine glass.

"No, thank you." The man walked away. Wendy drank deeply. "Your friends will be ready to leave soon," Smith said.

"I don't have any friends."

"What about Rob and Alan and the rest?"

"Jason's friends. Always Jason's friends." She finished the drink. "Get us a bottle, will you."

"How much have you had, Wendy?"

"Not enough for it to be any of your business." She hiccupped. The waiter passed with a tray overflowing with mugs of beer, and Wendy shouted at him to bring a bottle.

Smith touched the man's shoulder. "Cancel that." He shrugged and passed around the drinks. The table next to them was crowded with six young men packed around a table for four. They crashed their mugs together and cheered.

Smith leaned over and spoke into Wendy's ear. "It's too loud in here. I told the waiter to bring our drinks outside. Let's go."

"What?"

Smith lifted Wendy's elbow and guided her out of her chair. "I wanna another drink."

"He'll bring it outside."

"Okay." Wendy let herself be led. She was wearing ski boots and tripped over the chair leg. She stumbled against the young men's table. Beer mugs wobbled, and men grabbed for them. "Hey, watch it. Stupid drunk."

"It's all good." Smith gripped Wendy's arm, and with her other hand grabbed the girl's helmet off the table and jacket down from the hook.

The main room of the lodge was busy with families packing up at the end of the day. Smith spotted an unoccupied, battered old couch close to the center of the room, and led Wendy to it.

Through the big windows, Smith could see a line of cars heading down the mountain. The earlier promise of snow never arrived and the clouds had left to dump their load someplace else. The winter's night was closing in fast, although a full moon was low in the sky to the south.

She threw Wendy's things on the couch. "I'm going to look for your friends, okay? I saw Kathy downstairs earlier."

"Kathy thinks she's gonna get Rob just 'cause she wants him. Not gonna happen. Why are women so dis…disillusional?"

"You wait here, Wendy, okay?"

The girl's eyes were glazed and unfocused. She wasn't hearing anything Molly Smith was saying. "Rob's too polite to tell her to get lost."

Smith started to walk away. Over the din of the lounge, she caught one word that had her spinning around and crouching down beside Wendy.

"What was that?"

"I said Rob needs to be more like Ewan. And Ewan needed to be more like Rob. He was a fucker."

"So I've heard."

"No loss to the world now he's gone."

Smith took a deep breath and settled herself on the edge of the couch, beside Wendy. "It's tough when you like a guy like that, isn't it?"

Wendy started to cry. Although she wasn't really starting, just releasing another round of the tears that had been there all day. "Where's that damn bottle?"

"You told him you liked him, didn't you? What happened then? He laughed, I'll bet, right?" Smith had a feeling that perhaps she shouldn't be having this conversation. This was out of her league. She'd take Wendy to her friends, then call Sergeant Winters and ask for help.

She stood up. "Come on, let's find the others."

"I want another drink."

"Too late, I'm afraid. The bar's closing."

"Doesn't matter. We've ordered. Go get it."

"Where are you supposed to meet the others?"

"Didn't laugh."

"No one's going to laugh at you."

"He didn't laugh."

Wendy fumbled in the pocket of her ski pants and pulled out a tissue, tattered and worn from over-use. She blew her nose, but most of the snot ended up on her fingers. She wiped her hand on her right leg. The mucus spread across the thigh of her yellow ski pants.

"Didn't laugh," she repeated. "Said he'd give me a quick one."

"Who said?" Smith asked. Although she knew. She sat down again.

"I waited a long time, years, for Ewan to notice me. Ewan-Jason, Jason-Ewan, they were always together. It should have been Ewan-Wendy. Jason was my parents' favorite. Jason got everything I wanted. Even Ewan.

"He went away to university and I thought I'd lost him. Then Jason made plans for this holiday and I knew it'd be my chance." She hiccupped, and pounded her upper chest with her hand. "Oopsie. Here, away from Oakville where we'd been kids, Ewan would see that I've grown up. I look good, don't I?"

"You look very good." And wasn't that a lie. Tears and mucus streaked Wendy's face. Her eyes and nose were red and running, make-up either washed off or smeared, hair a tousled mess.

"I bought a bra and pantie set, lavender silk and lace, to wear for Ewan our first time. Someone touched them so I threw them away. I figured it was Lorraine, going through my things, but now I think it was Kathy. She's a snoop."

"What? Kathy goes though the guests' underwear?"

"Sad, eh? The miserable little mouse."

"But Ewan didn't care. He just wanted a screw, a cheap, nasty screw, in the cold and the snow, up against a tree." Wendy was crying so hard, Smith had trouble making out what she was saying.

She leaned closer. The girl smelled of good soap and too much alcohol. "When was that?"

"You think it's funny, don't you?"

"No, Wendy, I don't think any of this is funny."

Wendy closed one eye and peered at Smith through the other, trying to focus. "He said he didn't have time to go inside, said he had to meet someone. He wanted to have me up against a tree, so he could meet a cheap slut who operates a cash register."

The day he'd arranged to meet Marilyn Chow was the day Ewan had died. "Did you do it?" Smith asked.

Wendy covered her face with her hands and sobbed. People were looking at them. A security guard approached. Smith started to stand up.

"No," Wendy said, grabbing Smith's hand, and pulling her back down. "Don't leave me. I would have. Sad, eh?"

Sad? Oh, yes. It was all so sad.

"We went to the back of the B&B, to that patch of woods out of the view of the street. He told me he had to hurry 'cause he was meeting another girl. I didn't want it anymore and pushed him away. He fell down. He was pulling out his cock—that takes all their attention, doesn't it—so he didn't have a hand to catch himself with and fell real hard. I ran away."

She wiped her nose with the back of her hand. "You said you wouldn't tell anyone this, right?"

Smith was pretty sure she hadn't said any such thing. She had to get Wendy into town, to Sergeant Winters. But first, one more question. "Jason?"

"When Ewan didn't come back to the B&B, I figured he was with that slut. There was something wrong with him, you know. After…after I left him, I went for a long walk and thought about it, and realized that Ewan had a real problem. He didn't want nice, decent girls. He liked them cheap. So, in a way, it was a complement to me that Ewan didn't want to be with me."

Smith failed to see it that way, but she wasn't going to argue. "Jason?"

"I'd lost a glove. I'd taken it off to touch Ewan's cheek. I wanted some tenderness. Pretty dumb, eh? It was good, leather with a fur lining. On Christmas Eve, while everyone was getting ready for midnight, I went to look for it." Her body shuddered. "I figured the glove would be covered in snow, but thought I'd look anyway. The wind had created drifts around the trees where we'd been standing and some patches were bare. Instead of my glove, I found him. Ewan. He was lying on the ground, his head and shoulders covered with snow, but his lower body was bare. He was twisted to one side, with his hands still around his cock. Protecting his damn prick to the very last. I didn't know what to do. Do you understand? I didn't know what to do!"

"It's okay, calm down." Smith looked around. People were still watching them, but the security guard had disappeared. "I killed him. It was an accident. I didn't even know he was dead."

Wendy didn't know how right she was. What had Doctor Lee concluded? That Ewan had died, not of the injury to the back of his head, but of the cold that killed him while he was unconscious and concussed. If Wendy'd gone for help, he probably would have lived.

"I went for a walk, trying to decide what to do. Jason drove by. He picked me up, and could tell something was wrong, so I told him."

She wiped at her face. "He said not to worry, he'd take care of it."

"Come on, I'm going to get us a ride back to town." Smith pulled on Wendy's arm, but the girl resisted.

"Where's that damned bottle of wine?"

"Wait right here. I'm going to get it, okay?"

Swimming against the crowds, Smith took the stairs as fast as she could in her ski boots and burst into the security office. The old guy was typing something into the computer.

"Call the Mounties. I need a car for pick-up, and I need it now."

"What's up?"

"Then call the TCP, and ask them to contact Sergeant Winters. Tell them I'm bringing someone in about the Williams case."

"Why?" His fingers still hovered over the keyboard.

"Will you just do it! I don't have all day here."

He reached for the phone.

"Have one of your people meet me upstairs."

Smith ran out. She pushed her way through the crowd, saying "Excuse me, excuse me," at almost every step. A few people turned to glare, but everyone obliged.

The big old couch in the center of the room was empty. Smith looked around. No sign of Wendy. Thinking Wendy had given up waiting for someone to bring the bottle of wine, Smith ran into the bar. The room was packed, but it was very small, and Wendy wasn't there. She headed for the washrooms.

She glanced at the table in front of the couch as she passed. Wendy's helmet and jacket were gone.

A female security guard approached her. "Constable, what do you need?"

Smith described Wendy. "Check the washrooms and then every nook and cranny."

"You got it."

Smith crashed back through the crowds and down the stairs. "I've lost her," she said to the guard in the office. "Did you make that call?"

"On their way."

"She's got her equipment with her. Contact the lift operators." Smith described Wendy again.

"Lifts are closed."

"As of when?"

He looked at the big round clock on the wall. "Five minutes ago."

"Does that mean that anyone who was on the lift, say six minutes ago, made it to the top?"

"Yup."

"I need to know if that woman got on, and off, a chair."

The radio crackled. No sign of Wendy in any of the bathrooms.

"Ask Fred to meet me here. I want everyone you've got looking for her. This woman is a suspect in a murder investigation."

Fred Stockdale ran into the office. Smith explained the situation and he issued orders quickly and efficiently.

The radio spoke again. "Rick here. On Lift Three. I'm pretty sure I saw the woman you're looking for. One of the last to get on."

A big map of the resort filled the back wall of the office. Smith traced the path of Lift Three with her index finger, although she didn't have to. She knew it well. It led to the Double Black Diamonds.

"I'm going up," she said.

Chapter Twenty-six

John Winters wasn't happy to see Lucky Smith's battered Pontiac Firefly parked halfway into the road outside the Glacier Chalet B&B. He wasn't in the mood to put up with Lucky's attempts to run interference around the few questions he had for Ellie Carmine. He considered coming back another time, but decided that was the coward's way out, and reluctantly parked behind the old car. How Lucky managed to maneuver that thing down the snowy mountain roads between her home and town he didn't want to speculate.

The door opened as he mounted the porch steps. Ellie Carmine was holding a phone in her hand. "I haven't even pressed talk and here you are."

"Pardon?"

"Jeremy's upstairs packing," she explained. "When he showed up, straight from the jail I imagine, I told him to clear out. I was afraid he'd kick up a fuss, so I've punched 911 into the phone already. But he didn't say a word and I don't hear the sound of breakage." She stepped aside to invite him in.

As always the hallway was warm with heat from the kitchen and redolent with the odors of fresh baking. Today apple and cinnamon were prominent.

"I'm afraid I've been a coward," Ellie explained.

Winters closed the door against the cold winter air and hid a smile at how he used that word to describe himself just moments ago.

"I expected Jeremy would come here when he was released from jail and didn't want to be on my own, so I called Lucky and asked her to come over. She's upstairs, standing outside while Jeremy packs up. Sounds like them now."

Footsteps on the stairs and Jeremy, wearing winter coat and heavy scarf, dragging a wheeled suitcase behind him, with a tattered backpack tossed over one shoulder, came into the hall. Lucky followed.

"You didn't have to call the cops, lady," he said. "I wouldn't stay in this dump any longer if you paid me."

"I didn't…." Ellie began.

"But I'm glad to see your friend here. Saves me coming down to the station to make a complaint." He gave Ellie a mean smile and turned to Winters. "You see, Sergeant, when a member of the public checks into a fine establishment such as this we have an expectation of privacy."

Winters opened the door. "Good bye."

"Hear me out. Someone is snooping around here. Going through drawers, checking out the contents of pockets, rifling purses. You know—*touching* things. Now, me, I don't have any secrets." He gave Winters a big wink. "So as long as nothing was being stolen, not my problem. But it is *your* problem lady, and you can be sure my dad'll be mentioning it to the tourism authorities and perhaps the Chamber of Commerce. You might want to have a word with your daughter before you're run out of business. Have a nice day."

He left, dragging his suitcase behind him.

"Charming fellow," Lucky said. "Pay him no mind, Ellie. People like him like to make trouble, but if they can't punch someone's face in they're too lazy to do civilized things such as lay complaints. John, what brings you here?"

"I have a question for Mrs. Carmine."

Ellie Carmine didn't appear to be paying Jeremy Wozenack "no mind." She had gone very pale and her fingers pulled at the tassels decorating the hem of her Christmas apron. "I've been wanting to talk to you, Lucky, about…about what he said. But I don't know how." Tears spilled down her face.

A bell rang in the kitchen. "Perfect timing," Lucky announced. "The muffins are ready." She took her friend's arm and led Ellie into the kitchen. Feeling like an uninvited guest, Winters closed the front door, took off his outerwear and boots, and followed. Dirty bowls and baking implements were on the counter and pot handles stuck out from the mound of fluffy white soap suds in the sink. A broom leaned against one wall.

Lucky was lifting muffins out of the baking tin and placing them on a platter. Ellie sat at the table, her shoulders hunched and her head down. One of the red tassels had come off her apron, and she was weaving it between her fingers.

"Sit," Lucky ordered Winters. Obediently, he sat.

Lucky placed the plate of muffins on the table, followed by a mug of coffee. He selected a muffin and dropped a pat of butter onto it. It spread across the warm surface like a soft yellow river.

"What he...that Jeremy...said? About Kathy? I've been wanting to talk to you about it, Lucky, but I just didn't know what to say."

"We'll have a nice long chat, *later*," Lucky said, pushing the muffins toward her friend. "Once we've helped *Sergeant* Winters with his business and he's on his way."

"I'm looking for Wendy Wyatt-Yarmouth, but if there's something you need to talk to me about, go ahead."

"She's not here. Wendy I mean, although Kathy isn't here, either."

"He's not asking about Kathy," Lucky said.

"Do you know where Wendy's gone?" he asked, trying to ignore Lucky.

His cell phone rang.

It was the station, and he listened for only a moment before abandoning his coffee and muffin and heading for the door.

The lift ended at two black diamonds and three blues. The skiers who'd come up with her cranked their boot buckles down tight, settled goggles over faces, checked the direction of the wind, pointed the tips of their skis downhill and allowed themselves to fall forward. Family groups were slower at getting children off on the gentler runs but soon they too were gone. The sun was almost down leaving streaks of pink between the gray clouds, washing the snow in a light pink glow.

Wendy stepped out from behind a tree. The top of the hill was empty. Only a smattering of skiers had gotten onto the lift after her and she realized, not much caring, that the ski hills had closed. The lift attendant had his head down, and was writing something in a notebook.

She was alone.

Always alone.

Everything was so very quiet. Not even a bird was chirping. Only the wind roared in her ears.

She turned around. At the top of the hill, beyond the giant mechanism that moved the ski lift, the terrain was much gentler and heavily treed. She hadn't bothered to look at the map of the area when Jason and the others had been studying it so intently on their first day.

Was it only a week ago? Seemed like a lifetime ago.

It was a lifetime ago. Jason's lifetime.

He hadn't seemed all that surprised when she'd led him to Ewan's body beneath the tree. "Figured someone'd get the prick some day," he'd said.

Even through her shock and guilt, Wendy had looked at her brother in surprise.

"I didn't like him much, you know, once we weren't kids any longer. Ewan never gave a thought for anyone but himself. But he was my buddy, eh? My best buddy since Kindergarten.

"He raped a girl in high school. We were at a house party while the parents were on vacation. Ewan got her into a bedroom and raped her. I saw her when she came out of the room. Her clothes were ripped, her lip was cut, her cheek swollen. She was crying. Ewan stood in the doorway, zipping up his pants, laughing. He told her she'd be making a fool of herself if she went to the cops. She was hammered and everyone knew she put it out for the whole football team. He saw me watching, and winked."

Jason hadn't looked at his sister, just kept his eyes on the snow-covered body at his feet. "I turned and walked away. I wasn't going to back her up, not against my friend. I should have.

"If I'd told the cops what he'd done, maybe he would have learned something and wouldn't have tried it with you."

Jason thought Ewan had tried to rape her. If only he knew.

"I'll call the police," she said.

"No. They'll try to make it sound like you were responsible for this. They'll say you led him on and killed him when he rejected you."

Wendy hung her head and didn't look at her brother. The wind had shifted and snow was settling over Ewan's body like a shroud.

"Look," Jason said at last. "I didn't help that girl, but I can help you. I'll dump him in the woods. We'll say we haven't seen him since last night. There's nothing but wilderness around here. It'll be easy to hide a body. They'll never find him, and if they do, who's to say some jealous boyfriend didn't get rid of him."

And so Jason had carried Ewan to the SUV, while Wendy followed, arranging the snow to hide the imprint of Ewan's body and their footsteps. Which hadn't really been necessary, the snow was falling so fast, and the wind blowing so hard across the open yard, every trace of their passing was soon covered. Jason had difficulty getting the body into the SUV, but Ewan was slight and Jason strong. Wendy had thought someone would see them, come out, investigate. But it was Christmas Eve and people had better things to do than spy on the neighbors.

She'd killed Ewan. That she could live with, he deserved it. But she'd killed Jason as well. The police said he'd gone into the river minutes after midnight. He'd left her not long after ten o'clock. He must have driven around, looking for a spot to dump the body, wondering if he was doing the right thing.

There's nothing but wilderness around here, Jason had said. Yet he'd come back to town, still with Ewan. Had he changed his mind and decided to take the body to the hospital?

If Wendy had faced the consequences of her actions, Jason would still be alive.

There's nothing but wilderness around here.

She was past crying, past grieving. Time to do the right thing.

The area in front of her was roped off and signs warned skiers that this section was off-limits.

She ducked under the ropes.

Chapter Twenty-seven

Molly Smith jumped off the chair lift. A thump beside her told her that her companion, a member of ski patrol named Gareth, was on his feet as well. A round, fat full moon hung in the western sky, bathing the snow in a milky-white glow.

The resort's security guards were posted at the bottom of the runs, waiting for Wendy to come down. Outdoor staff had been told to look out for the woman in yellow while doing their regular sweep.

"What now?" Gareth asked.

"She isn't a good skier. This hill is no place for her." The official name of the major run was Black Powder, although the locals called it Hell's Vestibule, or just The Vestibule. Even the lesser runs that left from this spot were various degrees of challenging.

Other than the wind and the almost silent movement of the chair lift, all was quiet. A gust of wind lifted a breath of snow off a tree and tossed it into her face.

Smith skied to the top of the closest run and looked down. Impossible to distinguish one set of ski tracks from all the others that had been laid down during the day. She turned toward the out-of-bounds area. The traces of a few skis broke away from the mass of tracks, showing where people had walked to the edge to look at the view. Branches creaked and snow drifted off dark green needles.

A single line of skis, the snow on either side punctuated by the round imprint of poles, skirted the out-of-bounds signs and went under the rope. The tracks wobbled, looking as if they'd been laid by someone not too skillful, and snow hadn't begun to fill the depressions.

"Jerk," Gareth said, and Smith started, thinking for a moment he was calling her names. "There's always someone too clever for his own good." He pointed at the tracks. "There's a reason this area is posted. It's dangerous ground out there."

"She's got what, about a fifteen-twenty minute lead on us? She's not a good skier, but this section's pretty flat. What's it get like further in?"

"Heavily forested. It's never been used for a run, mostly because if you take a left there's a heck of a cliff."

"Molly, you there?" Radio.

"I'm here. She's gone into the backcountry behind Black Powder."

"Not good," Stockdale said. "That area's under an avalanche warning. Mountie with the dog's here."

She let out a grateful puff of air. "That was quick."

"Says he was nearby. He's getting a machine and coming up. Says for you to wait there."

"Will do."

<> <> <>

Skiing wasn't so bad, once you got away from the crowds and the clumsy little kids and teenage show-offs. There was no groomed trail here, no tracks laid down by earlier skiers. There was a rough sort of path cutting through the trees, used by deer and elk perhaps, and it went down at a gentle angle. That wasn't so bad either, not like the terrifying drops Jason and Ewan seemed to think she could be goaded into trying.

Wendy had fallen in a pile of soft snow almost as soon as she'd taken her first step past the boundary rope, and been afraid she wouldn't be able to keep on her feet long enough to disappear. Wouldn't that be embarrassing: to flounder around up to her waist in a pile of snow, like a fish flipped into a boat, and be rescued by some stuck-up, know-it-all ski patroller.

After only a few feet of careful going, she entered the woods. A solid line of trees uphill kept the snow from blowing too deep here. She no longer had to struggle in the powdered snow that everyone else seemed to love.

She had never heard such silence. Blissful silence. Not a sound but wind moving through the trees and snow settling on the branches. No one nagging her to do better in school, to work harder, to start saving some money, to ski faster. To keep up. Keep up with her mother the surgeon, her father the professor. With Jason, the prodigy. Jason the Perfect.

The cold winter moon lit up the path in front of her.

Chapter Twenty-eight

They heard the two-stroke whine of snowmobile engines coming toward them, and moments later two machines broke out of the trees. Adam Tocek was driving the first, large and bulky in the protective suit. Norman was tucked into the seat in front of him, protected by the driver's arms, wearing an orange avalanche-dog vest. They pulled up in a spray of powder, and Tocek lifted his visor. Another member of the ski patrol was driving the second snowmobile, which pulled a first-aid toboggan.

The driver tossed a pair of boots toward Smith. "Don't know if these'll fit, but we figured you'd be better off without your ski boots."

Smith caught the footwear. "Glad you could make it, Adam."

"What you got?"

"Woman on skis. We're pretty sure she went that way." Smith turned and pointed her pole toward the solid line of snow-wrapped trees. "She's involved in the Wyatt-Yarmouth and Williams deaths, you know about that?"

Tocek nodded.

Norman showed everyone his large pink tongue.

"She's not too good on skis, and she isn't out for a pleasure jaunt."

"Trying to run?"

"Not thinking, most likely. I spoke to her less than an hour ago and she was drinking heavily and close to a breakdown."

"Can you operate one of these things?"

"Been driving snow machines a lot longer than patrol cars." She released the bindings of her skis and stepped clear before planting the skis toes first into the snow. While Gareth supported her by one arm, she changed boots. "What's happening down below?" she asked, bending over to tie the laces.

"John Winters is on his way, and the helicopter is on standby. Norman and I were heading to the office when I heard the call."

"Tracks are visible as far as I followed them. She fell at least once. If we're lucky, she'll give up and wait for us."

"As long as that moon stays out, we can find her. Let's go."

Smith told the woman who'd come up with Adam to remain here and direct other searchers if needed. Then she pulled a helmet out of the snowmobile's storage compartment, put it on, swung her leg over the snow machine, and settled into the driver's seat. Gareth clambered on behind her. Smith dropped the visor, and reached for the controls to rev the engine. A low mumble came from the row of mountains ahead of them.

"Snowpack's moving," Tocek said. "Over that first ridge. Should be well beyond any ground our target can cover." His machine edged forward.

They went slowly and lay low to duck under the ropes. Tocek gave the engine a bit more gas, and they headed into the wilderness.

The moon threw the tracks of Wendy's skis into deep relief. Tocek tried to keep to one side of the trail, to preserve the track in case they needed to backtrack, but the trees soon closed in leaving them without much room to maneuver. Wendy's trail started off wobbly, veering off in all directions, rounding trees, turning back on itself, but it soon settled into a more-or-less straight line.

Smith watched Norman. The long hairs at the ruff of his neck and around his ears stood up under the force of the wind, and his nose was constantly twitching as he sniffed the air.

Adam Tocek had to go slowly, keeping his eyes on the trail. He came to a near stop and gave Norman a push. The dog jumped off the machine, gave himself a shake, and fell into pace to lope beside them. The moonlight was good but the forest was full of fallen branches and snow-covered boulders and deep shadows that could conceal a fallen skier.

Norman came to a sudden stop. He lifted his big head and barked. Just once. Darkness swallowed the lights of the snow machines. Ahead, there were no more trees, no more snow. Nothing but blackness. Smith pulled up beside Adam as he dismounted and got off her own machine. Her legs were heavy and the snow was deep beneath her ill-fitting boots. She could feel Gareth moving beside her.

They joined Adam and Norman at the edge of the cliff. The ski tracks didn't waver, they simply disappeared over the edge. Smith reached for the dog's head and felt Adam's glove. He turned his hand over and took hers. They stood together looking down. The side of the mountain had been cut away as smoothly as a knife slices off a piece of cake. It was at least a hundred feet, probably more, to the bottom. The remains of the ancient rock fall showed jagged black edges above the snow.

Far below, a tiny patch of yellow lay across the boulders, broken, twisted.

"Call for a helicopter," Adam said at last. "This isn't a rescue anymore, it's a recovery."

Chapter Twenty-nine

Red lights lit up the deep winter night. A stretcher was guided down the ramp and loaded into the back of the ambulance, and a man climbed in after it. It pulled into the street, sirens warning cars to get out of the way. Two police officers watched. A light snow was falling, but there was no wind and the night was calm.

"That was the hardest thing I've ever done," Molly Smith said.

"Yup."

"Do you get used to it?"

"Never," John Winters said.

It hadn't taken long for the helicopter rescue team to descend into the crack of the mountain and bring out the body of Wendy Wyatt-Yarmouth. Winters had joined Smith and Tocek at Blue Sky, before going back to town to break the news to Wendy's parents. Smith, overwhelmed by what she saw as her failure to protect the young woman, accompanied him.

Mrs. Wyatt-Yarmouth had, at first, simply refused to believe them. She insisted that the police had made a mistake. Winters gently persisted and offered to drive the couple to the hospital, whereupon Patricia had screamed and flown at him, ready to blindly take out all her rage and grief. Winters grabbed her hands, and spoke to her softly, until she was spent. Then he'd laid her on the bed and called an ambulance to take the inconsolable woman to the hospital. The entire time her husband stood at the window, looking out at the street lamps in the alley. Smith pressed her back against the wall, and felt useless.

"My wife has made friends with Mrs. Wyatt-Yarmouth," Winters said, fishing in his pocket for his cell phone, as the ambulance doors slammed shut. "She'll want to help, if she can. Can I give you a lift somewhere Molly?"

"No, thanks. I need to walk for a while."

He watched her walk down the street. At first she moved slowly, her head down, her hands stuffed into her pockets. She kicked at a lump of dirty snow. As she waited at the corner for the light to change, she straightened up, lifted her head and held her face to the falling snow. Then she punched the air with her fist, once, and dug into her pocket for her own cell phone. When the light was green, she ran across the street with a wave to a passing pedestrian.

She pulled up a stored number. "Hey," she said, "it's me." He'd given her his number earlier, in case she needed to talk. She didn't need to talk, not about Wendy Wyatt-Yarmouth and grief and sorrow. Enough sadness in the world; time to get back to living. "I haven't celebrated the New Year yet, and I'm starving. What time do you get a break? It's late so pretty much everything's closed, but we can probably get a sandwich at the Bishop. Want to meet me? Dinner's on me."

"I'd like that, Molly," Adam Tocek said. "Give me half an hour."

Chapter Thirty

Molly Smith came through the front doors into Alphonse's Bakery, and he smiled to see her. "Happy New Year, Molly."

"Happy New Year to you. I'd like to put in an order."

He lifted his eyebrows.

"For tomorrow," she said. "I'm on days, working until three, but I'd like to get a fresh baguette, maybe two, and some of that great cheese. Could you save some for me?"

"Having a friend over?"

She grinned. "Yeah, I am."

"I have one chocolate croissant left just for you." He rummaged behind the counter for the pastry.

As she'd closed out her shift, Winters had called her into his office to update her on the results of the forensic search behind the Glacier Chalet B&B. Ray Gavin and his team had found Wendy's leather glove in the woods. They had also found a rock with traces of blood on it right about where Molly had told them to look. Beside the rock there were some partially burned logs.

"A group of women," Winters said, "had a bonfire in the clearing not far from there to celebrate the solstice. Without getting a permit, I might add."

"I assume my mom was one of them. She's not a big one for bureaucratic regulations."

"No kidding. Not mentioning any names, but one of the women told me that when they'd extinguished the fire, they kicked the logs around and covered them with snow before leaving. The wind probably uncovered some of the wood, and Ewan Williams fell onto them. Thus the traces of singed wood and ash Doctor Lee found in his head wound."

It was all rather moot now, but had to be done.

Clutching the bag of baking, Smith went out the back of the bakery and ran upstairs to her apartment with a light step. After taking off her uniform, she lay down on the bed, just for a moment, to think about what she could make for dinner tomorrow. The cheese and French bread would be a good start. Adam looked like he was a big eater; he'd probably like a steak and baked potato with all the trimmings. And a big green salad tossed with Lucky's secret dressing.

Adam. She'd enjoyed his company the other night at the Bishop and Nun. Just a quick burger in the back of the bar before he had to get back to work, but she'd had fun. More fun than she'd had in a very long time.

No more sadness. It was time to say goodbye to Graham, knowing he'd always have a special place in her heart, and move on. She fell asleep with a smile on her face.

When she woke up, it was dark. The clock at her bedside said it was only eight o'clock.

She'd fallen asleep thinking about what to have for dinner, and was ravenous. As usual there wasn't much available, so she'd head for Trafalgar Thai and get a take-out.

She dressed quickly in jeans and T-shirt, pulled on her winter coat and gloves, stuffed her feet into her boots and ran down the stairs. She felt just great. Adam was working tonight, but starting tomorrow they were both off for a couple of days. They were going to take it easy, let things go where they wanted.

She threw open the front door and stepped into the alley.

It was snowing, again, and fat flakes drifted through the night. Someone was standing just outside the circle of light cast by the street light. It was a man, and she knew who it was. He watched her, but made no move to approach.

She slipped her key between her fingers and stepped into the alley.

"She's not here, Charlie. Which is too bad or I could arrest you for breaking parole conditions." She stopped, keeping herself out of striking range.

He spat into the snow between them. "If you mean Chrissie, I'm not interested in her. Guy wants to be friends and she freaks. What a bitch. Don't know why she thinks she can be so fuckin' fussy. It's not as if she's all that much to look at, and she sure doesn't have any money."

"Glad to hear it. You'll be leaving town, then. Nothing to keep you here."

"There is one little thing." His voice was low, the tone threatening, if not the words. Smith held her keys tighter.

"Chrissie didn't put me in jail. You did that, Molly. The way I see it, you and me have unfinished business."

His hand shot out and she flinched. But he punched only snowflakes and wind.

"Be seeing you around, Molly."

She watched him saunter away. He reached the street corner and turned to look at her. He lifted his right hand and held out his forefinger, the thumb holding the other three fingers, and pointed to the sky. The hand came down and aimed straight between her eyes.

And, with a grin, mean and ugly, he was gone.

To receive a free catalog of Poisoned Pen Press titles, please contact us in one of the following ways:

Phone: 1-800-421-3976
Facsimile: 1-480-949-1707
Email: info@poisonedpenpress.com
Website: www.poisonedpenpress.com

Poisoned Pen Press
6962 E. First Ave. Ste. 103
Scottsdale, AZ 85251

LaVergne, TN USA
25 October 2010
202196LV00003B/72/P